**Nate's own silence came**          
**closeness of Sarah.**

She had chosen to sit next to him on the wagon seat so James and Margaret could sit together. The children lay down in the bed of the wagon. At every bump and turn Sarah's skirt brushed against his knee, keeping him constantly aware of her presence.

She must have been as tired as all of them, though. She didn't say a word until they reached the cabin on Williams Street.

"Thank you for the wonderful day, Nate." Her voice was soft, and she smiled as she spoke.

"We sure appreciated your company." He tore his gaze away from those deep blue eyes. They had spent too much time together, walking across his land and making plans.

Plans that she wouldn't have any part in, if he had his way. Life with him—well, he wouldn't ask anyone to share the kind of life he h~~~~~~d so far. But he couldn't keep from w~~~~~~~~~lk into the cabin.

**Jan Drexler** enjoys living in the Black Hills of South Dakota with her husband of more than thirty years and their four adult children. Intrigued by history and stories from an early age, she loves delving into the world of "what if?" with her characters. If she isn't at her computer giving life to imaginary people, she's probably hiking in the Hills or the Badlands, enjoying the spectacular scenery.

### Books by Jan Drexler

#### Love Inspired Historical

*The Prodigal Son Returns*
*A Mother for His Children*
*A Home for His Family*

# JAN DREXLER

## A Home for His Family

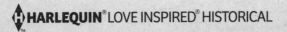

HARLEQUIN® LOVE INSPIRED® HISTORICAL

Recycling programs for this product may not exist in your area.

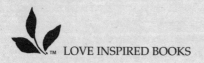

™ LOVE INSPIRED BOOKS

ISBN-13: 978-0-373-28328-6

A Home for His Family

Copyright © 2015 by Jan Drexler

www.Harlequin.com

**Printed in U.S.A.**

Lay not up for yourselves treasures upon earth, where moth and rust doth corrupt, and where thieves break through and steal: But lay up for yourselves treasures in heaven, where neither moth nor rust doth corrupt, and where thieves do not break through nor steal: For where your treasure is, there will your heart be also.

—*Matthew* 6:19–21

To my mother, Veva, 1929–2014.
Thank you for teaching me to love stories.
I miss you more than words can say.

# Chapter One

*Deadwood, Dakota Territory*
*May 1877*

"Sorry for the delay, folks. There's a bull train on the trail ahead of us, and they're hogging the road. It won't be long until we're moving again." The stage-coach guard acknowledged Sarah MacFarland and Aunt Margaret, the only ladies in the cramped stage, with a tip of his hat. Water sluiced off the brim onto the feet of the male passengers. "The good news is that we're only a few miles from Deadwood, and the rain is easing up a bit."

"Thank you." Sarah answered him with a nod, but kept her face classroom-firm. She had already learned women were few in this western country, and men were eager to take even a polite smile as permission to overstep the boundaries of propriety. Aunt Margaret had the notion Sarah might find a husband out here in the West, but Sarah had no such dreams. Twenty-eight years old put her firmly in the spinster category and she was more than happy to remain there.

"Excuse me, ma'am." Mr. Johnson shifted his bulk and reached under his seat. The man's cigar jammed between his teeth had bothered Aunt Margaret the entire journey from Sidney, Nebraska. "If you'll oblige, I'll take my bag. Since we're this close to the camp, I might as well walk the rest of the way."

He grabbed his satchel and squeezed out of the crowded coach. The other men spilled out after him like a half-dozen chicks from a grain sack.

"Are they all walking to Deadwood from here?" Aunt Margaret adjusted her hat as she peered through the open door.

Peder Swenson pushed himself up from his spot on the floor. "I'm not. But I am going to stretch my legs and see what's going on." The blond eighteen-year-old had kept them entertained with stories of his native Norway on the long journey.

As Sarah watched Peder stride away on his long legs, she couldn't sit still another minute. "I am, too."

Aunt Margaret grabbed her sleeve. "You will not. Who knows what you'll find out there? We've seen enough of those bullwhackers along the trail to know what kind of men they are."

Sarah held her handkerchief to her nose. Rainy weather kept the heavy canvas window covers closed, and even with the men gone, the heavy odor of unwashed bodies was overwhelming. "I'll be careful. I have to get some fresh air. I'll stay close by, and I won't go near the bull train."

Aunt Margaret released her sleeve, and Sarah climbed out of the stagecoach, aching for a deep breath. With a cough, she changed her mind. The air reeked of dung and smoke in this narrow, serpentine valley.

She held her handkerchief to her nose and coughed again. Thick with fog, the canyon rang with the crack of whips from the bull train strung out on the half-frozen trail ahead. She pulled her shawl closer around her shoulders and shook one boot, but the mud clung like gumbo.

A braying sound drew her attention to a wagon a few feet from the coach, leaning precariously close to the swollen, rocky creek at the side of the trail. She stepped closer to get a better look and nearly laughed out loud at the sight of a black mule tied to the back of the covered wagon. The creature sat in muddy slush as it tried to pull away from the rushing water and noise.

A tall man, soaking wet and covered in mud from his worn cavalry hat down to his boots, grabbed for the mule's halter. "Loretta, if you break that rope again, I'm going to sell you to the first butcher I find."

The mule shook her head, and he missed his grab, landing flat on his back and sliding down the slope toward the edge of the creek. As he fell, the animal flicked her gray nose toward him and snatched his hat in her teeth.

A giggle rose in Sarah's throat at the sight, and her shoulders shook as she fought to keep it in.

The man rolled over, lurching to his feet as he grabbed his hat from the mule. "You stupid, dumb, loco..." He muttered all kinds of insults at the animal, who only tossed her head as he slapped the hat against his legs in an effort to clean the mud off it.

A young boy appeared at the back of the wagon, pulling the canvas cover open. He couldn't have been older than eight or nine, with a straw-colored cowlick topping his forehead. Would he be one of the students in her new academy? Uncle James had written that several families lived in and around Deadwood and that some of the parents were desperate for a good school. Sarah had brought a trunk full of books and supplies for boys just like this one, and for the poor young women trapped in the saloons. She smiled at the thought. Dr. Amelia Bennett would be so proud of her.

The boy caught her attention again, shaking his head as he watched the man and the mule. "She was only trying to help."

"Charley, the day that mule helps me do anything will be the day I eat my hat. I've never seen a more useless…"

"Not Loretta." Charley's voice rang with boyish confidence. "She knows exactly what she's doing."

The man leaned one gloved hand on the corner of the wagon box while he raised a boot to dislodge the mud with a stick. "Then why does she keep fighting me every time I try to get her to do something?"

"Because she's smart. She doesn't want to go any closer to this creek."

The man stomped his foot back onto the ground and lifted the other one. "The horses don't have any problem with it."

Sarah glanced at the four-horse team at the front of the wagon. They stood with their backs hunched as the rain gave way to a cold wind that threatened to snatch her hat away. She pushed it down tight and turned back to the scene in front of her.

"The horses are stupid."

The flabbergasted expression on the man's face as Charley pronounced his judgment triggered another giggle. Sarah slapped a gloved hand over her mouth, but a snort of laughter escaped between her fingertips.

"Ma'am." The man locked eyes with her, then released his foot, stomping the heel on the ground. "I'm happy to see we amuse you."

"Oh, I'm…" She snorted again. "I'm so sorry. But the mule, and you and those poor…" She couldn't talk through her laughter. "Those poor horses. I think the mule is right."

"See, Uncle Nate? I told you."

"Charley, get back in the wagon." The boy ducked inside as the man called Nate strode across the few feet of trail toward her. "So you think the mule is right?"

Sarah's laughter died. No answering smile lit his dark eyes and his lips formed a thin, tight line. She was the only one who had found the incident funny, but he didn't need to condemn her. She lifted her chin. "You drove into a precarious spot. One misstep and your wagon and all its contents could end up in the creek."

"You think we ended up there on purpose? The stagecoach…" He looked at the coach, and then at her. "*Your* stagecoach about ran us off the road."

Sarah's face heated in the cold air. A muscle in one of his stubbled cheeks twitched. "I apologize. I should have realized you were at the mercy of the crowded trail."

He pulled his hat off and wiped a weary forearm across his brow. "Yes. The crowded trail, and the rain, and the forty freight wagons all trying to head into Deadwood today and the cold." He turned away, gazing into the fog-shrouded pines looming above them at the edge of the canyon, and then faced her again. "And now it's my turn to apologize. I'm letting my frustrations get the better of me."

Sarah observed him as he waited for her reply. His apology had turned the corner of his mouth up in a wry grin.

"Of course, you have my pardon." She smiled, breaking her self-imposed rule. "Anyone would be hard-pressed to let a day like today not frustrate him."

As he smiled back, a gust of wind ruffled his short dark hair.

"You and Charley are on your way to Deadwood?"

"Yes, ma'am, we are."

Sarah searched his eyes for that wild gleam of gold fever—the look that made the men she had traveled with lose all their common sense—but his brown eyes were calm and clear in spite of the tense lines framing them that spoke of exhaustion and many days on the trail. He met her gaze with his own interested one. Something foreign fluttered in her stomach.

"My uncle has started a church in town, and I'm a teacher. I'll be opening a school soon, and I hope Charley will be able to attend."

His smile disappeared. "Wouldn't count on us, ma'am. We'll be busy getting settled."

The flutter stilled. "But you can't let a boy like Charley grow up without any education."

"I don't intend to, miss. The children will get all the education they need."

Sarah pressed her lips together. Did this cowboy truly think a child could get a decent education while mining for gold or running wild in the streets?

Her reply was interrupted as the stagecoach driver climbed back up onto his seat. "You'd better take your place, miss," he said over his shoulder. "We have a way cleared and are going on into town now."

"Yes, all right." As she turned to the coach, Charley's uncle reached out to open the door for her. As he leaned near, she caught the scent of leather and horses.

"Thank you, Mr.…."

"Colby. Nate Colby."

He smiled as he offered his hand to steady her climb into the coach.

"I hope we'll be able to continue discussing Charley's education at another time."

He waited until she was seated and then leveled his gaze at her. "I think we've finished with that subject. The children's schooling is already taken care of."

Sarah opened her mouth, ready to deliver the stinging words that would put this cowboy in his place, but as her eyes locked with his, the argument died in her throat. He smiled, nodded to Aunt Margaret and closed the door. He was gone.

"Why, Sarah." Aunt Margaret began, straightening Sarah's skirt as she took her seat. "Who is that man? You promised you would stay away from the bull train."

Sarah rubbed at a splash of mud on the hem of her skirt, turning away from her aunt. She was certain her face held a telltale blush. "He was driving an immigrant wagon and has his nephew with him."

And he had mentioned children, so more than only his nephew.

"But still, you haven't been properly introduced. We don't know anything about the man, and you're letting him…"

"I allowed him to be a gentleman and open the door

for me. It isn't as if he is courting me." She patted Margaret's hand in assurance.

The driver called to the six-horse team and cracked his whip. She fell back in her seat as the coach started off with a jolt. The opposite door flew open, and Peder jumped in.

"*Uff da*, I made it!"

As Peder launched into his description of the stalled bull train for Aunt Margaret, Sarah turned in her seat and lifted the corner of the canvas window cover. Nate Colby stood in the center of the muddy trail, his feet planted far apart and his arms crossed over his chest, watching the stage. She let the curtain fall and braced herself against the rough road. He certainly wasn't the kind of man she had expected to meet in the notorious Deadwood.

Nate shook himself. He had no time to stand watching a stagecoach wind its way along the muddy trail between the freight wagons, even if it did carry the most intriguing woman west of the Mississippi. He had a family to take care of.

He turned to the wagon, tilted on the bank between the road and the creek, and that stubborn mule still pulling on the halter rope with all her might as if she could keep the whole outfit from tumbling into the water.

Olivia appeared in the opening of the wagon cover. At nine years old she was the image of her ma, from her upturned nose to her golden hair. "Uncle Nate, are we almost there?"

"We should be in town this afternoon." Nate tied down a corner of the canvas that had pulled loose in the rising wind. "You get back in the wagon and take care of Lucy. I've got to get us off the creek bank and back up on the trail. It's going to be bumpy."

Eight-year-old Charley popped his head up next to Olivia's. "Who was that, Uncle Nate? I've never seen a prettier lady."

Olivia gasped. "Charley, you can't say that. No one was prettier than Mama."

"Mama was a mama, not a lady."

Nate tightened the end of the canvas. "Your mama was a lady, Charley," he said, drawing the opening closed with a tug. "She was the prettiest lady who ever lived."

"I told you so."

Nate hardly heard Olivia's words as he moved around the wagon, checking every bolt, tightening every rope. She was right; no one had been prettier than Jenny, and no one had been happier to have her as a sister-in-law than him. But if anyone came close to Jenny, it was that girl from the stage. Instead of Jenny's golden light, she had the beauty of a rare, dark gem, with black curls framing her face. Her eyes had seemed nearly purple in the gray afternoon light, but no one really had purple eyes.

Olivia's voice drifted through the canvas cover, singing Lucy's favorite song. Nate pushed against the familiar worry. Lucy would get better soon. Once they were settled, she would get back to the bubbly and energetic five-year-old she had been before the fire. All she needed was a safe and secure home with her family, and she would be back to normal.

But how long would it take until they had a home again? He went through the steps in his head.

Find his land. Good land with plenty of meadow grass for the horses. That was first. Then file the homestead claim. Next would be to build a house, outbuildings, make sure water was accessible.

Nate worked a wet knot loose and pulled the canvas tight before tying it again. He moved on to the next knot.

Find more mares for his herd. Some of the mustangs he had seen here in the West had descended from quality stock, he could tell that. And with some work and gentling, they'd make fine broodmares. Their colts, with his Morgan as the sire, would make as fine a string of remounts as the US Cavalry could wish for.

Test the next tie-down. Loose. He pulled at the soaking knot. The plan had to work. What would become of the children if this chance didn't pay out?

He retied the rope, tightening the wet cover against the rising wind. The plan would work if it killed him.

Nate pressed his left cheek against the damp, cold canvas, easing the burn of the scars that covered his neck and shoulder and traveled down both arms to the backs of his hands. The constant reminder of his failure to save Andrew and Jenny. The reminder of what his cowardice had cost the children. A chill ran through him. What if he failed again? He couldn't. He wouldn't.

Olivia's song filtered through the canvas, a song of God's protection and care.

With a growl, Nate pushed away from the wagon and headed toward the horses. When had the Lord protected them? When he was nearly blown to pieces in Georgia during the war? When Ma and Pa died in '64, leaving Mattie alone to fend for herself? When Jenny and Andrew were burning to death? When three children were left homeless and orphaned?

He could live without that kind of protection. God had His chance, and He hadn't come through. They would just have to get along on their own.

And they'd get along without any busybody schoolteacher stepping in. As if he'd let some stranger take care of Andrew and Jenny's children. It didn't matter that the scent of violets curled like tendrils when he stepped close to her, pulling him deeper into those eyes.

He shook his head. The children were his responsibility, and he'd make sure they had everything they needed.

When he reached the team he checked the traces, and then each horse. Pete and Dan, the wheel horses, stood patiently. Ginger, his Morgan mare, tossed her head as he ran his hand over her legs. At just three years old and growing larger with her first foal, she had the lightest load of them all, but she'd have to throw her shoulders into the harness to get the wagon back on the trail. She could do it, though. Morgans were all heart.

Last was Scout. The stallion rested his nose on Nate's shoulder, mouthing at his neckerchief as Nate scratched behind the horse's left ear and smoothed the forelock back from his eyes. This horse had saved his life more times than he could count during the war and carried him all over the West as he had searched for Mattie the years since then. Nate owed him everything.

Scout nudged his shoulder.

"Sorry, boy. No carrots today. We've got work to do." He stroked the dark cheek under the bridle strap, holding Scout's gaze with his own. The horse understood. He would get the wagon back onto the trail.

With shouts from the bullwhackers and the crack of whips, the train started out. Nate called to his team, "Hi-yup, there!"

The horses strained, the wheels turned in the mud and the wagon lurched up and onto the road. But as it did, Nate heard a sickening crack. Halting the team, he stooped to look under the wagon, dreading to confirm his fears.

The front axle was splintered and twisted along a narrow crack from one end to the other. A stress fracture. But it was still in one piece. He'd have to try to drive the wagon into Deadwood for repairs.

He stamped his feet to get some feeling back into them. The weather was turning bitter, and fast. He had to get the children into some sort of shelter for the night. The wind seemed to take a fiendish delight in whistling down the length of the canyon. If he didn't know better, he'd think this weather was bringing snow behind it. But this was May. They couldn't have snow in May, could they?

He'd have to walk to keep the strain off the axle. He glanced up at the wagon. Should he have the children walk, too? He shivered and buttoned the top of his coat. No, they'd be better off in the wagon, out of the wind. He pulled at Scout's bridle, and the horses started off.

Glancing upward, he breathed out a single word. "Please." As if he really believed someone would hear him. The wind pulled water from his eyes, and he ducked his head into the blast. When the gust eased, gathering itself for another onslaught, he looked straight up into the pewter sky, at the light breaking through the gray clouds in golden rays. He had to keep the children safe. He had promised.

"Oh, not again!"

Sarah caught hold of the branch of a juniper shrub as her boot slipped on the muddy creek bank. The night spent in the snug cabin Uncle James had built when he came to Deadwood last summer had been a welcome relief after days in the stagecoach, but she was quickly getting chilled and miserable again on this afternoon's mission of mercy.

"Are you all right?" Aunt Margaret puffed as she tried to keep up with Uncle James's pace.

"Yes, I'm fine." Sarah pulled at the juniper until she was on the trail next to her aunt again and brushed a lank strand of wet hair out of her face. Uncle James reached out a hand to steady her, shuddering as a gust of wind struck them.

"This storm is getting worse, and it's starting to snow. We need to be getting home." Uncle James took Aunt Margaret's arm.

"I'm glad we went, though. Mr. Harders would have been frozen solid by morning in that cold cabin with no fire." Sarah buried her chin in her scarf.

"The poor man." Margaret clicked her tongue under her breath. "If he was this sickly, he should never have come to Deadwood."

James tucked her hand in the crook of his arm. "His doctor told him to come west for his health."

"And this place is healthy?"

"Wait until the weather clears, my dear. I know you'll love it as much as I do."

Sarah took her aunt's other arm. "Let's hurry and get home where it's warm."

"Wait." Margaret clutched at James. "What is that? An Indian?"

Sarah peered through the brush along the creek. "She doesn't look like a Sioux, unless they wear calico skirts." Sarah started toward the girl, who was now bending to dip a pail in the creek. A few steps took her around the bushes and face-to-face with the barrel of a shotgun.

"You stop right there." The gun barrel wavered as the eight-year-old boy holding it stepped into view. The same boy she had seen yesterday afternoon, peering out of the covered wagon. Charley, wasn't it? She looked past him to the empty trail. Her stomach flipped at the thought of seeing Nate Colby again.

"Young man, put that gun down right now." Margaret's voice was as commanding as if she was reprimanding one of the Sunday school boys.

"Uncle Nate said to keep a gun on any strangers coming around, and that's what I mean to do." Charley squinted down the barrel and raised it a bit higher to aim at Margaret's head.

This was getting nowhere, and Sarah was wet and cold.

"Come, now, surely you can see we're no threat." She smiled, but Charley only swung the gun barrel around to her. The gun wavered as he stared at her. "I know you, but I don't know them." He turned the shotgun back toward Uncle James.

"Charley, what are you doing?" The girl with the water pail came up the path behind him, and the boy tightened his grip on the gun.

"Keeping a gun on them, just like Uncle Nate said."

The girl, half a head taller than the boy and a little older, eyed Sarah as she pulled a dirty blanket tighter around her small body.

"Are you two out here alone?" Sarah smiled at them. "Where is your uncle?"

The children exchanged glances.

"No, ma'am, we aren't alone," the girl said. "Uncle Nate went hunting, but he'll be back soon." She pulled at her brother's sleeve. "Come on, Charley. We have to get back."

Charley let the gun barrel droop and backed away.

"There aren't any cabins around here." James sounded doubtful, as if these children would lie.

"We have a wagon. We've been traveling the longest time."

Charley turned on the girl. "Olivia, you know Uncle Nate said not to talk to strangers." His voice was a furious whisper.

"They aren't strangers. They're nice people." The girl's whispered answer made Sarah smile again.

"Why don't you bring your family to our cabin for a warm meal? You can wait there until this storm blows over."

The two looked at each other.

"Uncle Nate said to stay with the wagon." Sarah could hear doubt in the boy's voice.

His sister pulled on his sleeve again. "Lucy is already cold, and night's coming. It's just going to get colder."

"We have stew on the fire," Sarah said. The thought of the waiting meal made her stomach growl.

"Why are you even asking them?" Margaret stepped

forward and took each of the children's hands in her own. "Now take us to your wagon, and let us take care of the rest."

The children looked at each other and shrugged, giving in to Margaret's authority. They led the way to the covered wagon, listing on a broken axle, at the side of the trail. The canvas cover whipped in the wind. So Mr. Colby had made it almost all the way to town before breaking down. Another half mile and he would have reached safety. But where they were now... Sarah glanced at the bare slopes around them, peppered with tree stumps.

As they drew close, Olivia dropped Margaret's hand and ran to the wagon.

"Lucy! Lucy, where are you?"

A curly head popped over the side of the crippled wagon, and a young girl with round eyes stuck her thumb in her mouth and stared. Sarah guessed she looked about five years old.

Out here, away from the shelter of the trees and brush along the creek, the wind roared. Sarah marveled at its fury, and the children huddled against the gust.

Margaret stepped to the end of the wagon and looked in. "Is this all of you? Where is the rest of your family?"

Olivia's teeth chattered. "There's only Uncle Nate. We're supposed to wait here until he gets back."

Sarah stamped her feet to warm them. Mr. Colby should know how dangerous it was to wander around this area alone. Uncle James had warned her and Margaret to never go anywhere outside the mining camp without him after they had arrived last evening. Between claim jumpers and Sioux warriors scouring the hills, even visiting a sick neighbor was a risk.

She stepped forward and put her own warm cloak around Olivia's shoulders. "He can find you at our cabin. We need to get in out of the weather, and you need a hot meal."

Charley looked at her, his lips blue in the rapidly falling temperatures. "How will Uncle Nate find us?"

"I'll leave him a note."

Olivia and Charley exchanged glances, and then Olivia nodded. "All right, I think he'll be able to find us there, if it isn't too far."

Sarah scratched a brief message on a broken board she found near the trail and put it in a prominent place next to the campfire. She raked ashes over the low coals with a stick and stirred. The fire would die on its own.

She took Olivia's hand in hers as Margaret lifted Lucy out of the wagon. Uncle James untied the horses, Charley took his mule and they started up the trail toward home.

Sarah's breath puffed as they climbed the steep hill, her mind flitting between worry and irritation with the children's uncle Nate. These children needed her, no matter what their uncle said. Somehow she would see that they received the care and education they deserved.

As the snowfall grew heavier, obscuring the distant mountains, Nate gave up. He'd been wandering these bare, brown hills since midmorning and hadn't seen any sign of game. He and the children would just have to make do with the few biscuits left from last night's supper.

When the wagon axle had finally broken yesterday

afternoon, he thought the freight master would have helped them make repairs, but the man had only moved the crippled wagon off the trail and then set on his way with the bull train again.

"We're less than a mile from town—you'll be fine until we send help back for you. Just keep an eye out for those Indians."

And then they were gone, leaving Nate and the children alone.

Less than a mile from Deadwood? It might as well be twenty, or fifty, when everything they owned was lying by the side of the road. By the time the gray light of the cloudy afternoon started fading, Nate knew the bull train driver had forgotten them.

They had spent the night on their own with little food and a fitful fire. Morning had brought clouds building in the northwest and he'd hoped he'd be able to find a turkey or squirrel before too long. But here he was coming home empty-handed.

As he hurried over the last rise, Nate's empty stomach plummeted like a stone at the sight of the wagon. The wind had torn one corner of the canvas cover and it flapped wildly. Why hadn't Charley tied that down? Didn't he know his sisters and all their supplies were exposed to this weather?

And why hadn't they kept the fire going? They had to be freezing.

The hair on the back of Nate's neck prickled. The wagon tilted with the blasting gusts of wind. It was too quiet. The horses were missing. Even Loretta was nowhere in sight.

Nate broke into a run.

When he reached the wagon, he closed his eyes,

dreading what he might see inside. They were just children. He had been so stupid to leave them. He had let his brother down again.

He gripped the worn wooden end gate and slowly opened his eyes. Nothing. Just the barrels and boxes of supplies. The children were gone.

Why had he taken so long? He should have stayed closer to the wagon. He had been warned about the Indians in the area, attacking any settlers who were foolish enough to venture out without being heavily armed.

He knew why he had taken the risk. No game. No food. He had had to leave them for a few hours.

He turned into the wind and scanned the hills rising above.

"Charley!" A gust snatched his voice away. "Olivia! Lucy!"

A wolf's howl floating on the wild wind was his only answer as he slumped against the wagon box, his eyes blurred with the cold. It had been the same when he and Andrew had returned from the war, back home to the abandoned farm. The wind had howled that afternoon, too, with a fierce thunderstorm. But they were gone. Ma, Pa, Mattie... Ma and Pa were dead, but Mattie was lost. None of the neighbors knew where she had gone, or even when. Years of searching had brought him only wisps of clues, rumors that this cowboy or that miner had seen her in Tombstone, or Denver or Abilene, but she was gone without a trace.

Nate's legs gave way as he sank to the ground.

The wolf's howl came again, answered by several others. A pack on the hunt? Or a Sioux raiding party?

Nate scrambled to the fire, pulling his rifle with him. He blew the coals to life again and fed the flames with a few small sticks left near the wagon and a stray board that he threw on when the blaze was strong enough. A fire should keep the wolves away, at least until dark. Until then, he could search for some sign of which way the children had gone.

He took a deep breath, shutting down the panic that threatened to consume him. The panic that would make him freeze in a shuddering mess if he gave in to it. Closing his eyes, he whooshed out the breath and filled his lungs again. *Where could they be? Think.*

The wind gusted again with a force strong enough to send the canvas wagon cover flapping. With the rising wind, perhaps the children had gone to seek a better shelter than the crippled wagon. He clung to that hope. The alternative—that they had been stolen along with the horses—was too horrible to consider.

## Chapter Two

The walk back to the cabin wasn't more than a half mile, but Sarah's feet were frozen by the time they climbed the final slope up from the trail at the edge of town. The wind pierced her wool dress.

Charley and Uncle James took the horses and mule into the lean-to where they would get some shelter, as Aunt Margaret led the way into the house. Warmth enveloped Sarah as she stopped just inside the door. She took the cloak from Olivia and guided the girls closer to the fireplace.

Lucy watched the glowing coals while Olivia folded the blanket her sister had been using as a wrap and laid it on the wood plank floor.

"You girls must be frozen." Aunt Margaret added a few sticks to the fire and swung the kettle over the flames. "Sit right here while we warm up the stew. Supper will be ready soon enough."

She left the girls to get settled on the blanket while she pulled Sarah to the side of the cabin where Uncle James had built a cupboard and small table.

"What can we feed them? I do wish we had been

able to bring Cook out West with us, and Susan. They'd know what to do."

She wrung her hands, but Sarah stopped her with a touch. "You said you wouldn't complain about leaving the servants behind in Boston."

"That was before I found out we would be cooking over an open fireplace. How can we have guests in conditions like this?"

Sarah put one arm around the shorter woman's shoulders. "We'll put another can of vegetables in the pot and some water to stretch it out. Meanwhile, we'll make a batch of biscuits. That will fill everyone's stomachs."

"I'm so glad you know your way around a kitchen." Margaret glanced at the girls, content to sit near the fire. "I'll learn as quickly as I can, but I don't think I could make a biscuit if my life depended on it!"

"Then we'll do it together." Sarah put a bowl on the table, along with a can of flour and Uncle James's jar of sourdough starter. She squelched the irritation that always rose whenever Aunt Margaret's helplessness showed its face. One thing Dr. Amelia Bennett had expounded upon frequently at her Sunday afternoon meetings was the careless way women of the privileged classes in Boston wasted the hours of their days, while their less fortunate sisters in the mills and saloons longed for the advantages denied them because of lack of education. But with all the education available to her, Aunt Margaret had never even learned to do a simple task like baking.

Sarah took a deep breath. Dr. Bennett wasn't here, but she was. She would help her aunt in any way she could, even if it was only to teach her how to make sourdough biscuits.

While they mixed the dough, James and Charley came in the door, bringing a fresh blast of cold air and stomping feet.

"It's getting even colder out there as the sun goes down." James sat in his chair near the fireplace and pulled off his boots.

"But Loretta and the horses will be safe in the lean-to, won't they?" Charley hung his coat on a hook and joined his sisters by the fireplace.

"Sure they will. Animals can survive pretty well as long as they have food and shelter."

"What about Uncle Nate?" Olivia turned to Uncle James, and then looked at Sarah. "Will he be all right?"

Sarah smiled at her. "We'll pray he will be."

A dull ache spread across her forehead as she rolled out the dough and cut biscuits. Nate's crooked smile swam in her memory. Was he warm enough? Would he be able to find the cabin? She didn't have any choice but to trust God for his safety.

"What made your uncle decide to bring you to Deadwood?" Uncle James asked.

The two children exchanged glances.

"There were some ladies in our church who wanted us to go to the orphans' home," Olivia said. "Uncle Nate said he wouldn't do that. He said he could take care of us."

"They called the sheriff to arrest Uncle Nate." Charley scooted closer to the fire.

"Charley, don't exaggerate. They only said they might. They said will's fare was at stake." Olivia looked at Sarah. "What does that mean?"

Sarah laid the biscuits in the bottom of the Dutch oven. "I think they meant welfare. That your welfare was at stake. It sounds like they wanted what was best for you."

"Yes, that's it. That's what they said. But Uncle Nate said they didn't know the situation and he'd see what was what if they tried to take us away from him."

Aunt Margaret cleared her throat and Sarah saw her exchange glances with Uncle James.

"What was your situation?" Uncle James leaned back in his chair, ready to hear the children's version of the event.

"There was a fire…" Olivia bit her lip.

"Our house burned." Charley picked up the story as Olivia fell silent. "Pa and Uncle Nate got the three of us out of the house and then went back in to get Mama."

The children stared at the fireplace. Sarah set the Dutch oven in the coals and then sat next to Olivia with her arm around the girl's shoulders.

"You don't have to tell us the rest, if you don't want to."

Charley went on. "When Uncle Nate came out of the house, his clothes were on fire." His voice was hollow, remembering.

Olivia hid her face in Sarah's dress. "I could hear Mama," she whispered. "She and Papa were still in the house."

"But Uncle Nate," Charley said, his voice strengthening, "he didn't want to give up. He kept trying to go back inside, to save them, but the neighbors were there, and they wouldn't let him. And then the roof fell down and everything was gone."

"Uncle Nate was hurt awful bad." Olivia sat up and took Charley's hand. "He almost died, too."

"That's when the ladies at church said we should go to the home." Charley wiped at his eyes. "But Uncle Nate just kept saying no."

"It sounds like your uncle loves you very much." James laid his hand on Charley's shoulder.

Charley leaned against Uncle James's knee. The children fell silent, looking into the fire.

Sarah watched Lucy. She didn't look at her sister or brother, and she hadn't seemed to hear what they had been talking about. She sat on the folded blanket, staring at the flames, lost in a world of her own. During their walk from the crippled wagon to the cabin, the little girl hadn't made a sound, but had passively held Sarah's hand as they walked.

At the time, Sarah had thought Lucy was cold and only wanted to get to the cabin. But now with the others talking and in the warm room, she was still closed into her own thoughts. Could it be that she was deaf? Or was something else wrong?

The biscuits baked quickly in the Dutch oven, and supper was soon ready. Everyone ate in front of the fire, and Sarah was glad to see how quickly the biscuits disappeared, except the ones Olivia had insisted they save for their uncle along with a portion of the stew.

After they were done eating, Lucy climbed into Sarah's lap. The little one melted into her arms without a word, the ever-present thumb stuck in her mouth.

"You stay where you are," Margaret said as Sarah started to put Lucy back on the floor so she could help clean up from the meal. "Her eyes are closing already."

Sarah settled back in her chair, enjoying the soft sweetness of holding a child in her arms. These children had suffered so much, and their story brought memories of her own losses to the surface. How well she remembered the awful loneliness the day her parents had died, even though she had been much younger than Olivia and Charley. She had been about Lucy's age when she had gone to the orphanage.

She laid her cheek on Lucy's head, the girl's curly hair tickling Sarah's skin, pulling an old longing out from the corner where she had buried it long ago. The room blurred as she held Lucy tighter.

All those years in the orphanage, until Uncle James returned from the mission field when she was seventeen years old, she had never had the thought that she would marry and have children. She had changed enough diapers, cleaned enough dirty ears and soothed enough sore hearts to have been mother to a dozen families.

Marriage and children meant opening her heart to love, and she refused to consider that possibility. Loving someone meant only pain and heartache when they died. She wouldn't willingly put herself through that misery again.

She still enjoyed children, but only when they belonged to someone else. Teaching filled that desire quite nicely.

Sarah hummed under her breath as Lucy relaxed into sleep. Charley and Olivia had settled on the floor in front of the fire, where they were setting up Uncle James's checkers game.

Where was their uncle? She prayed again for his safety in the blowing storm.

Nate stood in the abandoned camp. His hastily built fire was already dying down, and the empty canvas flapped behind him. Snow swirled. Before too long any traces of where the children had gone would be covered.

The wind swung around to the north, bringing the smell of wood smoke. A fire. People. Friends? A mining camp?

Or an Indian encampment.

He needed to find the children. He had to take the risk.

Setting his face to the wind, he followed the smoke trail to a line of cottonwoods along Whitewood Creek. He had reached the outskirts of the mining camp, and the thin thread of smoke had turned into a heavy cloud hanging in the gulch. He paused on the creek bank. Ice lined the edges of the water. The children had either been taken away, or they had run off to hide. It wouldn't take long for them to freeze to death on an evening like this one.

There. Hoofprints in the mud. Nate followed the trail up away from the creek until he came to a cabin sheltered among a few trees at the edge of the rimrock. A lean-to built against the steep hill behind the cabin was crowded with horses. Even in the fading light, he recognized Scout and Ginger. Pete's and Dan's bay rumps were next to them, and then the mule's black flank.

Nate tried not to think of what kind of men he might find in this cabin. This was where the horses were, so horse thieves, most likely. But were they kidnappers? Murderers?

He pounded on the heavy wooden door and then stepped back, gripping his rifle.

The middle-aged man who cracked open the door

wasn't the rough outlaw he expected. The white shirt, wool vest and string tie would fit in back home in Michigan, but Nate hadn't seen a man dressed this fancy since they left Chicago in March.

"Yes, can I help you?" The man poked his head out the door.

"I'm looking for some children."

"Uncle Nate! That's Uncle Nate out there!"

Charley's voice. Relief washed over Nate, leaving his knees weak.

The man smiled and he opened the door. "Come in. We've been expecting you."

Nate stepped into the warmth. Charley jumped up from a checkers game on the floor in front of the fireplace and ran toward him, wrapping his arms around Nate's middle without regard to his soaking and icy clothes. Olivia joined her brother in a hug, but Lucy stayed where she was, asleep on the lap of…

Nate dropped his gaze to the floor. Lucy was in the lap of the young woman from the stagecoach. Willowy, soft, her dark hair gleaming in the lamplight, the young woman held the sleeping child close in a loving embrace. He couldn't think of a more peaceful scene.

A round woman dressed in stylish brown bustled up to the little group. "Oh my, you must be frozen. You just come right in and change out of those wet clothes. We saved some supper for you."

Nate ran his fingers over the cheeks of both the older children. Yes, they were here, safe, sound and warm. It was hard to see their faces, his eyes had filled so suddenly.

"I thank you, ma'am, for caring for the children like

this. I can't tell you how I felt when I got back to the wagon and they were gone."

"Didn't you get our note?"

Nate met the young woman's deep blue eyes.

"Uh, no, miss. I didn't see any note."

"We found the children alone with the storm coming up, so we brought them here." Pink tinged her cheeks as she spoke, her voice as soft as feathers. "I left word of where we were going on a broken plank. I leaned it against the rocks around the fire."

"A piece of wood?" The piece of wood he had laid on the fire when the wolves were howling. He could have saved himself some worry if only he had taken the time. Then Nate looked back at Charley and Olivia, their arms still holding him tight around the waist. If he had lost them, after all they had been through, he would never have forgiven himself.

"No matter. You're here now," said the man. He put his arm around the shorter woman. "I suppose some introductions are in order. I'm James MacFarland, and this is my wife, Margaret."

"Ma'am." Nate snatched the worn hat off his head and nodded to her.

"And our niece, Sarah MacFarland."

She had a name. He nodded in her direction.

"I'm Nate Colby."

"Well, Mr. Colby, there are dry clothes waiting for you behind that curtain. While you're changing, I'll dish up some stew for you." Mrs. MacFarland waved her hand toward the corner of the little cabin where a space had been curtained off.

Nate untangled himself from Charley's and Olivia's arms and ducked behind the curtains. On the small bed were a shirt and trousers, faded and worn, but clean. When he slipped the faded gray shirt over his head, he paused. There was no collar. Nothing to cover his neck.

The children had gotten used to the angry red scars left by the burns that had nearly killed him, but these people—Sarah... Miss MacFarland—what would they say?

"Uncle Nate, aren't you hungry?" Charley was waiting for him.

Nate pulled the collarless shirt up as high as he could and gathered his wet things. He didn't really have a choice.

Sarah stroked Lucy's soft hair, surprised she still slept after all the noise Olivia and Charley had made when Nate came in. She had felt like shouting along with the children, she was so relieved to see him safe.

When he stepped out from behind the makeshift curtain, Sarah couldn't keep her gaze from flitting to his collar line. When the children had told of how their uncle had been burned in the fire, she hadn't realized how badly he had been injured. Scars covered the backs of his hands and the left side of his neck like splashes of blood shining bright red in the light. Suddenly aware she was staring, Sarah turned her attention back to the girl in her lap, but not before she saw Nate's self-conscious tug at the shirt's neckline, as if he were ashamed of the evidence of his heroism.

"Come sit here, Uncle Nate." Charley directed his uncle to the chair closest to the fireplace and Olivia gave him a plate of stew and two biscuits she had saved for him. Nate didn't hesitate, but dug his spoon into the rich, brown gravy and chunks of potato.

Uncle James pulled a footstool closer to the fire while Olivia and Charley went back to their checkers game on the floor, relaxed and happy now that their uncle was here. Aunt Margaret settled in the rocking chair with her ever-present knitting.

"The children tell us you've had quite a trip," James said after their visitor had wiped the bottom of his plate with the biscuit. "You've come to get your share of the gold?"

Nate reached out to tousle Charley's hair. The boy leaned his head against his uncle's knee.

"Not gold, but land. My plan is to raise horses, and this is the perfect place. When the government opened up western Dakota to homesteading, I knew it was time."

"You've been out here before?"

Nate's eyes narrowed as he stared at the fire. "I've made a few trips out West since the war." He glanced at the children. "It's a different world out here than it is back East. A man can live on his own terms."

"I'm gonna be a first-class cowboy." Charley grinned up at Nate.

When Nate caressed the boy's head, Sarah's eyes filled. No one could question that he loved the children as much as they loved him.

"That's the boy's dream." Nate leaned back in his chair and smiled at his nephew. "Providing remounts for the cavalry is my goal, but I need a stake first. We'll start out with cattle. With the gold rush, I won't have to go far to sell the beef."

"There's plenty of land around here, if you're look-ing for a ranch." James was warming up to his favor-ite subject—the settling of the Western desert. "The government has opened this part of Dakota Territory up to homesteading, but with the gold rush going on, not too many are interested in land or cattle."

Margaret rose to refill Nate's plate, her face pinched with disapproval. She hated the greed ruling and ruining the lives of the men they had met on their journey to Deadwood. Would she keep her comments to herself this time?

"Have you struck it rich yet?" Nate asked James between bites of stew.

James glanced at Margaret. His work here had been a bone of contention between them ever since Uncle James had decided to move west. "It depends on what you mean by *rich*. I'm a preacher, seeking to bring the gospel to lost souls."

"If Deadwood is like other gold towns I've heard about, there are plenty of those here."

Margaret let loose with one of her "humphs" and Lucy stirred on Sarah's lap. The little girl opened her eyes and gazed at Sarah's face with a solemn stare before sticking her thumb in her mouth again and settling back to watch Nate eat. There was still no sound from her. Sarah smoothed her dress and buried her nose in her soft curls again.

Nate saw Lucy was awake and winked at her, and then his eyes met Sarah's. His smile softened before he went back to eating his stew.

James went on. "Deadwood is the worst of the worst. Too many murders, too many thieves, too many claim jumpers, too many..." He paused when Margaret cleared her throat. "Ah, yes," he said, glancing at the children, "too many professional ladies."

Oh yes, those "professional ladies." Sarah had heard

Aunt Margaret's opinion of them all the way from Boston. There were few enough women in a mining camp like Deadwood, but most of them wouldn't think to darken the door of a church. Sarah shifted Lucy on her lap and glanced at Margaret. What would her aunt do if one of those poor girls showed up on a Sunday morning? Or if she knew of Sarah's plan to provide an education for them?

"Have you had any success?"

"We have a small group of settlers, families like yours, who meet together. I've recently rented a building in town, and now that Margaret and Sarah have arrived, I hope more families will come. You and the children are welcome to join us."

Nate shoveled another spoonful into his mouth.

"Could we?" Olivia looked into Nate's face. "Oh, could we? We haven't been to church ever since…"

Charley gave his sister a jab with his elbow, but Nate, scraping the bottom of his second plate of stew, didn't seem to notice. Aunt Margaret took the empty dish.

What had happened? One moment Nate was discussing Uncle James's work, and the next Olivia and Charley were fidgeting in the uncomfortable silence. Lucy slid off Sarah's lap and crossed to Nate. He took her onto his lap and stroked her hair while he stared at the fire.

"We'll be busy building the ranch," he said, looking sideways at James. "I doubt if we'll have time for church."

He shifted his left shoulder up, as if he wanted to hide the scars, and glanced at Sarah. It sounded as if going to church was the last thing he wanted to do.

* * *

Nate woke with a jerk, the familiar metallic taste in his mouth. He willed his breathing to slow, forcing his eyes open, trying to get his bearings. The MacFarlands' cabin. They were safe.

Head aching from the ravaging nightmare, he rolled onto his back, waiting for his trembling muscles to relax. He might go one, or even two, nights without the sight of the fire haunting him. Before Jenny and Andrew died last fall, the nightmares had almost stopped—but now they were back with a vengeance. Whenever he closed his eyes, he knew what he would see and hear: the cavalry supply barn going up in flames. Horses screaming. The distant puff and boom of cannon fire. The fire devouring hay, wood, boxes of supplies, reaching ever closer to the ammunition he had managed to load onto the wagon. And those mules. Those ridiculous mules hitched to that wagon, refusing to budge. Over and over, night after night, he fought with those mules. And night after night the flames drew ever closer to the barrels of gunpowder. And since last fall, Andrew had been part of the nightmare. He stood behind the wagon, in the flames, yelling at him, telling him to hurry…hurry…to leave him…don't look back…

And then Nate would jerk awake, shaking and sweaty.

He glanced at Charley, lying beside him on the pallet in front of the fireplace. At least the boy hadn't woken up this time.

Nate looked around the cabin. Still dark, but with a gray light showing through a crack in the wooden shutters. Close to dawn. Almost time to get the day started.

Above him, in the loft, the girls slept with Sarah MacFarland. He hadn't missed how quickly Olivia and Lucy had become attached to her. Lucy had even let Sarah hold her, something she hadn't let anyone do except himself in more than six months. They were safe here. Safer and warmer than they had been since they left home eight weeks ago.

Was he wrong to bring the children to Deadwood? Was this any place to raise them?

The women of their church back in Michigan had made it clear the only right thing for him to do would be to put the children in the orphanage. The Roberts Home for Orphaned and Abandoned Children. As if they had no one to care for them.

Absolutely not. They would take these children from him over his dead body.

Charley turned toward him in his sleep and snuggled close. Nate put his arm around the boy and pulled him in to share the warmth of his blanket.

The sound of dripping water outside the cabin caught his attention. The wind had died down, and the temperature was climbing. The storm was over, and from the sounds of things, the snow was melting already. And that meant mud. As if he didn't have enough problems.

Shifting away from Charley, Nate sat up. He pulled on his boots and stepped to the door, opening it as quietly as he could. No use waking everyone else up. Standing on the flat stone James used for a front step, he surveyed the little clearing.

Last night, James had told him he had been in Deadwood since last summer, building this cabin before sending for the women back in Boston. He had built on the side of the gulch, since every inch of ground near the creek at the bottom had already been claimed by the gold seekers. This cabin and a few others were perched on the rimrock above the mining camp, as if at the edge of a cesspool. Up here the sun was just lifting over the tops of the eastern mountains, while the mining camp below was still shrouded in predawn darkness.

Saloons lined the dirt street that wound through the narrow gulch. The sight was too familiar. Every Western town he had been in had been the same, and he had stopped in every saloon and other unsavory business looking for his sister. But Mattie's trail had gone cold a few years ago. No one had seen her since that place in Dodge City where the madam had recognized the picture he carried. She had to be somewhere. Could she have made her way to Deadwood? Fire smoldered in his gut at the thought of where Mattie's choices had taken her.

The door opened behind him.

"Oh, Mr. Colby. I didn't realize you were out here."

Nate moved aside to make room for Sarah on the step. The only dry spot in sight. She had already dressed with care, her black hair caught up in a soft bun. Her cheeks were dewy fresh and she smelled of violets. He resisted the urge to lean closer to her.

"I'm an early riser, I guess." He chanced a glance at her. "I heard water moving and thought I'd check on the state of things. Our wagon is still on the trail back there, mired in the mud by now."

"I had to see what the weather was like, too." She smiled at him, and his breath caught. "After yesterday's storm, this morning seems like a different world. I've never seen weather change so quickly."

"That's the Northern Plains for you. It can be balmy spring one day, and then below zero the next."

"I suppose we'll have to get used to it." Sarah pushed at a pile of slush with one toe. She wore stylish kid-leather boots with jet buttons in a row up the side. They would be ruined with her first step off the porch. "Your children are so sweet. I've enjoyed getting to know them."

Nate rubbed at his whiskers. "They seem to like you, too. You have a way with children. I've never seen Lucy take to anyone so quickly."

"I hope you'll reconsider sending them to school when I open the academy next week."

He shot another glance at her, wary. "They won't have time to attend any school. They'll be with me all day. I'll see they get the learning they need."

She leveled her gaze at him, tilting her chin up slightly. Nate straightened to his full height, forcing her chin up farther. "Mr. Colby, I'm sure you know children do best when learning in a safe, secure environment. Can you provide that for them while you work to find your ranch?"

"I can provide the best environment they need, and that's with me." Nate felt the familiar bile rising in his throat. The busybodies back in Michigan had used the same arguments.

"But what about school?"

"President Lincoln learned at night after a day's work. Charley and Olivia can do the same."

"But surely you don't think—"

"Surely I do think I know what's best for these children. They're my responsibility, and I'm going to take care of them."

She stared at him, her eyes growing bluer as the sun rose higher over the distant hills. And here he'd thought he'd escape these do-gooders when he came west. No one was going to take his children away from him. He slammed his hat on his head.

"I'll be waking the children up now. We need to work on getting the wagon repaired and head on into town."

"You can leave the girls here, if you like, while you and Charley take care of the wagon." She reached out one slim hand and laid it on his sleeve. "You are right, that the children are your responsibility, but that doesn't mean you can't let others help you now and then."

Nate considered her words. She was right, of course. With all the mud and the slogging to town and back to get that axle repaired, it would be best for the girls to stay here and enjoy a day in the company of women, in a clean, safe house. But it galled him to admit it.

He nodded his agreement to her plan. "I'll take Charley with me. But only for today." He lifted a warning finger, shielding him from those gentle eyes. "The children stay with me. They're my responsibility and I aim to do my best by them."

"Of course you want the best for them. So do I."

She turned to look down into the mining camp as it stirred to life in the early-morning light. Somehow, he didn't think her version of what was best for the children would be the same as his.

## Chapter Three

"I can help. Let me help." Charley hopped on one foot, a flutter of movement in Nate's peripheral vision.

Shifting his left foot closer to the wagon, Nate shoved again, sliding the wagon box onto the make-shift jack. He ran a shaking hand across the back of his neck.

"Charley, some jobs are just too big for an eight-year-old." Who was he trying to kid? This job was too big for a thirty-year-old. If Andrew was here…

Nate looked into Charley's disappointed face. If Andrew was here, they'd still be living in Michigan, and Charley would still have his pa. But a man couldn't bring back the past, and he couldn't always fix the mistakes he'd made, no matter how much he wanted to.

He squeezed Charley's shoulder. "I'll need your help with the next part, though." Charley's face brightened. "We need to get that broken axle off there and find a new one."

"Loretta can help, too, can't she?"

Nate looked at the mule, tied to the back of the crippled wagon. It flipped its ears back and stomped its front foot in response.

"I suppose she could carry the axle to town."

"Sure she could. Loretta can do anything."

Nate glanced at Charley as he knocked the wheel off the broken axle. Where did the boy get such an attachment to a mule? The animals were outright dangerous when they took it into their heads to go their own way.

He knew the answer to his own question. Andrew had given Loretta to the boy years ago, when Charley was barely old enough to ride. Andrew held that mules had more sense than horses and that she'd keep Charley safe wherever he wanted to take her. Nate had argued, tried to change Andrew's mind, but Loretta became one of the family.

And now? Charley had already lost so much. He wasn't going to be the one to take the mule away from the boy. No matter how much he hated it.

Nate fumbled with the ironing that held the axle to the bolster above it. Sometimes he could use a third hand.

"What can I do? I want to help."

Nate glanced at the boy again.

"Here you go, Charley. Hold the axle up against the bolster while I get it unfastened."

With Charley's help, Nate released the ironings with a quick twist, and the axle was free. He glanced at the mule again. It was wearing the pack harness that Charley used for a saddle. It had come in handy on the trail when Nate needed to bring some game back to camp or haul water. Would the thing carry the axle for him?

Nate approached the mule, hefting one part of the

heavy axle in his hands. "Whoa there, stupid animal, whoa there."

The mule rolled its eyes and aimed a vicious bite at his shoulder.

"She knows you don't like her." Charley stood off to the side, watching.

"Of course I don't like her. Help me get these axle pieces on her harness, will you?"

When Charley climbed up onto the animal, Nate was sure the mule winked at him. But it let him load the axle on the harness, and Charley fastened the straps, balancing with his weight on the other side of the mule. Nate looked at Charley's grin as he perched on the pack saddle. In spite of the work still ahead to get the wagon back on its wheels, Nate had to grin back at him. What he wouldn't give to be a boy again.

He fixed his eyes on the trail ahead. Those days were long gone.

Sarah scrubbed the hem of her traveling dress on the washboard. Mud seemed to be everywhere in this place.

"Here's some more hot water for you." Aunt Margaret came out the back door of the cabin to the sheltered porch where Sarah and Olivia bent over tubs of soapy water.

"Thank you." Sarah pushed a lock of hair out of her face with the back of her arm. "It's so wonderful to be able to do laundry in the fresh air this morning." She smiled at Olivia as she took the steaming kettle from Margaret. "I would imagine it was hard for you and your uncle to keep up with chores like this along the trail."

"We didn't take time for anything," Olivia answered, swishing a pair of socks in her tub. "Uncle Nate said we had to keep up with the bull train."

Sarah turned the heavy skirt in the water and tackled another muddy stain. Her thoughts wandered to Nate Colby. Again. Was he having any success with his wagon? Would he be able to get the axle fixed? He'd have to take it into Deadwood to find someone to repair it.

"Did Uncle James say when he was going to show us the building he rented?" she asked Margaret.

Her aunt looked toward the roofs of the mining camp below them. "He said we would go this afternoon although I can't see why we need a building down there."

"Because that's where the people are. And the academy needs to have a place, unless you want the children studying in the cabin."

And with the church and school in the center of the mining camp, she would have ready access to the unfortunate young ladies she intended to find and educate.

Sarah looked up at the towering pine trees that climbed the steep hill behind the cabin. On those Sunday afternoons last winter in Dr. Amelia Bennett's crowded parlor on Beacon Hill, she had never imagined the fire that had been lit in her would bring her to such a place as this.

Dr. Bennett was a pioneer. A visionary. Her plans for educating the women of the docks and brothels of Boston were becoming reality in the opening of her Women's Educational Institution, and Dr. Bennett had urged Sarah to spread the work to the untamed wilderness of the American West, as she had called it. Sarah intended to make her mentor proud.

A sniff was Margaret's only reply as she went back into the house. Lucy stopped playing with the pine-cones she had found and stared after her.

Olivia wiped an arm across her forehead. "Is she always so…"

"Disapproving?" Sarah finished Olivia's question. She wrung the water out of her skirt. "My aunt didn't want to come out West. She's trying to make the best of things, but it is hard for her to adjust to this life."

"Why did she come, then? Why didn't she stay at home?"

Sarah looked from Olivia's earnest face to Lucy's wide eyes. Why did any of them leave their homes? "My uncle said God was calling him to preach to the gold seekers." She put one of her uncle's shirts into the warm water. "Aunt Margaret came because he asked her to."

"Why did you come?"

Olivia's question struck deep. Sarah moved the shirt through the gray water and smiled at the girl. "I wanted adventure, and I wanted a purpose in my life. When Uncle James wrote that there were families here with children, I knew what this town would need is a school." A great center of learning, for young and old. That was how Dr. Bennett phrased it.

"Can I go to your school?"

"May I…"

"May I go to your school?"

Sarah thought back to her conversation with Nate. Olivia would be such a charming pupil in the academy, one she would love to share the knowledge of the world with, but could she promise such a thing if the girl's uncle was opposed to it?

"We'll have to see what your uncle says." Olivia's face showed her disappointment as she went back to her scrubbing. "But even if you can't come, I'll certainly share my books with you and help you learn."

"Would you, really?" Olivia's face shone as if the sun had come clear of a swift cloud. "And will you help me teach Lucy to read?"

Sarah glanced at the five-year-old, who had gone back to her pinecones. It looked as if she was building a house with them. She leaned closer to Olivia. "I've never heard your sister say anything. Does she talk?"

Olivia shook her head. "She used to. Before Mama and Papa…" She bit her lip, and Sarah put an arm around her narrow shoulders.

"She hasn't spoken since you lost your parents?"

At the shake of Olivia's head, Sarah pulled the girl into a closer embrace. There had been a boy at the orphanage who had never spoken, from the time he came to live there until he passed away a few months later. The matron had said he died of a broken heart, but Sarah had known better. He had died because he couldn't face life with no hope and no family.

She watched Lucy put the pinecones in lines, framing the rooms of her house. She put rocks into the spaces for furniture and used small pinecones for people that she walked in and out of the doors.

She could learn to speak again. Surely her life wasn't as hopeless as the boy at the orphanage. Lucy was still surrounded by family, and she was healthy. Surely with love and nurturing she had hope for a normal, happy life. Resolve to assist these children filled her heart.

"I'll help you teach Lucy to read, and we'll make sure Charley works on his studies, too."

Sarah held tight as Olivia's arms squeezed around her waist. Had she just made a rash promise she couldn't keep?

By the time Nate found a wheelwright who could make a new axle, noon had passed. He fingered the coins in his pocket.

"Is there any place to buy something to eat?" he asked the wheelwright.

"The Shoo Fly Café has good pie." The burly man gestured with his head up Main Street.

"What about a grocer's?"

"The closest is Hung Cho's, right across the way there."

"Thank you. We'll be back to pick the axle up around midafternoon."

Nate guided Charley across the muddy street with one hand on the boy's shoulder, making sure he stepped wide over the gutter in the middle. Hung Cho's was a solid wood building with a laundry on one side and what looked like a hotel on the other. Some of the signs were in English, but most had what Nate guessed were Chinese characters.

Charley stared at the short, round Chinese man who approached them as Nate sorted through the wares on the tables outside the store.

"Yes, yes, sir." The man bowed slightly. "You want some good food for your boy, yes? Hung Cho carries only the best. Only the best for our friends."

Nate glanced at the man. He had run across men from China before, but Charley hadn't. Hung Cho's smile seemed genuine, his expression friendly.

He fingered the coins in his pocket again and looked at the items on the table. He recognized some apples, dry and wrinkled from being stored all winter, but apples nonetheless.

"How much for one of these?"

"Oh, these apples. They are very fine. Make a boy very healthy, yes? Only one dollar."

"I only want to buy one, not all of them."

"Yes, yes. I understand." Hung Cho's head bobbed as he nodded. "Apples are very dear. One dollar."

Nate pulled out a dollar coin, along with a two-bit piece. I'll take one. Do you have any crackers, and maybe some cheese?"

Hung Cho leaned forward to peer at the coins in his hand, and then slid his look up to Nate's face. His smile grew wider. "You have coin money, not gold? You are new in Deadwood."

At Nate's nod, Hung Cho reached under the table and brought out two apples in much better shape than the ones he had on display. "For cash money, I give you two apples, one pound crackers and cheese. Nice cheese, from back East."

They followed the little man into the dim interior of his store. The odor of dried fish in one barrel overpowered the close room. Hung Cho squeezed between it and another barrel filled with rice. He scooped crackers out of a third barrel and weighed them in a hanging scale, then sliced a generous wedge of cheese from a wheel behind the counter. He wrapped it all in a clean cloth and handed the bundle to Charley.

"One dollar and two bits, please."

"Why the change in price?"

"Cash money is hard to come by. Bull train drivers want cash from the Chinese instead of gold." The man's smile disappeared as he shook his head. "They do not trust the Chinese. Will not accept gold dust from us for fear it is not pure."

Nate handed over the coins in his hand.

Hung Cho bowed as he slipped the money into some folds in his robe. "Thank you, sir. Thank you very much."

They left the store and then turned right, toward the center of the mining camp. As they crossed an alley and stepped back up on the boardwalk in front of a row of businesses, Charley tilted his head up to look at him. "Where are we going to eat, Uncle Nate?"

They were passing an empty space between two canvas tents. A couple barrels stood close to the boardwalk. "How about right here?"

They settled themselves on the barrels and divided the food between them. Charley shoved the crackers into his mouth two at a time.

"Whoa there, boy. Those crackers won't disappear. Take your time."

Charley grinned at him and Nate took a bite of his apple as he settled in to watch the traffic on Main Street.

Two doors down was a saloon, and beyond that were signs for several more. Across the street, a large building had a sign, The Mystic Theater, but from the look of the young women leaning over the rail of the balcony, much more than theatrical entertainment was available there. James MacFarland had been right about the saloon girls—they seemed to be everywhere. This must be the Badlands of Deadwood he had heard the bullwhackers mention.

Nate took another bite of his apple and looked closely at the women on the balcony. The youngest seemed to be no more than sixteen, while a couple of them wore the bored look of years of experience in their business. The apple turned sour in his mouth. He swallowed that bite and then offered the rest to Charley.

Mattie, if she was still alive, would be the age of those older women. Did her face bear that same expression? She would be thirty-two years old by now, and it had been almost fourteen years since she had disappeared.

He watched the two women, their mouths red slashes against their pale, white faces. The dresses they wore had been brightly colored at one time, but now looked sadly faded next to the younger girls, like roses that clung to a few blown and sun-bleached petals.

He hoped that Mattie had found her way out of that life.

He sighed and took a cracker. Turned it in his hands. The last time he had searched for his sister and come home again with no news, Andrew had told him to give it up. If she wanted to come home, she'd find her way.

But Andrew didn't live with the memory of her face the night he told her he was running away to join the army. The hard, crystalline planes that shut him out.

"You'll kill Ma and Pa," she had whispered as she tried to wrest his bundle of clothes from him. "And then what will I do?"

He had turned from her, bent on following Andrew, but she had been right. By the time he had come home after the war was over, Ma and Pa were dead, and Mattie was gone.

He looked back up at the balcony of the Mystic. He'd never give up looking, hoping that someday he'd find her before… The cracker snapped between his fingers. He refused to listen to that voice inside that kept telling him it was too late.

When Charley finished his lunch, Nate wrapped up the rest of the crackers and cheese.

"Let's go see what the town looks like."

The street was crowded with men all going nowhere in particular and Nate pulled Charley closer to his side. Between the coarse language and the open bottles of liquor, he knew this wasn't a place Andrew and Jenny would want their son to be. But this was where they were.

The businesses crowded together between the hills rising behind them and the narrow mudhole that passed for a street. Nate slowed his pace as the storefronts turned from the saloons to a printing office. Next came a general store and a clothing store, with a tobacconist wedged in between. Across the street was Star and Bullock, a large hardware store that filled almost an entire block.

And in the middle of it all, just where the street took a steep slope up to a higher level on the hill, men worked a mining claim. Nate shook his head. In all his travels through the West, he had never seen anything quite like Deadwood.

"Look, Uncle Nate. There's Miss Sarah!"

Charley ran ahead to where the MacFarlands stood at the end of the block. Nate halted, watching Sarah's face as she greeted the boy. She looked truly happy to see him. From what he had seen, busybodies from schools and orphanages never seemed to like the children they claimed to care so much about.

She didn't fit the mold. She didn't fit any mold.

Charley pointed his way and she looked for him. Another smile. The crowded streets seemed to fall silent, and Nate saw several of the men on the boardwalk look in her direction. He hurried to catch up with Charley.

"Miss MacFarland." He found himself smiling, and he turned to the elder MacFarlands. "Mrs. MacFarland. James." Lucy reached for him and he lifted her into his arms.

Sarah's wide skirts swung as she turned toward him. "Was your errand a success?"

"The broken axle is being repaired as we speak."

"We were just on our way to see the new storefront Uncle James rented. Would you and Charley like to come along?"

"Say yes, Uncle Nate. Please?" Charley clung to his free hand, while Olivia hopped up and down. He couldn't say no to them.

"We'll be pleased to accompany you."

They all followed James as he turned down a side street and led the way toward a boarded-up saloon. Nate let Sarah go ahead of him, Charley and Olivia each holding on to one of her hands, while he followed with Lucy. Anyone watching would think they were a family.

Nate let that idea sift through until it soured his stomach. A family? He hugged Lucy close as he carried her. These children were all the family he needed, and he didn't deserve even this.

When they reached the building on Lee Street, a few doors from the corner at Main, Sarah took Lucy's and Olivia's hands while Nate and Uncle James pulled the slats from the boarded-up door. Once there was an opening, Uncle James led them in.

"This is a church?" Olivia let go of Sarah's hand and stepped farther into the room. "It looks like a saloon."

Uncle James cleared his throat as Margaret followed Olivia to the bar that extended from one end of the room to the other. "The latest tenants ran a drinking establishment, and it needs work."

Aunt Margaret stared at him. "You said you had found a storefront."

Lucy tightened her grasp on Sarah's other hand at the ice in Margaret's voice. Sarah gave her small hand a reassuring squeeze. "It does need a lot of work, but I can see the possibilities." She led Lucy to the center of the room to get a feeling for the size of the space. "If that bar is removed…"

"And that hideous mirror behind it." Aunt Margaret waved her hand in the direction of the gold-flecked monstrosity on the wall. A narrow hole in the center radiated spiderweb cracks in all directions.

"There will be room enough for whoever comes to worship." Sarah glanced around the room again. A piano listed to the side in one corner. Perhaps there would be someone in town who knew how to repair it.

She glanced back at Nate, standing in the doorway. He was removing nails from the wood slats, one by one. He didn't seem to want to come any farther into the dusty building.

Margaret sniffed as she ran one finger along the top of the bar and inspected her glove.

"You need to see this place as I do, dear." Uncle James crossed the room to his wife and pulled both of her hands into his own. "With some effort, we can redeem this place for the Lord's work." He turned to look around the room. Sarah had to smile at the grin on his face. Uncle James was a hopeless optimist.

No, not hopeless. He had confidence in the Lord's leading.

"What I see is a den of iniquity." Margaret's voice softened. "But if anyone can make a silk purse out of a sow's ear, it's you, James MacFarland."

"When we started the church in China, we didn't even have a building. Only a stone slab and rubble." James sighed, the smile still on his face. "Here we have a good roof, a good floor and two large rooms. The Lord has blessed us, indeed."

"Two rooms?" Sarah had planned to teach in this room, but if there was another…

"Right through that door." James nodded toward the far end of the bar.

Sarah picked up Lucy and started across the dirty floor, skirting a broken chair on the way. Olivia and Charley came behind them. When she opened the door, Charley crowding past, she nearly dropped Lucy. A man stood in the center of the room, a white felt hat and cane in one hand and a sheaf of papers in the other. He looked up when she gasped.

"Oh, I'm sorry. I thought this room was vacant." Sarah stepped back, pulling Charley with her.

The man smiled as he took a step toward her. "There's no need to go. I am to meet my client here. A Mr. MacFarland?"

Uncle James was at her side. "Mr. Montgomery." The two men shook hands. "You're early. I was just showing the building to my wife and niece."

"Wilson Montgomery, at your service, Mrs. Mac-Farland. Miss MacFarland." He bowed his head in Margaret's direction and then in Sarah's. His voice was cultured and his manners impeccable, except that his gaze lingered on Sarah a little too long before he turned back to Uncle James.

"Mr. Montgomery is from the bank. He's handling the lease on this building."

"Why don't we ladies inspect this room while you and Mr. Montgomery attend to your business?" Aunt Margaret shooed Sarah and the children into the back room and closed the door behind them.

"Well, what do you think?"

Sarah looked around the room. It had its own entrance from the alley on the side of the building, and with a window next to the outer door, the room was light and airy.

"I like it." She walked from one wall to the other, mentally placing benches and a chalkboard.

"No, no. Not the room. Mr. Montgomery." Aunt Margaret's words hissed in a loud whisper.

"Mr. Montgomery?" Sarah eased Lucy down to the floor. Olivia took her sister to the window to join Charley.

"Don't you think he's perfect? James told me about him last night. He's from Boston."

Aunt Margaret ended her pronouncement with a smile. Sarah grasped her aunt's meaning.

"You don't mean you think that he…" Sarah shook her head. "Don't start matchmaking, Aunt Margaret. You know I'm too old to marry, and no man will appreciate a spinster being thrown at him."

"Oh, now," Aunt Margaret sputtered, "I would never

throw you at him. He attends the church and is a very eligible bachelor. He is the manager of the First National Bank of Deadwood, and his father is the owner."

As she ended her sales pitch, Sarah sighed. "If he is that eligible, don't you have to ask yourself why he isn't already married? In my experience, once a man reaches a certain age without being married, there is usually a good reason for it."

"In your experience? My dear, you haven't had that much experience."

Sarah watched the children at the window. Charley had found a spider and the three of them were engrossed in its meal of an insect caught in its web. She would rather not talk about men with Aunt Margaret. Her aunt had been thirty-five when she met Uncle James, fresh from the mission field in China. Since she had married late in life, she held that there was hope for every woman. But a man, at least a good man, was a rare bird.

Nate opened the door between the two rooms and stepped in.

"It's time for Charley and me to head back to the wheelwright's. The axle should be done by now."

Sarah turned to greet him. His timing couldn't have been better. Maybe he would take Aunt Margaret's mind off Wilson Montgomery.

"I'm so glad we met in town so you could inspect the new church and school with us." She crossed the room, slipped one hand into the crook of his elbow and swept the other across the room with a grand gesture. "This is our academy. What do you think?"

His gaze followed the sweep of her hand. "It's a right

fine room. But you'll need desks, won't you? And a chalkboard? And books?"

Margaret was watching them, so she leaned a little closer. "I brought books with me, and Uncle James will build benches for the students to use." She looked up at him. "I'm not sure what to do about the chalkboard. Do you have any ideas?" She considered batting her eyes, but she had never done that to any man, and she wasn't about to start now.

He lifted her hand off his arm and stepped away. "I'm sure you'll think of something, Miss MacFarland." When he grinned, a dimple appeared in his chin. She hadn't noticed it yesterday. Shaving certainly made a difference in a man's looks.

Nate walked over to the window. "Charley, it's time to go."

He ushered the boy toward the door leading to the alley and turned to Sarah. The shadow of his smile still lingered. "We'll come for the girls as soon as we get the wagon fixed."

"You'll stay for supper tonight, of course." Aunt Margaret's voice denied any argument.

Nate turned his hat between his hands and looked at Charley. "I appreciate it, ma'am, I surely do. But the children and I need to set up our camp."

Sarah's throat tightened. Once he left with the children, would she ever see him again?

Her face heated with a sudden flush. Where had that thought come from? But still, something made her want to have more time with him. And the children.

"You must eat supper with us tonight." His eyes met hers. "And I think I know where there is a perfect spot for you to camp, right near the cabin."

He glanced at the children, watching him. They were waiting for his decision with bated breath, just like she was.

Finally he shoved his hat on his head. "I know when I'm outnumbered." He turned to Aunt Margaret. "I'm certainly beholden to you for your hospitality, ma'am. I don't know how I'll be able to repay you."

"Pishposh." Aunt Margaret waved her hand in the air. "You don't need to repay anything. We're glad to have the company."

Sarah followed him to the door and stepped outside. Charley wandered toward the front of the building, but Nate turned to her. Sunshine had chased all the morning clouds away, and it shone brightly into the alley. She shaded her eyes with her hand as she looked up at him.

"I'm glad you decided to have supper another night with us. I would hate to give up the children's company so soon."

"Is it their company, or are you still going to try to talk me into letting them come to your school?"

"You know already that I would love for them to attend and that I think it is the best thing for them." Nate started to turn away, but she stopped him with a hand on his arm. "But I will respect your wishes concerning them."

He looked at her, his chin tilted just enough for her to see she hadn't convinced him, but his teasing grin lingered.

"You won't mention the school, to me or to the children?"

Could she just give up on making sure those children had an education? On the other hand, Nate was their uncle. Maybe she could convince him that they both had the children's best interests in mind.

Without mentioning the school.

"I promise. As long as you promise we can be friends."

One corner of his mouth turned up. "Friends? All right, friend." He stepped backward. "I'll see you at suppertime." He caught up with Charley at the corner of the building and disappeared.

Yes, he certainly was a rare bird.

## Chapter Four

Replacing the axle was easier now that Nate had figured out how to work with Charley. The boy's nimble fingers slipped the ironings into place as Nate held the axle against the bolster. Even so, it was late afternoon before he had the horses hitched up and they were ready to drive to the MacFarlands' cabin.

Instead of the shorter route up the steep hill on the north end of Williams Street, James had recommended the more gradual ascent up Main Street to Shine, and then to Williams. Nate and Charley had led the team down that route before picking up the new axle, and it was still going to be a hard pull for the horses with the loaded wagon.

Charley climbed up onto the seat next to him and Nate chirruped to the horses. Before too long they reached the outskirts of the mining camp, where tents crowded along the road. Miners of all description watched them pass. Groups of young men, old sour-doughs, even a couple families. Soon they'd be heading to their claims, now that the snow in the hills was melting. Men who had secured claims along Whitewood Creek were already at work, standing knee-deep in the rushing water with their pans, or shoveling dirt and gravel into rockers.

Nate glanced at Charley, who watched the miners with wide eyes.

"They're sure working hard, aren't they?"

The boy nodded. "I thought gold miners just picked nuggets up off the ground, but what they're doing doesn't look like much fun."

"Mining is dirty, backbreaking work. And not too many find success."

"Then why do they do it?"

Nate watched two men shovel gravel into a sluice. "They're looking for an easy way to get rich, but they're learning the only way to success is hard work. The ones who keep at it will do okay, but others will give up before the month is over."

"That's why we're going to be cowboys, right?"

Nate nudged Charley's knee with his own. "That's right. We'll be working hard, too, but at the end, we know we'll have something to show for it."

They passed the wheelwright's shop and Chinatown. The street was crowded as they approached the Badlands and Nate slowed the horses to a walk, threading their way between freight wagons unloading their goods and the crowds spilling off the board sidewalks into the mud.

Once they moved past the Badlands, the crowds grew thinner and the going was a bit easier. A flash of color on the board sidewalk caught Nate's eye. Three girls dressed in red, yellow and purple silk dresses jostled each other as they paraded down the walk. High-pitched laughter rose above the general noise of the street. With their attention all on themselves, they pretended not to notice the stares they were garnishing from the crowds of men around them.

Nate's stomach roiled, but out of habit he studied each face, looking for the familiar features. He looked again at the girl in red. She was too young to be Mattie, but she looked so much like his sister that he stared. She wasn't laughing along with her friends, but glanced this way and that, a frightened rabbit surrounded by hounds.

Just as the wagon drew close to the girls, the team halted, unable to move past a freight wagon stopped in front of them. At the same time, a large, balding man approached the three women. When they saw him, their laughter died. The girl in red stepped behind her friends.

"Good afternoon, girls," the man said in a loud voice, commanding the attention of everyone in the vicinity.

The girl in purple giggled as the one in yellow, the older one, sidled up to the man, caressing his arm. "Hello, Tom."

The man shrugged her away. "That's Mr. Harris to you, Irene. What are you girls doing out here on the street this time of the afternoon?"

Irene pushed away from him as the purple girl giggled again and dangled a package in front of him. "We've been shopping, Mr. Harris. But we're on our way back to the Mystic right now." She waved at the crowd of men around them. "And maybe we'll bring some customers with us."

Nate turned his head away. The girl was inebriated, or drugged. He had seen her kind too often in his search for Mattie. Past the watching crowd, crossing the intersection of Main and Lee, were the Mac-Farlands with Olivia and Lucy. As Sarah stopped to watch the altercation, Nate's attention was pulled back.

"Fern, I want you and Irene to head back to the Mystic right now." The girls did his bidding, pushing past him. Fern and Irene waved to the men as they made their way down the boardwalk toward the Badlands, but Harris reached out and grabbed the girl in red. "Not you, Dovey." He pulled her closer than a man properly should. "I'll escort you back. We wouldn't want you to get lost now, would we?"

The look on Dovey's face as she tried to pull away from Harris was more than Nate could stand. Girls like Fern and Irene were one thing—they seemed to be having a good time—but Dovey wanted no part of Harris's plan for her.

He handed the reins to Charley. "Stay here."

Nate jumped onto the boardwalk, facing Harris. "It looks to me like the young lady doesn't want to go with you."

Over Harris's shoulder, Sarah's face caught his eye. She urged him on with a nod.

Harris looked at Nate and then turned to the surrounding crowd. He laughed with the tone of a man who knew he had the upper hand. "I don't know who you are, but this matter is none of your concern."

Dovey looked at him with Mattie's eyes, pleading. "It's all right." Her voice was almost a whisper. "Don't…"

"Do you want to go with this man?"

Harris laughed again. "Of course she does, don't you, my dear?" His right hand was in his pocket, where the outline of a derringer showed through the fabric. Harris's face grew hard. "And truly, it's none of your business." He held Nate's eyes with his own as he pushed past, pulling Dovey along with him.

The crowd closed around the pair and they disappeared. Nate pulled at the handkerchief knotted around his neck. If it had been Mattie, that confrontation might have been different. He liked to think he would have risked a shot from that derringer to get her away from Harris.

Sarah appeared at his side as the crowds of men dissipated, holding Lucy by one hand. "Do you know that girl?"

Nate picked up his niece and held her close. The little girl snuggled in on his right side, away from the scars. "No. She reminds me of someone, though."

"I applaud you for stepping in like that. Those poor girls need a champion." Sarah had a fire in her eyes he hadn't seen before. She looked down the street where Harris and Dovey had disappeared.

James and Mrs. MacFarland caught up with Sarah, Margaret ushering Olivia in front of her. "Sarah, this just isn't proper. Not at all." Margaret hissed her words, reaching out for Sarah's arm.

"But, Aunt Margaret, this is just the kind of situation Dr. Bennett told us we may run into in this wild town. Can't you see? That poor girl obviously needs someone's help."

Margaret's head switched this way and that, daring any of the men still watching the scene to say anything. "That may be true. But not here, and not now."

Sarah bit her lower lip and Nate smiled. In any other woman, he'd take that to mean that she was unsure of herself. But Sarah MacFarland? She was holding back whatever words were dancing on the tip of her tongue.

James put his arms around both women and turned them toward the city stairs that led between Lee Street and Williams, where the cabin stood.

"We need to go home, ladies. We'll meet you up above, Nate, and we'll lead you to a fine camping place."

Nate touched his fingers to the brim of his hat in answer and climbed back up onto the wagon seat, settling Lucy next to Charley. He'd hate to be on the receiving end of whatever comments were waiting to come out of Sarah's mouth.

Sarah held Olivia's hand as they climbed up the steps leading to Williams Street. Partway up, Olivia stopped to look behind them and clutched Sarah's hand even tighter.

"We're already as high as the roofs on Main Street."

Sarah looked back. Even here the noise and dirt of the mining camp seemed far away. "We need to hurry if we're going to get back to the cabin before your uncle Nate."

Olivia started climbing again, taking one step at a time. "Will we get to stay with you again tonight?"

"I think your uncle will be setting up your camp, but you can eat supper with us." Sarah paused for breath at the top of the steps. Uncle James and Aunt Margaret were far ahead, walking arm in arm past the cabins perched along the trail. Their cabin was farther on, around the bend of the hill.

It was just as well. Arguing with Aunt Margaret about the scene down below wouldn't be fruitful. She let Dr. Bennett's words bolster her strength. *Choose your battles wisely,* she had said many times during the Sunday afternoon meetings in her parlor on Beacon Hill. *We fight against a formidable enemy. One who is not willing that any of these unfortunate souls would slip from his grasping fingers.* Sarah smiled at the memory. What fire that woman had, and what a way with words!

"Is our campsite far away from you?"

Sarah looked down into Olivia's face and smoothed back a wisp of blond hair that had escaped her braid. "No, not very far at all. We'll be able to see each other often."

Olivia smiled at that and turned to follow James and Margaret. She was a sweet girl. Sarah hurried to catch up with her. "We'll have to ask your uncle about the reading lessons. At the very least, I'll be able to loan you some books to use."

"Do you have the Third Reader? That's the one I was reading from at home."

"Yes, I do. How far along are you?"

"Nearly finished. I memorized 'The Snowbird's Song' for our Christmas program, but that was our last day at school."

"I know that poem. It's all about how God takes care of the birds and provides for them."

"Yes, that's right." Olivia fiddled with the end of one braid. "But Uncle Nate said we have to take care of ourselves." She flung the braid back over her shoulder and looked up at Sarah. "Is he right? Won't God take care of us?"

Sarah stopped and faced the girl. "What makes you think He wouldn't?"

Olivia blinked her eyes, as if she was trying to hold back tears. "Mama always said He would, but then she died. If God was taking care of her, wouldn't He have rescued her from the fire?"

Feeling her own tears threatening, Sarah looked past Olivia to the buildings below them. But Olivia took her hand, bringing Sarah's gaze back to her.

"And when Lucy cries, I tell her what Mama always told me, but how can I know?"

Sarah pulled Olivia to a log lying along the trail and motioned for her to sit next to her. "One thing I always hold on to is that God promised He would be with us. Jesus said that in the book of Matthew. And God always keeps His promises." She swallowed past the lump forming in her throat. She remembered questioning God just like Olivia was doing. How did she get past the questions to the faith she had now?

"But what about Mama?"

Sarah smiled and squeezed Olivia's hand. "You can be certain that God is still taking care of your mama. I don't know why she died, and I don't know why God didn't rescue her then, but I do know that He never abandoned her. Sometimes it's very hard to understand, but you can trust that God's ways are best."

"Then Uncle Nate is wrong?"

"I'm not sure I'd say he's wrong, but maybe he doesn't understand about God the way we do."

Olivia frowned as she concentrated on Sarah's words. The sound of a wagon coming up the trail traveled toward them. It had to be Nate.

"Then I should pray for him, right?"

Sarah gave the girl a quick hug. "Yes, you can pray for him, and I will, too."

Olivia grinned and hugged her back. "I hear the wagon coming. We'll have to run to beat them to the cabin."

"Then let's run. I'll race you!"

Sarah ran as fast as she could, but Olivia was ahead of her the rest of the way to the cabin. She collapsed against a tree, breathless and gasping, but laughing at the way Olivia danced around her. Suddenly the wagon appeared around the bend of the hill, and she caught Nate watching her. At the sight of the grin on his face, she straightened up and tried to control her laughter, but she couldn't keep from smiling as Charley jumped off the wagon seat and joined Olivia in a game of tag.

Sarah glanced at Nate again, his chiseled features soft as he watched the children's game. She frowned. Noticing a handsome Westerner was far from the tasks Dr. Amelia Bennett had challenged her with when she left Boston. But Dr. Bennett had never met someone like Nate Colby.

Nate was watching her, that grin still on his face. She felt flushed and windblown from her race with Olivia.

She walked toward the wagon. "This morning Uncle James showed me a spot that might make a good camp for you. It's just a little farther along the trail. I can take you to it."

"Come on up." He patted the seat next to Lucy, where Charley had been sitting.

She climbed into the seat, taking Lucy onto her lap. The little girl stuck her thumb in her mouth and relaxed in her arms.

"Olivia and Charley are fast runners. I'm glad I'm not trying to catch them." She glanced up again. He shifted in his seat and pulled at his neckerchief. Were his scars bothering him?

"They like to play tag, that's for sure. Almost every night on the trail they'd start a game like that. I don't know where they get the energy."

Nate clucked to the horses, and the team went on up the trail and through a stand of young pine trees.

"There it is, to the left there. Do you see the creek, and the clearing next to it?"

A stream tumbled down from the hills in a narrow gulch of its own before falling over the rimrock and joining Whitewood Creek below. As the creek reached this spot, it slowed, forming a little eddy. A small meadow with lush grass filled the rest of the space.

"Here it is. This is where we get our water. Uncle James says the stream will dry up to almost nothing later in the summer, but it's so much better than going down to get water at the bottom of the gulch."

Nate turned the horses into the meadow and then circled around so the wagon rested parallel to the creek, up against the rising hill behind it.

"This will make a good camp. Plenty of grass for the animals and convenient with the water close by."

Nate jumped to the ground and then reached back for Lucy. Before Sarah could jump down on her own, he turned to help her. She rested her hands on his shoulders, and he grasped her waist, guiding her to the soft grass as she hopped down. As soon as she was steady, he moved his hands away. The place where his hands had rested burned with the memory of his touch.

Sarah stepped away from him, her mind a blank. What had they been talking about?

"This is a lovely sound with the water falling and

jumping down the slope." She turned back to look at him. "How long do you think you'll be here?"

Nate started unhitching the horses. "As long as it takes to find a homestead and file on it."

"I'll enjoy having you and the children living close by for a while."

"I know the children will like it, too."

"It will give us all an opportunity to learn to know each other better." She bit her lip. Her words sounded forward, even to her own ears.

Now would be the perfect time to bring up loaning her reading books to the children, and she had promised Olivia. Then she saw something moving on his shoulder. A daddy longlegs spider was creeping toward his collar.

She stepped close to him, and Nate froze. His gaze made her knees quiver. She took a deep breath of leather, pine and horses. Swiping her hand across his jacket sleeve, she brushed the culprit to the ground.

"There," she said, stepping back again. "I was afraid that spider would crawl down your shirt, as fast as he was going."

She cast about in her mind to find the words to mention how she could help the children with their reading, but he turned back to the horses and the moment was gone. Sarah balled her hands into fists at her own cowardice.

"I'll go get the children. I know they'll want to help you set up camp."

She nearly ran back to the cabin, brushing past the young pines at the edge of the trail. What was it about Nate Colby that made her lose her senses when she was around him?

* * *

With Charley's and Olivia's help, camp setup was quick. Of course, they had all had plenty of practice on the trail. Nate had built a lean-to for a quick shelter for the horses and the mule while the children set stones in a ring for their fire.

"Since we're going to be camping here for a long time, we can make it look real nice," Olivia had said.

"Do you think it will take me that long to find our homestead?" Nate tied the lean-to poles together with strips of rawhide. No use wasting nails on such a temporary structure.

Olivia had looked toward the MacFarland cabin then, but hadn't answered. She wanted to stay near Sarah for as long as possible, and Nate didn't blame her. He had finished the lean-to in silence, his stomach roiling. If he was ever tempted to look for a woman to spend the rest of his life with, Sarah MacFarland fit the bill. But a woman like Sarah deserved a real man, not someone like him.

The thought came back to him again after supper, while the children helped Margaret with the chores. James had gone back to the mining camp for a meeting with his banker.

Nate and Sarah sat on the bench next to the cabin door. Nate whittled on a bit of pine, watching the evening darken the trail under the trees. As the hour grew later, the noise from the mining camp increased.

Sarah cleared her throat and he turned toward her.

"I was talking with Olivia, and she's anxious to start her schooling again."

"I told you, I'm going to see to their education."

She turned to face him. "Oh, I know. But I can help."

Nate tapped the bit of wood against his knee. These busybodies never accepted his answer, did they?

"The children are going to stay with me." He could feel his teeth grinding.

"Of course they are. What I'm offering is to loan them books and to help tutor if they need it. Lucy is old enough to start learning to read."

"Do you think she'll ever be able to learn anything?" he interrupted her. Women like her never came up with practical plans. She knew what Lucy was like.

Sarah sat in silence for a moment. "We'll never know if we don't try." Her voice was gentle.

"I've tried everything I can think of, but she hasn't spoken—hasn't hardly noticed anyone else is around—ever since her ma and pa died."

"I know about that. The children told us what happened."

Nate didn't want her pity, but he waited for it. Waited for the condescending comments he had heard from the church people back in Michigan, about how the fire that killed his brother was God's will. He couldn't have done anything. God would help him get through the hard times. He shoved at a pile of pine needles with his boot. What god would put him through this misery?

He waited, but Sarah sat in silence. Glancing at her, he saw that she was watching the ground in front of his foot, and then looked out over the gulch, where tendrils of smoke rose from the buildings and tents on Main Street. She sighed and then looked at his face, and when she saw him looking at her, she gave him a little smile.

"Uncle James always says that when one direction

isn't working, maybe it's time to turn around and try something else."

A snort escaped. "Something else? How? What?"

She shrugged her slim shoulders. "I really don't know. But I know who does."

Ah, here it came. The preaching. He braced himself for the argument, but she only laid her hand on his.

"You'll figure it out."

"You're not going to tell me to just pray and the answer will come?"

She shrugged again. "Praying will help, and God will answer, but I'm not telling you anything you don't already know."

He turned back to the pine needles. He had scuffed them aside so that the yellow quartz of the rimrock showed underneath. He knew about God, all right.

"What I know is that I could have done something to save Andrew and Jenny, but I didn't. The children think I tried to go back in the house, but I know better. I could have tried harder—I should have tried harder to rescue them, but I froze. Andrew needed me and I did nothing to help him."

She started to say something, but he kept going. "God stopped caring about me when I abandoned my parents to go to war, and He sure doesn't care about me now." He stood and walked toward the edge of the gulch. Anywhere to be away from those violet eyes. "We're on our own, and the children will survive or not because of me. Me and no one else. They're my responsibility and I'll take care of them." He watched the haze of smoke shift in a fitful breeze.

Somehow, he'd take care of them.

He heard her walk up beside him. "You're not alone, Nate."

Her voice was so soft, he almost missed the words.

"You may think God has left you on your own, but you're here, and we're here." She motioned toward the gulch. "Like it or not, you're part of this community, just because you're here. Anytime you need help, you'll get it." She turned to face him. "And the children will survive, with or without you. They may be scarred, but they're ready to face the future."

He looked down at the town. Rough and dirty, like an open wound cut in the wilderness. Like the open wound in his heart. What future could she see for them?

Sarah pushed some hair back with one hand and twisted it into her bun, all without looking away from the scene below them. She was beautiful. Disheveled from playing with the children, tired from a long day of work, and yet she glowed with beauty. She glanced at him and smiled before turning back to watch the lamps being lit in the mining camp. Lanterns on poles lined Main Street, and one by one they came to life.

A gnawing hunger prodded him. A future? The long-forgotten dream pulled at him. A home. Not just a ranch, not just a cabin in the wilderness, but the kind of home Pa had made when he married Ma. With a woman like Sarah, could a future like that be a possibility?

But how could he even think that when he knew what kind of man he really was? He chafed his arms with his hands, trying to ease the tense muscles. No woman would marry a coward.

"What you did today, with that girl—that was very brave."

"It was foolhardy. That man—Harris—he could have shot me down right there on the street and no one would have thought twice about it. I poked my nose into his business."

She turned to face him again. "You said she reminded you of someone."

"My sister, Mattie." He swallowed. Hard. He had failed Mattie, too.

Sarah laid a soft hand on his sleeve. "Tell me about her."

Nate shrugged, careful not to disturb her touch. "Mattie ran away from home soon after I went to war. When Andrew and I got home again, she was gone. Ma and Pa were in the churchyard. Andrew moved on, married Jenny, started his life. But I couldn't leave it alone."

He paused, listening to the sounds drifting up the hill from the saloons.

"Andrew and Jenny said I'd always have a home with them, but I can't—couldn't—stay in one place. Not while Mattie was out there somewhere."

"Do you have any idea where she went?"

Nate pulled at his neckerchief. "I found out she went with some man to Saint Louis. And then to Saint Joe. And the man abandoned her there. After that she headed farther west, to the mining towns in California, Colorado, Montana."

Sarah listened without a word.

"I'd spend months traveling, searching for any trace of her. I'd show her picture around, and people would tell me they had seen her here or there. Then I'd lose track again and I'd head back to Michigan. But it wouldn't last. A few months later I'd be off looking for her again."

"How long have you been searching?"

Nate thought back over the span of time since the war. "Twelve years, off and on. I lost the drive to look any more the last couple years. I'm afraid I've lost her."

He couldn't say that he feared she must be dead. Gone from him forever.

"And she is a saloon girl?"

Nate managed to get one word past the lump in his throat. "Yes."

Her hand on his arm tightened. "You're just the person I've been looking for."

Nate shook his head to clear the fog of memories. "What do you mean?"

"I've been looking—praying—for someone who feels as strongly as I do about these poor saloon girls. They need my help, Nate. You can be the one to help me contact them, to tell them about the school I'm starting for them."

He took a step back. "You're planning to teach the children and the saloon girls together?"

She laughed, but he couldn't tell if she was laughing at him or at her own ludicrous idea.

"Oh no. Of course not."

Nate felt his shoulders relax.

"I would teach the saloon girls at a different time. Like at night, or on Saturday morning."

"Sarah, you know these girls work at night, don't you?"

She waved her hand in the air. "Don't you think they'd rather go to school and learn a skill that will get them out of that life?"

Nate rubbed at his whiskers. "You're assuming they want to leave the life they have now."

"Well, maybe some of them don't. But you saw that girl this afternoon. The one they called Dovey. You can't tell me she isn't looking for a way out."

Dovey's eyes haunted him. Had Mattie longed for a way out of the trap she ended up in? Had she wished for someone to help her? He sighed.

"What kinds of things would you teach them?"

"Oh, how to read and write, if they don't already know. And a skill, like sewing or housekeeping. Dr. Bennett says—"

"Hold on there. Who is this Dr. Bennett?"

"She's just the most wonderful person!" Sarah paced back and forth, her hands animated. "Dr. Amelia Bennett is a medical doctor, trained in London. I joined her Committee for the Betterment of Women last autumn and learned so much about the importance of education in a person's life. Not only children, but adults, too. Dr. Bennett says that even the poorest, most unfortunate woman can rise above her circumstances with the right education. She says that the reason there is poverty and disease in the world is because there isn't enough education."

Nate lifted one foot onto a nearby stump and leaned on his knee. "And you're going to fix all the evils of the world by educating saloon girls?"

That laugh again. "Of course not. Only the evils of Deadwood."

"Sarah."

She stepped close enough that he could see her smile in the growing dusk. "Don't worry about me. I know the evils that exist down there won't be eradicated in a year or two. It's a process. But someone has to do something, don't you think?"

Nate gazed down on the roofs of the saloons of the Badlands. If Mattie was down there, he'd be doing something, but he had no idea what.

"I'll help you, but only to give a chance to those girls who want it. Most of them have chosen the life they're in for a reason."

Sarah looked beyond him, down the trail. "Uncle James is coming. Please don't say anything to him, or to Aunt Margaret. Not until I have a chance to make some plans."

"All right, I won't."

She squeezed his arm again, gently this time. "Thank you, Nate. I'd better go inside and see if Aunt Margaret needs help with the children."

Even in the dusky light, Nate couldn't help following her with his eyes as she opened the door and stepped into the cabin. Had he just promised to help Sarah in her wild scheme to help saloon girls? What was it about that woman that made him lose his senses when he was around her?

## Chapter Five

Two weeks later, Sarah had nine children enrolled in the academy, all of them between six and twelve years old. Any boy older than twelve was already working on a mining claim, and the girls worked just as hard in stores or in one of the many boardinghouses that had appeared as summer approached and the mining camp's population exploded.

Nine children, even without the Colbys. Nate insisted on taking his children with him on his daily hunts for land, sometimes even camping out overnight if they had traveled too far. When she had protested, reminding him of the dangers, he had assured her that with the finer weather, and the new peace treaty signed with the Indians, the only danger they needed to worry about was going too far up the wrong gulch and having to backtrack.

Still, Sarah smiled to herself. The Academy for Young Children, tucked away down the alley behind the church on Lee Street, was thriving. It might be too early to count the school a success after only one full week of classes, but they were doing well. Very well.

At least, until today. She tapped the end of her pencil on her desk. Only the Woodrow children had come to school this morning. The Fergusons had sent word that their four children wouldn't be attending school until the summer was over, which she could almost understand. The Fergusons had a claim in Two-Bit Gulch, and with the warm weather and long days, they needed all four of their boys to help work. But the Radcliffes, with their two girls, would certainly let her know if something was wrong, wouldn't they?

With only three students, she had given the Woodrow children permission to work their arithmetic problems on the big chalkboard at the front of the room. Laura Woodrow finished her sums first. A bright nine-year-old, she was quick with both reading and arithmetic. Sarah wished there was a way for her to meet Olivia. The two girls would be good friends.

Bernie, Laura's older brother, raced to finish his work as quickly as his sister.

"Slow down, Bernie. You're making too many errors." Sarah leaned over him to erase his last problem, scribbled so quickly she couldn't even read it. "Now, write that one over again. And take your time."

The eleven-year-old sighed but wrote the numbers again.

Seven-year-old Alan, the youngest of the family to attend school, slowly wrote his numbers on the board, his tongue stuck through the gap in his front teeth as he concentrated. When he finished writing the number six, he turned to Sarah.

"Is that right, Miss MacFarland?" His missing teeth gave him a lisp, so when he said her name, it came out "Mith MacFarland."

"Yes, Alan, that's just right. You can go back to your seat now. As soon as Bernie is done, we'll have our history lesson."

Sarah retrieved the history book from the shelf behind her desk and opened it to the page they ended on yesterday. She brought her chair to the front, where she could sit facing the children as she read.

Where were the Radcliffe girls?

Bernie joined his brother and sister on their benches and Sarah started reading. The narrative told the story of the Battle of Hastings in 1066, and the children listened, spellbound.

When she finished the chapter, she closed the book and looked at her watch, pinned to her shirtwaist.

"It's dinner time. I'll see you in an hour."

The children left quietly enough, but as soon as the boys were out the door, Bernie shouted to Alan that he would race him home, and they were gone.

Sarah returned the history book to the shelf and reached for her shawl. She and Uncle James walked home for dinner together. She hoped he was ready.

Just then noise from the front room of the building caught her attention. Someone had come in and was talking to Uncle James. The door between the two rooms opened and Celia and Nancy Radcliffe ran in, followed by their mother.

"Miss MacFarland," Celia said. "We've come to tell you goodbye."

"Goodbye?" Sarah glanced at their mother, Tina, who nodded, her eyes red from crying.

"I'm afraid so. We're going back East and only stopped here to make our farewells."

"But why?" The Radcliffes had only been in Deadwood for a month. Surely they wouldn't be giving up already.

Tina glanced at the girls, who were listening to their conversation. "My husband feels it is best for the girls to live closer to their grandparents." She turned to the girls. "All right, you've said goodbye. Go back to the other room with your pa."

Sarah gave each of the girls a hug. "God go with you both." She smiled as she said it, but she could feel the tears standing in her eyes. She would miss these pupils.

After the girls closed the door between the two rooms, she turned to Tina. "There's more to this story, isn't there?"

Tina nodded and Sarah laid her hand on the other woman's arm. In just a few weeks they had become good friends, and now she had to say farewell so soon?

"What is wrong?"

"There were men who came to our claim last night. I had the girls in the cabin with me, but I could hear them talking to Will. They threatened..." Tina took a deep breath, holding her handkerchief to her lips. "They threatened such awful things if Will didn't give them the deed to his claim."

"You must tell the sheriff about this. That isn't right."

"Will doesn't want to take a chance." Tina leaned closer as she lowered her voice. "Those men work for Tom Harris, the man who runs the saloon in the Badlands. I'm afraid of what they might do if Will fights them."

"Then you must leave. But where will you go?"

Tina wiped a tear off her cheek. "We'll go live with my parents. They still have their farm, and Pa will let

Will work with him until he can find something else."
She blew her nose. "We had such dreams when we
came here. Times are so hard. There were no jobs in
Chicago, and nowhere else to turn. Will thought he
could find enough gold to start over. That was all he
wanted."

Sarah pulled her friend into her arms. "I'll miss you.
And I'll miss the girls."

Tina gave her a swift, tight hug. "I'll miss you, too.
I have to leave. I told Will I'd only take a minute to say
goodbye. You're a good friend, Sarah."

They went into the front room, where Uncle James
and Will were shaking hands.

"I'm sorry to see you go, and your family. Deadwood is a rough place, and we need families like yours
to help tame it and make it into a town we can be proud
of. But I understand. I'd be going back East, too, if I
were in your shoes." Uncle James shook hands with
Celia and Nancy, while Sarah gave Tina a last hug.

"Be careful on your way," she said to Will.

"We're traveling with one of the bull trains. It's safer
that way."

Sarah stood in the doorway of the church, watching as the family climbed into their wagon and set
off down the street. They turned onto Main and were
gone from sight.

"Well, that leaves only the Woodrow children in the
academy." Sarah turned back inside.

"You're not giving up, are you?"

Sarah shook her head. "We'll keep going. When autumn comes and more families move back into town
from their claims, we'll grow again. Until then, the

Woodrow children will have me to themselves." Sarah smiled at Uncle James, hoping she looked brave.

Then she remembered. With fewer students, she would have time to plan an institute for the saloon girls.

"Don't worry. I have plenty of projects to keep me busy."

Sarah dressed carefully the next day after their noon meal, slipping her calling cards into her reticule, along with the list Uncle James had prepared for her. There were almost a dozen families in town that had school-age children, and she planned to visit each one in her quest to build up the numbers of students.

She peered at her image in the small mirror and straightened her shoulders. Her green silk day dress might be a bit warm for today, but it was the best she owned. Making a good first impression was para-mount. Dr. Bennett had drilled that into her. She pinched her cheeks to bring some color into them and picked up her reticule.

"I'll be back in time for supper, Aunt Margaret," she said as she opened the door.

"I wish I could go with you, but this suit of your uncle's needs to be finished before church tomorrow."

"I understand, and it's all right. I'll be able to find my way around town, and I'll be home long before dark."

Sarah closed the door behind her and started down the trail toward the Lee Street steps. The first of the families on her list were the Samuelsons. Uncle James had given her directions to their house in Ingleside, on the other side of the gulch.

But as she started down the steps she paused. It was

still early in the afternoon. Perhaps now would be a good time to call on some of the ladies in the Badlands. She would still have time to visit the names on her list afterward.

She smoothed her skirt and continued down to Main Street. This time of the day would be the best for visiting the Badlands, she argued, trying to convince herself of the wisdom of her plan. The town should be quiet, and the girls would be...unoccupied. Her face heated at the thought she might find one of them working, even at this early hour. But that wouldn't happen. Evil deeds were done under cover of darkness, weren't they? As long as it was still midday, she wouldn't run into any trouble.

As she turned left on Main, toward the Badlands, Sarah took a deep breath, but her hands still shook. She grasped her reticule in both hands and took one step, then another. She stopped to look in the window of a dry goods store. Bolts of fabric lined the shelves behind the counter. Perhaps she should buy fabric for a new dress instead.

Dr. Bennett's voice rang in her head. *You're just delaying what you know needs to be done.*

Sarah squared her shoulders and continued down the boardwalk.

As she descended the steps to Lower Main Street, the crowd grew larger and rowdier. Uncle James had said the men loitering in town were looking for jobs in the mines, since most of the tracts near last year's successful strikes had already been claimed. Until then, though, they idled in the streets, gambling and drinking, and who knew what else. Sarah walked near the buildings, away from the mudhole that passed for a

street, careful to avoid eye contact with anyone. She
had been foolhardy to think the camp would be quiet
after the dinner hour. Should she turn back and head
to the calmer neighborhoods?

Then ahead she saw the largest of the saloons that
comprised the Badlands. Girls in bright dresses lined
the rail of the balcony above the street, leaning out
and calling to the men below them. Sarah's steps faltered. Their laughter was brittle, their words coarse.
She steeled herself. Dr. Bennett had said these girls
were calling out for help, that they were longing for a
savior and that moving to Deadwood was her opportunity to rescue them.

The girl on the end of the balcony spotted her. Sarah
turned her eyes away.

"Hey, lady!"

The girl's salutation caught the attention of her
friends and several of the men in the street. Sarah's
mouth went dry.

The girl leaned over the balcony rail toward her,
and Sarah looked up, then away again. Sarah had never
seen so much of a person's figure in public.

"Hey, lady! What are you staring at?"

Several of the other girls came to watch.

"Maybe she's here to join in the fun," one of them
said.

"Not dressed like that she isn't," said another. "Hey,
sweetheart, come on up here. Trixie will help you find
a new frock to wear."

The girls all laughed, and the men joined in.

"That's what the Mystic needs, all right," called out
a man in the crowd, "some new blood."

Another of the men stepped up onto the boardwalk

next to her, mud caking his boots and trousers. Sarah took a step back.

"Look at how shy she is, boys." The man spit onto the boards near her skirt and leaned closer, lifting his hat brim with a dirty thumb. "What do you say, girly? Come on in and I'll buy you a drink."

More of the men stepped onto to the boardwalk next to him, crowding close.

Sarah's stomach plummeted. She could not—she would not—get sick right here in the middle of this crowd. She scanned the ring of laughing faces, looking for someone familiar. Someone friendly. Her hands shook so hard her reticule nearly slipped from her fingers.

Heart pounding, she took a deep breath and looked up and away from the crowd of men circling her to the girls on the balcony. Only one face mirrored her panic. Dovey stood in the background, behind the girls lining the rail. Their eyes met, and then the girl turned and disappeared into the building.

Turning on her heel, Sarah pushed past the men crowding behind her and headed for the wooden stairs leading to Upper Main. She wouldn't cry. She wouldn't faint. She would just go home. Her chin quivered and she walked faster. The men roared with laughter as she went, but footsteps sounded behind her, along with coarse comments from the men who still followed her.

They were dogs, all of them. Worse than dogs. Her chin stilled and a rod of steel formed in her spine. Suddenly she was angry. She turned on her heel, stamping her foot as she faced her pursuers.

"Leave me be."

The three men stopped but swayed. They were as drunk as the proverbial skunk. Smelled like it, too.

"Ho, girly. No need to be so sassy. We're just looking for some fun."

A tall man appeared at her side and she heard a pistol cocked. "You heard the lady. Leave her be."

Sarah bit her lip to keep from crying out in relief. Nate. Swirling gray clouded her vision and she took a deep breath to keep from fainting. Nate was here. She was safe.

"You wait your turn, fella. We saw her first."

Nate moved his hand with a slight motion and planted a bullet at the men's feet. "I said, leave her be. Turn around and go back where you came from."

The men backed away.

"All right, all right. There's plenty more to choose from. You can have her this time." The man pointed toward Sarah. "But if you ever get hankering for the kind of fun a real man can give you, just head on down to the Mystic. I'll be lookin' for you." He grinned and then slipped away with his friends as Nate lifted his pistol again.

Sarah leaned against the closest storefront. Beyond Nate were his horse and Charley's mule, with the children perched on their backs. They had seen everything. Heard the coarse language. Witnessed Nate nearly shooting those men.

She started to slip down the wall, but Nate grabbed her arm and set her upright again.

"What in the world do you think you're doing?"

Nate guided Sarah over to the edge of the walk where the children waited. They watched with wide eyes. Olivia looked as if she might cry, but the only telltale sign was her blotchy cheeks.

At least Sarah didn't resist him. If she lit into him the way he had seen her face down those coyotes, he wasn't sure what he'd do. He patted Lucy's leg as she perched on Scout's back and smiled at Charley and Olivia to reassure them, then turned to Sarah.

"What do you think you were doing back there? You shouldn't be in this part of the camp alone. Ever."

"I thought I'd invite some of the ladies to my school." Her voice faded away as she glanced back down Main Street toward the Mystic.

Nate resisted the urge to try to shake some sense into her. Didn't she know how dangerous going to the Mystic by herself was? But watching her face as she regained her composure, he could tell she did. Or she did now.

"I'll take you home. We're going up that way now." He reached up and pulled Lucy off Scout's saddle. "Charley, you and Olivia take Scout and the mule back to our campsite. Lucy and I will walk with Miss Mac-Farland."

Charley took Scout's reins and started up Main Street with Olivia hanging on behind him. The mule made her sure-footed way up the slope between Lower and Upper Main, climbing past the mine in the middle of the thoroughfare.

"Will they be all right by themselves?" Sarah's voice shook a little.

"They'll be fine. Upper Main isn't as crowded as it is here, and Loretta will make sure they get home safely." That was one thing he could say for that mule. She always took care of Charley.

Nate shifted Lucy onto his left hip and felt Sarah's slim hand slip into the crook of his elbow as they started up the steps to Upper Main Street. She relaxed as they put distance between them and the Mystic.

"Where have you been today?"

Nate hitched Lucy farther up on his hip. "We've been scouting out land for our homestead."

"Did you find anything?"

"We looked at a few places, but the problem is water. Everywhere there's a creek, miners have made their claims already. But on our way back into town, one man told me about a place near Two-Bit Gulch. The prospectors didn't find any color there last year, so they've abandoned it. We'll head that way next week."

They passed the dry goods store and the newspaper office and then turned up toward the steps leading toward home. Sarah's face was thoughtful as they walked.

"You aren't planning to go back to the Badlands again, are you?"

She looked at him, startled. "Of course not." She chewed on her bottom lip. "But how can I get word to those girls about the school?"

"Give it some time. Sometimes people are a lot like horses. They have to figure out if they can trust you and if you have anything worthwhile to offer before they let you approach."

"And how will they find out?"

"I'll pass the word around, and they'll hear about it. It may take a while, but eventually, if they want to, they'll come find you."

"Meanwhile, I have the academy to think about."

She sighed. "But I refuse to be discouraged. Dr. Bennett's ideas are sound. I just don't want to let her down."

"Your Dr. Bennett doesn't know what you're up against here in Deadwood. Has she ever been outside of Boston?"

"I don't think she's ever been to a place like this." She turned toward him. "But it all sounds so logical and reasonable. Wouldn't anyone want to make their lives better?"

Nate's thoughts went to Mattie, to the places he had followed her to. She could have come home at any time. She could have turned to anyone for help. In Denver there had been a mission society that was trying to do just what Sarah had planned. Mattie could have gone to them during the months she was there. But no, she moved on again, just weeks before he made his way to the city.

"I think Dr. Bennett has that part wrong. For some reason, there are some who are happy enough where they are. It isn't logical, and it isn't reasonable."

"Uncle James would say that they've turned their backs on God."

Was that what had happened to Mattie? She turned her back on her family, but did she turn her back on God, also?

When they reached the top of the steps, Charley and Olivia were far ahead of them, just disappearing around the last bend before the MacFarlands' cabin.

"What about you?" Sarah's voice trailed, as if she was asking the question of the air, but she glanced at him, waiting for his answer. "Are you happy where you are?"

Nate let Lucy down as he thought of how to answer

her. Lucy took his hand and walked next to him, compliant as always.

"There are things I would change."

"Like what?"

He nodded toward Lucy. "The effect of the last six months. I'd change that if I could."

"Anything else?"

"I'd have the ranch going already. The children need a home again, but it's going to take months just to build up a herd of cattle so we have money coming in. And time to build a house to live in." He slowed his steps so Lucy could keep up. "If I had time, I could catch some mustangs and break them, too. Then I'd have remounts to sell to the army post at Camp Sturgis."

"But you need help."

"I mean to do it on my own, with Charley's help."

"Charley is still a boy. You can't expect him to do a man's work." She bit her lip.

"Go ahead. Finish what you were going to say."

She tightened the hand that lay in his elbow. "I was going to say he needs to be in school, but we've already talked about that." A few more steps took them around the bend, and the MacFarlands' cabin was in front of them. "Bring the children over to the cabin tonight. I can help them with a lesson in reading, and in arithmetic, too. I could spend some time with them each evening, until you're ready to move to your homestead."

Nate stopped and turned toward her. She looked up at him expectantly. The thought of teaching the children had wiped away any traces of the trouble she'd had in the mining camp this afternoon. He had to laugh at her eagerness.

"All right. I don't want to keep the children from

learning. And I can see how you do it, so that when we do move out to the homestead, I'll know how to teach them myself."

She bounced a little on her toes, the way Olivia did when she was excited. "Thank you, Nate." Her smile was beautiful. "I know the children will appreciate it, too."

# Chapter Six

The next Friday afternoon, Sarah sent the Woodrow children home early. Their mother, Lucretia, had requested the early release, and since they were the only children in school right now, it didn't make a difference.

She gathered books and slates from the benches of her schoolroom. Three children came to the academy. Three, out of the dozens she had seen around town.

She plopped the books on the table she used as a desk and started erasing the chalkboard. The children in this town ran wild, or worked with their families, like Olivia, Charley and Lucy. But even her visits to the homes of those families hadn't convinced them to send the children to her school any more than Nate Colby had been convinced. How could she communicate the importance of education when people were trying to earn enough to feed their children?

Uncle James popped his head in the door. "Are you almost ready to go? Margaret will be glad to see us home early today."

"Nearly. I just need to finish cleaning the chalkboard." Sarah wrung water out of a rag she kept for cleaning and wiped the dusty board. "I heard you talking to someone earlier. Do you think he might come to services on Sunday?"

"He might." James took the broom and started sweeping the floor. "He was certainly a greenhorn, just off the stage and ready to strike it rich. Someone had sold him a bill of goods, though, making him think gold nuggets are lying on the ground waiting to be picked up."

"How did he end up here?"

"Nate Colby sent him."

Sarah turned and stared at her uncle. "Nate? Why?"

"Nate and I have talked about the problem of these young men who are being swindled by thieves back East who call themselves 'outfitters.' I asked him to send them to me when he ran across them. Most of them, like this young man, are naive and easy prey for confidence men."

"What did you tell him?"

"The truth. He said he might stay in town anyway. There are plenty of businesses hiring eager young men who can keep the gold fever at bay."

Sarah rinsed her rag and tackled the dusty board again. She had spent every evening this past week with Olivia and Charley around the small table in the cabin while Nate sat with James and Margaret next to the fireplace. He may have been visiting with them, but she often caught him watching her. There was something about the man that wouldn't get out of her mind. She rubbed at a chalk mark with more force than necessary. She had never been one to be easily swayed by a handsome face. But no, it wasn't only his appearance, it was the gentle way he cared for those children.

Even if he was wrong in how he did it. Olivia and Charley were so eager to learn. What a difference it would make if she taught them here at the academy instead of an hour around a table at night!

Sarah took the bucket to the door and tossed the dirty water into the gutter. As she did every day, she looked past the crowded streets and crooked roofs of the neighboring buildings to the towering hills beyond. She let the bucket dangle and leaned against the door frame as she gazed at the white rocks at the top of Boot Hill. What would it be like to climb that mountain someday? What dangers lurked up there? She had often heard the scream of a mountain lion at night, and there were rumors of bands of Sioux warriors combing the hills for miners foolish enough to strike out on their own—although Nate still maintained that the danger from the Indians was over.

The clunk of the broom handle against the wall brought her thoughts back to Uncle James.

"The floor is clean," James said, taking the bucket from her hand. "Let's go."

Sarah gathered her books and waited outside the door while Uncle James locked it behind them. He had tried leaving the church unlocked one afternoon, but the next morning he had to evict a man who had taken advantage of the empty building and set up a saloon overnight. Since then, his motto had been, "We will be as harmless as doves but as wise as serpents," and he had been careful to lock the door each night.

Lee Street, where the church was located, was more of an alley than a street. Sarah had learned to step carefully around muddy spots and debris in the thoroughfare and to avoid looking at men. Any man. She didn't want a repeat of last Saturday. That experience was the only thing that kept her from pressing on with her plans for the saloon girls.

She held tightly to Uncle James's arm and kept her gaze on the path in front of her. Somehow, she must find a way to contact the girls who would welcome her help.

At the bottom of the Lee Street steps, Uncle James paused. "I need to have a few words with someone, and I want to pick up a copy of the *Black Hills Gazette*. Will you find your way home all right without me?"

Sarah always felt safer once she was on the steps. "I'll be fine. We'll see you at supper."

When she reached the cabin, Margaret was making sourdough bread, and Lucy sat at the table, her thumb in her mouth, watching.

"Hello, Lucy." Sarah gave the little girl a hug, but as usual, there was no response. She hoped the child would come out of her silence on her own once love and stability returned to her life. Sarah prayed she would, but meanwhile, she felt it was important to treat Lucy as if everything was normal.

"You're getting to be quite the hand with that bread, Aunt Margaret." She sat next to Lucy and the little girl climbed onto her lap.

Margaret pushed a strand of hair out of her face. "I can't believe it, myself. If you had told me a month ago that I'd be able to cook in this kitchen, I'd have thought you were destined for Bedlam."

"Uncle James always says that where God calls us to work, He equips us for that work." Sarah buried her nose in Lucy's curls. She was so sweet it was easy to love her.

No, not love. She'd promised herself long ago that she would never love again, never leave herself open to the aching grief when death or other circumstances took loved ones away. Still, that didn't keep her from giving Lucy another quick hug.

"James certainly had his work cut out for him when it came to convincing me that this was my calling." Margaret kneaded the stiff dough and then patted it into a circle.

"I know you didn't want to come west."

Margaret stopped patting the dough and looked at Sarah. "I'm ashamed of myself. I acted like a spoiled child, when I should have known James knew exactly what he was doing. I don't know what God has planned for our future, but I'm so glad we're here now."

"What has caused you to change your mind?"

Margaret smiled at her and then placed the loaf of bread into the reflector oven standing in front of the fireplace. "It was the sunrise last week. I stepped outside, and the sky was glorious, with the sun still below the tops of the mountains and the sky all shades of pink, orange and purple. It reminded me of the verses from Psalm 139, 'If I take the wings of the morning, and dwell in the uttermost parts of the sea, even there shall Thy hand lead me, and Thy right hand shall hold me.' I knew then that I am where God wants me to be. Here, in Deadwood, at this time." She smiled at Sarah again. "There is nothing that compares with that feeling. I knew the same thing when I married James, and also when he found you in the orphanage and wanted to bring you home."

She put her floury hand over Sarah's. "We have been so blessed. I'll always thank God for bringing you to us."

Sarah turned her hand so she could squeeze Margaret's. She remembered that cold November day when a strange man had appeared at the orphanage looking for her. Her! She had given up hope of ever being adopted long before, and by the time Uncle James had come she was seventeen years old and making plans for life outside the orphanage.

Her eyes misted over as she remembered her hopelessness. She had no experience, except her years as a teacher's helper. But there was no money to further her education, no positions open to her except working as a domestic. She knew she only had two choices—spend the rest of her life working in other people's homes or find her own way on the streets. If not for God's grace and His plan to bring Uncle James home at the right time, she could very easily have ended up like one of the girls in the Badlands.

But then Uncle James had come. He knew her name and had been searching for her through all the orphanages in the state. Papa's brother had been called to the mission field as a young man, before Sarah had even been born, and when he returned from China eighteen years later, looking for her became his first priority. Meanwhile, he had married Margaret, and they became a family of three.

The only problem was that no one had asked her if she wanted to live with these strangers. At seventeen, she thought she was an adult and didn't need a family. The memory of those stormy years still haunted her. But somehow they had gotten through that time. James and Margaret were the only people Sarah had made an exception for. She loved them, but only because they had persevered in their love for her. They had shown her what God's love was like.

"How did you end up with Lucy today?"

"I forgot to tell you, Nate found his ranch! He took Olivia and Charley with him to file the papers at the land office. I convinced him the errand would be too much for Lucy and we'd get along just fine this afternoon." She caressed the little girl's head. "And we've had a wonderful time, haven't we, dear?"

Lucy looked up at Aunt Margaret but didn't say anything.

Margaret filled the teakettle and hung it over the fire. "I thought we could all go out to look at Nate's new homestead. What would you think of an outing tomorrow?"

"That sounds wonderful. We haven't been outside of the mining camp since the stage brought us here." Sarah turned Lucy sideways on her lap so she could look into her face. "What do you think, Lucy? Do you want to have an adventure tomorrow?" Lucy's expression didn't change. Sarah gave her a hug. "We should pack a picnic."

"Oh, yes, that would be fun." Margaret poured cups of tea for the two of them and paused, the teapot in her hand. "Do you think Lucy would like some cambric tea?"

Sarah felt a slight inclination of the little girl's head.

"Let's try some."

Margaret got another cup and poured a small amount of tea in it. Then she retrieved the can of milk Uncle James used for his coffee from the cold box he had made outside the back door, and poured it in the cup. "A bit of sugar to sweeten it and we're all set." She placed the cup in front of Lucy, and they both watched her to see what she would do.

Lucy removed her thumb from her mouth and took the cup in both hands. She tasted one swallow and then another. She looked up at Margaret, grinned just as wide as any five-year-old with a treat and took another drink. Sarah exchanged triumphant looks with Margaret.

"It looks like we have a girl who likes cambric tea." Sarah felt like shouting but only took a sip of her own tea. She could celebrate Lucy's smile later.

Sarah and Margaret planned what to fix for the next day's picnic while Aunt Margaret worked on her knitting. As suppertime drew near, Charley came into the cabin.

"Uncle Nate asked me to come get Lucy."

Sarah helped the little girl slide off her lap. "You're home already?"

"We got back a little while ago. Supper is cooking, and the horses are taken care of, too."

Margaret looked up from her knitting. "I thought you might eat supper here tonight."

Charley shook his head. "Uncle Nate said you'd want us to, but we're fine on our own."

"We need to discuss plans for tomorrow." Aunt Margaret laid her knitting in her basket.

Sarah stood and took her shawl from the hook by the door. "I'll go back with the children and tell Nate what we've planned. I'll be home by the time supper is ready."

When she reached the campsite with Charley and Lucy, Nate looked surprised, but happy to see her. The camp was neat and orderly. The pine needles had even been swept away from around the fire ring Nate had built with rocks, and the horses stood under a shelter of pine boughs. Nate had made a home in the wilderness. Was there anything he couldn't do?

"I hear you're an official homesteader now."

He grinned, causing her stomach to flip. It did that too often these days.

"We sure are."

"You should see our ranch, Miss Sarah," Charley said from his seat next to the fire. "Uncle Nate says the horses are going to love it."

"Only the horses?"

Olivia looked up from the biscuits she was placing in their Dutch oven. "I love it, too, and so do you, Charley. I wish you could see it, Miss Sarah."

Sarah turned to Nate. "That's why I walked over here with the children. I wanted to ask you what your plans were for tomorrow."

Nate walked with her partway down the trail.

"I had planned to take the children up to the homestead to start figuring out where to build the house and barn. Why?"

"Margaret and I were hoping we could go along, since it is Saturday and I don't have school. We've planned a picnic lunch, and we can make a day of it."

Nate's eyes were dark under the shadow of the trees. The sun was nearly below the western hills, and the light was soft.

"You would want to go traipsing through the hills with us?" He shifted so his face was in the light. One side of his mouth twitched up.

"Don't you think we'd enjoy the adventure?"

Nate didn't answer but kept looking at her. She shifted her gaze away, to where the children were gathered around Olivia as she sat on a log, opening a book.

"The children look so happy." She hadn't meant to speak, but the scene pulled the words from her. She looked back at Nate.

He watched them, the muscles in his jaw clenching. "Do you think so? Do you think they could ever be happy again?"

Sarah laid her hand on Nate's arm, and he turned to her. "I lost my parents in an accident, much like they did. I learned to be happy again, even though I missed them terribly."

"I'm afraid I'll never be able to make it up to them."

"You don't have to make up anything to them. Just love them and take care of them."

He looked down at the ground, then back to the children. "I think a fun day for them tomorrow would be perfect. A picnic sounds like something they'd enjoy."

"Would you enjoy it, too?"

Nate laid his hand on top of hers, still resting on his arm. "I think I will." The corner of his mouth twitched again. "We'll have to leave at first light, though. Can you and Margaret be ready?"

"You just wait and see." Sarah gave his arm a slight squeeze and then started down the trail toward the cabin.

"Remember," he called after her, "first light."

"We'll be ready." Sarah hugged herself as she hurried to the cabin door, but then stopped with her hand on the latch. What was she doing? God had shown her what her future was, hadn't He? A life of teaching and caring for other people's children. There was no room for a man in that life.

She glanced back at the camp, where firelight danced between the tree trunks. Perhaps there was room for this man.

Sarah and Aunt Margaret had the table set for three when James came home with a visitor.

"You ladies remember Wilson Montgomery, don't you?"

"Of course we do." Margaret went to the door to greet him with a sweeping walk that reminded Sarah of the society balls they had attended in Boston. "Mr. Montgomery, what a wonderful surprise. You will stay for supper, won't you?"

"If you insist." Mr. Montgomery turned his smile from Aunt Margaret to Sarah. "I don't wish to intrude."

Margaret reminded Sarah of a hen after a beetle. "Oh my, no! It will be a privilege to enjoy your company."

Mr. Montgomery bowed his head slightly. "In that case, I accept."

Sarah set another place at the table as Uncle James and their guest sat in the chairs at the side of the fireplace.

"I wish we had more elegant fare this evening," Margaret said in a whisper, coming to Sarah's side.

"He'll have to be happy with the stew and bread. He knows we're living in a frontier town, not back in Boston."

Margaret sighed, her face worried. "I do hope you're right."

If Wilson Montgomery thought there was anything

inappropriate about their meal, his appetite didn't show it. Sarah refilled his bowl twice before he leaned back in his chair.

"That was a fine meal, Mrs. MacFarland."

Margaret blushed. "I hope you'll be able to try Sarah's cooking one day. She's the finest cook in the family."

Sarah rose to clear the table, avoiding their visitor's eye. Surely he hadn't come to endure Aunt Margaret's attempts at matchmaking.

The men rose from the table.

"You wanted to discuss something with me?" Uncle James moved to the chairs near the fire. Sarah set the dishes aside to wash later, and she and Margaret joined the men.

"Yes." Mr. Montgomery glanced at Sarah. "I hope the subject isn't too delicate for the ladies."

"Do go on, Mr. Montgomery." Aunt Margaret picked up her knitting. "Sarah and I are involved in most aspects of Reverend MacFarland's work."

"It's concerning the businesses of ill repute." Mr. Montgomery flicked a bit of lint off his knee. "There is a group of us whose intent is to drive that sort of business out of Deadwood. With the riches coming out of the ground, the miners are poorly equipped to resist the temptations offered to them by these establishments. Our goal is to remove the temptation, thereby making our fledgling town into a center of culture and civilization."

"That has been attempted in other towns, without success."

"In other towns the populace allowed the dens of iniquity take root and grow. We want to nip this problem in the bud, before it becomes too big to handle."

James paused before answering. "I think you're too late. Have you been to Deadwood's Badlands? Have you seen the number of establishments already there?"

Mr. Montgomery brushed at his other knee. "I wouldn't think of setting foot in that part of town. I only know them by reputation, and by the notoriety they are giving our fair city."

Sarah couldn't keep quiet any longer. "But what about the people working in those establishments?"

Wilson Montgomery turned to her with a condescending smile. "Those people are just the sort we don't want to have here. They will move on to other towns and set up their businesses there. They will survive. There are plenty of other places that will welcome them." He turned back to Uncle James. "We hope we have your support. We need the voices of all the decent people in the gulch and surrounding areas."

Sarah leaned forward in her chair. "In my experience, Mr. Montgomery, the best way to rid a community of undesirable activities is to change the people who are involved in them."

He leaned back. "You mean arresting the leaders of the illicit businesses? Publishing the names of the citizens who frequent them in the local papers?"

"Not at all." She scooted her chair toward him slightly. "I mean by reaching the hearts of the people involved. Teaching them new ways to earn a living and to become part of the community. Teach them about the love of Christ."

"Doesn't the Bible tell us not to throw pearls before swine? These people are sinners, Miss MacFarland, not the kind of upstanding citizens we want in a community."

Uncle James shifted in his chair. "I think you both have a point. Sarah—" he looked her direction with an intent gaze that told her she had carried her point a little too far "—is right. We need to work to bring the gospel to such people. And, Mr. Montgomery, you are also right, in that some of the people involved in these activities are hardened to their lives and will never accept the gospel. That doesn't mean we should do nothing to help them, though. I will consider your ideas."

He steered the conversation toward bringing more businesses into the community, and Sarah settled back in her chair to listen. Wilson Montgomery was an intelligent man, and he had some well-thought-out plans to attract various tradesmen and shops to town. As she watched him discuss his ideas with Uncle James, his face lost its bored look and lit up with enthusiasm. His narrow mustache took on a life of its own as he talked, and when he glanced at her, his blue eyes twinkled. She smiled back at him. It seemed that he had enjoyed their earlier discussion, even though they disagreed. But where did his real feelings lie in regard to the men and women who populated the Badlands?

Before very long, though, he rose from his chair.

"I'm afraid I'm keeping you good people from your evening activities, and I have an appointment in town I must keep. Thank you again, Mrs. MacFarland, for the delicious meal." He turned to Sarah. "I hope we can continue our conversation at a future time. Perhaps you would like to join me for dinner some evening?"

Sarah worked to keep her mouth from dropping open. Was he asking to keep company with her?

Margaret stood up, taking Mr. Montgomery's arm as he walked toward the door. "I'm sure Sarah would love to accompany you to dinner, whenever it's convenient for you."

"Well, then," he said, taking his hat from the hook by the door, "I'll be in touch, Miss MacFarland."

With another quick bow, he was off.

Aunt Margaret spun around, her hands clasping together. "Oh, Sarah! What a wonderful opportunity for you! I was certain you had lost your chance with him when you were so outspoken, but it seems he thinks well of you."

Sarah took the kettle from the fire to the kitchen corner and poured it into the waiting dishpan. "But I don't know if I want to have dinner with him. I hardly know him."

"But James knows him and approves." Margaret turned to her husband, who was scanning the titles on his small bookshelf to find the book he had been reading. "Don't you, James?"

Uncle James turned to her. "I suppose so. He comes from a good family and seems a likely chap."

Sarah picked up the bucket next to the sink. "We need more water. I'll go fill the pail from the creek before the children go to bed so I won't disturb them."

Margaret waved her on as she shaved soap flakes into the dishpan. Sarah pulled her shawl around her shoulders and went out. Aunt Margaret was completely wrong. Mr. Montgomery was intelligent enough, and certainly handsome, but she wasn't about to open her heart to anyone.

Nate stood as she approached his camp, Lucy asleep in his arms. Charley and Olivia ran to greet her.

"Did you come to say good-night?" Olivia gave her a tight hug.

"I came to get some water, but I can say good-night, too. Is it your bedtime?"

Charley kicked at the ground. "Uncle Nate says we've had a long day and he's tired."

"And we have an early morning tomorrow." Nate had put Lucy into the wagon and came to join Sarah and the children. "Say good-night, now, and hop into bed." He reached for Sarah's pail and took it to the stream.

"Good night, Olivia." Sarah bent down to give her a hug. "And you, too, Charley." He shied away from her hug, so she tousled his hair.

The children went to the wagon as Nate brought the dripping pail. Sarah reached for it, but he wouldn't let her take it.

"I'll carry it back to the cabin for you."

"The children will be all right?"

The corner of his mouth twitched in the firelight. "It isn't that far."

As Sarah turned to walk back, he fell in beside her. "You had company for supper?"

"How did you know?"

"Like I said, it isn't that far from our camp to your cabin. I could hear someone talking, and it wasn't James."

"Yes, we did. It was Mr. Montgomery from the bank."

"The fancy man with the suit and white hat?"

Sarah smiled at his description. "Fancy man" fit Wilson Montgomery perfectly.

"He's a gentleman from Boston, and Aunt Margaret likes him very much."

They walked up to the doorstep in silence, and Nate

handed her the pail. He paused, but his face was shadowed and Sarah couldn't see his expression.

"You said Margaret likes him. What about you?"

"He's nice, and he was good company at supper."

Nate looked off toward the gulch but made no move to leave. "Is he courting you?"

Suddenly, Mr. Montgomery's manners seemed polished and civilized. "I don't know if that's any of your concern."

"I just thought…" Nate took a step back and ran his finger under his neckerchief.

Sarah's face grew hot. "What had you thought?"

"I didn't think he would be the kind of man that would appeal to you."

He took another step backward and Sarah followed him.

"You didn't think a well educated, polite man would appeal to me?" Did he think she only liked mountain men and miners?

"No, that isn't what I meant." He took another step, shaking his head.

Sarah watched his profile against the evening sky as he stood with his head bowed.

He looked up and moved a step toward her. "I know I'm not the kind of man you're used to keeping company with, but I don't think he is, either. I've seen Montgomery around town, and I don't like him."

Of course Nate wouldn't like Wilson Montgomery. When did country rustic ever get along with cultured and civilized?

"I don't need your approval on every man Uncle James brings home for dinner, Mr. Colby. I don't think you have any right to tell me who I may talk to and who I must avoid."

He sputtered and then stopped, running his finger under his neckerchief again. "You're right. It's no concern of mine." He reached up to tug at his hat brim. "Until the morning, then, Miss MacFarland."

"Until morning."

She watched him fade into the trees lining the trail, her stomach churning as if she had lost a friend.

# Chapter Seven

Nate hitched the horses to the wagon as Olivia and Charley washed up from breakfast. The sun had already risen on the prairies behind the hills, lighting the sky with the yellowish pink that came just before dawn. When Charley tied Loretta to the back corner of the wagon, Nate bit back his objection. If the boy wanted to bring the mule, he could.

"Is Miss Sarah coming, too, Uncle Nate?" Olivia helped Lucy into the wagon.

"We're all going, even Miss Sarah." He patted Scout's nose as he moved around the horses.

Charley jumped up to the wagon seat. "Are we moving to the homestead today?"

"Not yet, Charley." Nate straightened Dan's harness. "We need to make plans. Decide where the house will sit and where the best place will be for the corrals."

"And then I can be a real cowboy?" Charley's voice rose an octave in his excitement.

Nate climbed onto the wagon seat next to Charley and reached into the wagon behind him for the boy's hat. "We have to get some cattle before you start being a cowboy." He plopped the hat on Charley's head.

He clucked to the horses, and they started down the trail to the MacFarlands' cabin. His stomach churned at the thought of seeing Sarah again. He could tell he had been rude last night by the hard edge to her voice as she said good-night, but the news of that dandy Montgomery courting her had come like a punch in the stomach. He pushed the memory away. This was a new day and he intended to give the children a good time.

James came out of the cabin with a large basket when they arrived.

"Good morning, James. That's quite a picnic the ladies have packed."

He lowered the back gate and helped lift it into the wagon. Once the basket was settled next to Lucy, James wiped his handkerchief across his forehead.

"I think Margaret and Sarah packed enough food to feed these children twelve times over."

Margaret came out the door, pulling on her gloves. "You know how hungry children get in the fresh air, dear. If we have any left over, we'll just bring it home."

Nate took a deep breath of the enticing aroma coming from the basket. "Do I smell fried chicken?"

"I ran into Peder Swenson yesterday afternoon, and he gave me a brace of prairie chickens." James grinned. "He figured we'd appreciate it, and he was right."

"Dear Peder," Margaret said. "I'm so glad he's attending church. Has he found a job yet?"

"Odd jobs around town, from what he says. He said he found some fellows to go prospecting with, though. They're heading over Bear Mountain next week to have a look at the canyons on the other side. He still hopes to strike it rich." James held Margaret's hand as she climbed into the back of the wagon. Nate had taken the canvas cover off and placed boards across the bed to serve as seats.

He searched the clearing, but Sarah was nowhere in sight. Had she decided not to come with them after their conversation last night? He didn't know he was holding his breath until it whooshed when she came out the door, swinging her shawl around her shoulders. While Margaret's burgundy dress looked as if she was planning to spend the day calling on friends in Boston, Sarah had dressed for a day in the hills, wearing a dark blue cotton dress and boots that were much more practical than the kid shoes she normally wore.

"Are we ready to go?" She climbed into the wagon box and sat next to Margaret. She greeted the children with smiles and returned Olivia's hug.

She had barely looked at him. Maybe she had decided that Montgomery was the right man for her after all.

"We're all set." Nate lifted the wagon gate and shot the bolts home to fasten it closed.

Olivia bounced on her seat. "Uncle Nate said you wouldn't be ready to go, but you were."

Sarah flashed a smile at him, making his knees go weak. "Your uncle was wrong, then, wasn't he? He underestimated our eagerness to see your new home."

It seemed she had forgotten all about Wilson Montgomery this morning. Nate whistled a tune as he walked to the front of the wagon and climbed up next to James and Charley.

Nate had the route to his land memorized. He had never felt satisfaction like that feeling that washed over him when he signed his name on the homesteading papers. He had earned two years' exemption for his time in the army, so he only had to wait three years for the land to be his.

He headed out of the mining camp on Main Street toward the northeast, down the valley that widened out after they passed Chinatown. The banks of Whitewood Creek were filled with men digging in the dirt, shoveling gravel into rockers or standing knee-deep in the cold water, bent over their pans. A few looked up as they passed, but most kept their attention on the specks of gold they were gleaning from the gravel.

Their route climbed out of the valley and up toward the hills, following the freight route that led through Boulder Canyon and on toward Camp Sturgis. When they reached Two-Bit Gulch, Nate turned the team up the narrow trail along the creek bed, then to the right, up a scree of loose rocks and then pulled the horses to a halt.

"This is the edge of the homestead." Even though he had walked through this land several times in the past week, he couldn't wait to see it again.

"Do we have to walk from here?" Sarah had stood up in the wagon box and was looking over Charley's shoulder.

"No. We'll drive on, but from here to those hills you're on Colby land." He grinned at Sarah as Charley let loose with a cowboy yell.

"Can I ride Loretta?" Charley asked.

"Go ahead. Meet us at the pond, in that grove of cottonwoods."

Nate waited while Charley untied Loretta and mounted her. The boy urged the mule to a trot and quickly outpaced the slower team. Then Loretta slowed to a walk and kept Charley within shouting distance. At least, it looked as if Loretta had decided that for herself. He'd never figure mules out.

He drove the team along a natural shelf on the side of the slope and then turned up. As they crested the rise, the sight that greeted him still took his breath away.

Green meadows stretched away in a wide swath at least a half mile across and twice that long, curving around the wooded slopes that crowded close to the open space. An eagle drifted above them against the clear blue sky.

Sarah whispered, "It's perfect."

Nate chirruped to the horses, driving them slowly through the knee-deep grass, heading for the grove of trees at the far edge. In his mind the mountain valley was dotted with horses—brown, black, white, gray— all grazing on the rich green grass that grew in a thick carpet everywhere he looked. Across the meadow, a meandering line of cottonwood trees followed a fold in the grass. That stream cutting through the land was the crowning touch.

He glanced at Sarah, still standing in the wagon bed, holding on to the seat between him and James. Her face was bright in the clear sunshine, the wind pulling loose hair from her bun. Her gaze went up to the tops of the hills surrounding them.

When she looked at him she smiled, and his heart swelled. Everywhere he looked he saw his future, waiting for him to reach out and grasp it. It was as if the past twelve years had never happened and he was just starting out, full of promise.

He ran a finger between his neckerchief and the scars. Could he hope that this time he could make something out of his life?

"May I get out and walk the rest of the way?" Sarah touched Nate's shoulder as she spoke. Would he understand her need to get down from the wagon? To feel the grass under her feet?

Nate turned with a grin. "I wish I could join you." He pulled the horses to a halt.

"May I take the girls with me?"

"Sure thing. We'll meet you at the cottonwoods."

Sarah grasped Olivia's and Lucy's hands, and they walked through the meadow toward the far side. Her skirt swished through the thick grass, and little yellow wildflowers were everywhere. Olivia soon had a handful of them.

Nate drove the wagon with James and Margaret on through the grass toward the grove of trees on the far side of the meadow. His voice carried across the distance as he talked with Uncle James, and although she couldn't make out the words, their gestures and excited tones told her what they were discussing—Nate's future ranch.

The look on Nate's face when they had reached the edge of the meadow stayed with her. In the time she had known him, she had never seen him so confident and happy. Ever since she had met him a few weeks ago, Nate had seemed driven, anxious and determined to accomplish his goals. But now, in the sunny, open field with the cobalt sky above them, he was a man who was settled. Like a top that suddenly righted itself and spun true, he was at home.

"Oh, Miss Sarah, look at this one!"

Olivia's voice drew her attention back to the girls, kneeling in a spot where the grass gave way to a rock surface. They were captured by the sight of small, bright purple flowers growing out of a fissure in the stony ground. Olivia turned and beckoned to her.

"It's like a shooting star, isn't it?"

Sarah laughed at the joy in Olivia's voice. "You're right. That's exactly what it looks like." She looked closer at the cluster of flowers, each one a yellow star pointing toward the earth with purple petals trailing behind it toward the blue above. "How lovely they are!"

"These are real shooting stars. Somehow they've been caught here in the meadow as they fell from the sky." Olivia's words caught at Sarah's imagination, and her explanation seemed perfectly plausible.

As Olivia reached out to pluck some of the flowers, Lucy grabbed her hand.

"No." The word was raspy but clear. "No."

Olivia stared at her sister. Lucy's face was twisted with the effort of words fighting to get out of her mouth.

Sarah fell to her knees next to the little girl. "Why don't you want Olivia to pick the flowers?"

Lucy looked at her, and Sarah's eyes stung as she struggled. The little girl took a deep breath. "They're too pretty."

Sarah smiled at Lucy. "We won't pick them. Olivia will leave them where they are." She reached out and Lucy leaned into her arms without another word. "You're right. They're too pretty to watch them wilt and die."

Olivia rocked back on her heels. "Do you think we

could plant them in a garden, so they can grow by our house?"

Sarah tucked a blond strand of hair behind Olivia's ear. "I don't see why not. Back in Boston, Aunt Margaret's garden club transplanted many wildflowers like this one. When you have the right place for it, we'll dig one up and plant it near your house."

Olivia smiled. "When Uncle Nate builds one for us." She looked at Lucy. "Will that be all right, Luce?"

The little girl nodded, her thumb back in her mouth. She had run out of words for now, but Sarah was confident she would talk again.

By noon they had reached the far edge of the meadow where the small stream widened out into an old beaver pond. The cottonwood trees grew in an awkward circle in the marshy grass and shaded a small rise. Nate and Uncle James had spread a blanket on the soft grass and Aunt Margaret unpacked the fried chicken and corn bread. The children gathered around the blanket, taking seats along the edge, but Nate stood staring at the surrounding hills as if they would disappear.

Finally, just as Margaret lifted the plate of cookies from the basket, he joined them, sitting between Sarah and Charley.

After grace, Sarah took a piece of fried chicken. The walk across the mountain meadow had whetted her appetite. She took two bites from the meaty breast before seeing that Nate was watching her.

"I don't mean to be greedy. It's all so delicious." She wiped her fingers on a napkin.

Nate grinned. "I was just thinking how I'm glad I'm not that chicken." He blushed red and took a piece of corn bread. "This would make a good place for a cabin, wouldn't it?"

Uncle James looked around them. "You're close to the pond here, and there is a nice level spot."

"Plenty of wood around, and a good view of the rest of the place." Nate stared into the distance, the bread forgotten in his hand.

Sarah scanned the meadow in front of them. She could imagine a cabin nestled under the shoulder of the hill. What would it be like to step out on the front porch every morning and be greeted by the sight of the vast meadow with the hills rising up behind it? That would be one sight she would never tire of.

Nate pulled a scrap of paper out of his pocket and smoothed it on the ground. Sarah leaned over to watch as he sketched in the hills, the stream and the meadows.

"I could only claim half of this valley for a homestead. It is at least two sections."

Sarah took a piece of corn bread and broke a small corner off. "But if you're only allowed one section, how could you choose which part to claim?"

"It had to be this one, with the pond, but I hate to give up the rest of the grazing land."

"I wonder if you'd be able to file on the other section as a tree claim," Uncle James said.

Nate took another drumstick. "I'll have to ask. The tree claim program was created for the prairies, though. I'm not sure if they'll allow one up here in the hills."

The children finished their dinners and started a game of tag in the meadow. Even Lucy ran after her brother and sister with all her might. This valley, swept by a clean wind and studded with wildflowers, was a wonderful place for the children to grow up. Such a difference from her childhood in the city.

"This is a perfect spot to raise your horses." Sarah handed Nate a cookie.

Nate nodded, his eyes on the children. As they ran toward the far end of the meadow, a herd of deer bounded away from them, across the valley and into the trees on the other side.

"Look at that," he said, gesturing with the cookie in his hand. "With game like that, we'll never go hungry here."

Sarah watched for the deer to reappear, but when they didn't, she focused on the children. Olivia and Lucy were picking wildflowers while Charley roamed through the grass around them, brushing the long stems with a stick.

"I wanted to tell you something while the children aren't here." She turned to Nate. "Lucy spoke this morning."

"She did? She started talking?"

Sarah shook her head. "Not really talking, but she said a couple words. It's a beginning."

Nate smiled and settled back on his elbows, watching the children again.

She gathered the dishes and placed them back in the basket. Uncle James was lying on his back, his hat over his face. Aunt Margaret leaned against a tree, her knitting in her lap, but her eyes closed.

Suddenly Nate stood and held his hand to her. "Come. Let's go explore a little while James and Margaret rest. We'll celebrate Lucy's progress."

Sarah let him tuck her hand in his elbow, and they walked across the meadow toward the children.

"Six months ago, I thought I had lost everything." Nate picked the head off a stalk of grass and stuck the stem between his teeth.

"Not everything. You had the children."

He shook his head. "Yes, I had the children, but how could I ever take care of them? I couldn't see our future. Without Andrew and Jenny, and Andrew's dry goods store, how could I provide for them? Besides, Andrew was the storekeeper, not me." Nate halted, looking up into the hills around them. "You said that sometimes God just wants us to change directions." He glanced at her, then back at the hills. "Do you really think there's a God who even cares what we do?"

Sarah bit her lip while she tried to think of a reply. If Nate didn't believe in God, what hope did he have in his life? She thought back to all the times when she had listened to Uncle James in these situations, when he was helping someone understand the difficult questions about God. He always found a way to help the other person reason their way through the problem.

"What makes you think there isn't?"

Nate didn't look at her, but dropped her hand and stepped away, still looking at the hills. "If you had seen what we went through during the war…" He turned toward her, but didn't meet her eyes. "How could any god have allowed that to happen?" His voice dropped. "If He was real, don't you think He would have intervened? Prevented the horror we experienced?"

Sarah's eyes stung. The pain in his voice was too awful to imagine. She hadn't witnessed any battles during the war, but she had seen soldiers who had returned home with lost arms or legs. Broken in body and spirit. But not all of them had turned away from

God. Nate had survived the war in one piece, but how many wounds did he carry beneath the surface, where no one could see them? She couldn't imagine the things he had experienced that caused his pain to continue so many years after the fighting was over.

"I don't have an answer for you, Nate." She stepped closer to him. "But I do know that God has not abandoned you." Nate appeared to be listening, even though he still hadn't looked at her. "Everything that happens has a reason, and God works through every circumstance of our lives." When he started to take a step back from her with a shake of his head, she stopped. He wasn't ready to hear more. She silently prayed that he would, and soon.

When he spoke, it was a whisper. "A reason?" He looked up at the surrounding hills again until she thought he had forgotten she was there. And then he turned toward her, running a finger along the kerchief tied around his neck. "I'll think on it." He nodded and lifted one corner of his mouth in a quick grin. "I'll think on it."

The sun still lingered far above the tops of the hills when they returned to Deadwood, but it had been hours since their noon meal. A pleasant exhaustion settled over Nate as he guided the horses back through the mining camp and up to the MacFarlands' cabin. That same happy weariness seemed to have claimed them all. There had been little conversation on the drive.

But part of Nate's own silence came from the closeness of Sarah. She had chosen to sit next to him on the wagon seat so James and Margaret could sit together. The children lay down in the bed of the wagon. At every bump and turn Sarah's skirt brushed against his knee, keeping him constantly aware of her presence.

She must have been as tired as all of them, though. She didn't say a word until they reached the cabin on Williams Street.

"Thank you for the wonderful day, Nate." Her voice was soft, and she smiled as she spoke.

"We sure appreciated your company." He tore his gaze away from those deep blue eyes. They had spent too much time together, walking across his land and making plans.

Plans that she wouldn't have any part in, if he had his way. Life with him—well, he wouldn't ask anyone to share the kind of life he had lived so far. But he couldn't keep from watching her walk into the cabin with James and Margaret, and he gave a nod to her small wave as she closed the door. He sat, staring, until Charley climbed up on the wagon seat in her place.

"What's for supper?"

Supper. Of course the children would be hungry.

"Do we have stew left from last night?" Nate looked at Olivia, the cook of the family.

"We ate it all for breakfast this morning, remember? You had the last bowl."

"That's right. Then it's beans and corn bread."

Nate's announcement brought no response, and he didn't blame them. Last night's stew had been a treat, after finding a squirrel near their camp, but meat was scarce close to town.

"Do you think we can read a story from the reader Miss MacFarland loaned us?" Olivia stood, clinging to the back of the seat.

"You can read one while supper is cooking, while we still have good light." Nate smiled at Olivia's grin.

"Really?" Her eyes shone.

"Sure thing. I want you to practice as much as you can."

As soon as they reached camp, Olivia climbed out of the wagon and went to the pile of supplies Nate had covered with the canvas that morning. She found the book and settled on a stump near the fire circle while she leafed through the pages.

"What are you doing? What about supper?" Charley was all boy, and food was always the first thing on his mind.

Nate reached over and ruffled Charley's hair. "Don't worry about supper. I'm Cookie tonight."

Charley grinned at him. "Cookie? Like cowboys on a trail drive?"

"Mosey up to the fire and we'll get the beans cooking," Nate said in his best dime-novel cowpoke voice. Charley had devoured the one he had found in Chicago, all about "Yellowstone Jack" and his adventures. What more did a boy need?

Lucy settled on an upturned log while Nate stirred up the ashes and brought the morning's fire back to life. A pot of beans had been sitting in the coals, and now Nate lifted it by its bail handle and pulled it to the flat rock they used for a work surface, glad for his leather gloves. Even so, drawing close to the growing fire brought pain, his scars searing in answer to the heat of the flame. Nate ignored the pain and gave the beans a stir. He got a bit of salt pork from the keg in the wagon and cut it into smaller pieces, stirred them into the beans and put the pot next to the fire again.

Olivia took a seat next to Lucy and started reading from her book. "Persev…persev… Uncle Nate? What is this word?"

Nate leaned over to look at the page she showed him. *"Perseverance."*

"What does it mean?"

Nate thought for a minute. "It means to keep trying, no matter what."

"You mean, like we're doing now?"

He looked at his niece. She had endured so much over the past year. He stirred the corn-bread batter, taking his time before he answered. Were they persevering?

"Yes. Like we're doing now. We've had some rough times, but we're persevering. We keep working toward our goals. Making our dreams come true. That's what that word means."

Nate poured the batter into the Dutch oven and set it in the coals at the side of the fire. Charley pitched in, using the small camp shovel to pile coals on top of the oven while they both listened to Olivia read the story about some children trying to fly a kite. One line echoed in his head. *A few disappointments ought not to discourage us.*

Disappointments? They'd had their share, all right. But were they discouraged? Nate looked at the children's faces, listening intently to Olivia's voice as she read. He had to admit it. Some days they were. But as long as he kept working, he'd make it. The children would have a home on the ranch, just as he'd promised.

When the corn bread was done, Olivia put the book away and got out their tin plates. Nate put a piece of corn bread on each one and ladled a scoop of beans on top. He took his spoon and dug in, pausing only to blow on the hot, fragrant beans.

Olivia stared at him.

"What's wrong?"

"At home we used to say grace. And at the MacFarlands' we always say grace. Why don't we say grace now?"

Nate shifted. Charley and Lucy both stared at him, too, waiting for his answer. What could he say? He didn't want his battle with God to become theirs, but he couldn't say thank-you to a God who didn't care about them.

But he had told Sarah he'd think about God. Her peaceful face came to his mind. She would give thanks. She would teach the children to pray before meals, and at bedtime. What would she think if he refused to let the children give thanks for their meal?

"Go ahead." Nate cleared his throat. "Charley, why don't you say the grace?"

He bowed his head while the boy prayed, sounding like Andrew. Of course he would. He had heard his pa pray at every meal since he was born.

During other prayers, the words had run off Nate's head and heart like water off a duck's back. He might as well have been made of wood. But not this time. Charley's clear voice was as confident as if he was talking to someone who was right here in the circle with them. The boy's trust made Nate open his eyes and look to make sure they were alone.

A verse from his childhood came back, echoing behind Charley's words—*For where two or three are gathered together in My name, there am I in the midst of them.*

Was God here? Did He really care what happened to them, as Sarah said?

When the prayer was over, they ate quickly. Even Lucy seemed hungry tonight and looked as if she was enjoying her simple supper.

"Tomorrow is Sunday," Olivia said when she had finished. "Can we go to church with Miss Sarah?"

"I don't know." Nate scraped at the last of the beans in the pot. "We'll see what tomorrow brings."

"I can see their cabin from here." Charley pointed through the trees to the clearing.

"Yeah, you're right." He looked in the direction Charley pointed, to the soft glow of light he knew came from the cabin windows. Every night he had watched that glow until the MacFarlands put out their lamps when they went to bed.

That gentle light drew him like a beacon. Like a lighthouse warning of rocky shoals ahead, pointing out the safe, narrow path he should take. A safe, narrow path with a dark-haired beauty. Why wouldn't he jump at the chance?

Nate stared at the fire as Olivia took his empty plate. That path wasn't for a man like him. That path was for a man like Andrew. A man who could follow through with his commitments. A man who had what it took to make a home for his family.

A man who hadn't watched everything he touched crumble in his hands.

He tossed the last of his coffee, thick with grounds, on the fire and watched the liquid disappear in the coals.

He couldn't ask Sarah, or any woman, to endure going through life with him.

Lucy crawled onto his lap, her thumb in her mouth and eyes half-closed. Nate pulled her close and rocked a little as the sleepy girl relaxed in the warmth of the fire.

And yet, with all his faults, he had ended up with these children. God sure had a strange way of giving a man what he deserved.

As Sarah entered the cabin behind Uncle James, he took a deep breath. "My, oh, my. That smells like good old New England boiled dinner."

Aunt Margaret blushed. "I thought it would be a good way to use the salt pork you brought home a couple days ago. We had a few potatoes and a can of carrots. It was simple to put the pot in the banked coals while we were gone for the day."

"It smells wonderful." Sarah lifted the Dutch oven out of the coals and removed the lid, then she ladled the meat and vegetables into a serving bowl that Aunt Margaret put on the table. "And it looks delicious, too."

"Thank you, dear." Aunt Margaret stood back to admire the table. "It isn't quite as elegant as our Boston dining room, but the food will fill us up."

After saying grace, Uncle James shook out his napkin. "I forgot to tell you, I had a conversation with an interesting man yesterday afternoon, before I ran into Wilson Montgomery."

"Who was that, dear?" Aunt Margaret spooned some vegetables and broth onto Uncle James's plate.

"There's a new merchant in Chinatown. He's recently come to Deadwood and has opened a grocery."

Margaret passed the bread. "Why did he want to talk to you?"

Sarah handed her plate to Aunt Margaret. When Uncle James had left her at the bottom of the steps, she had wondered where he had gone. With his experiences in China as a missionary, he enjoyed his visits to the Chinese section of Deadwood.

"He heard that I had spent time in Ningbo and thought I might know Charles Williams. It turns out that Charles is the man who taught Hung Cho the Bible. He's a Christian."

"I thought all those people in Chinatown were heathens." Aunt Margaret sniffed. "With their opium dens and such."

"You've been talking to Mrs. Brewster again." Uncle James pointed his fork at her. "You know that woman is a gossip." He cut a potato in two. "It is true. Most of the Chinese are Buddhists, and some of them do run opium dens and other unsavory businesses, but there are more who provide good services for the town, and even a few Christians."

"Will they be coming to our church?" Sarah broke a bite off her bread.

Uncle James shook his head. "Hung Cho speaks English fairly well, but a lot of them, especially the women, only speak Mandarin. He wants to start a Christian church in Chinatown and asked if I'd be willing to preach on occasion."

"You haven't spoken Mandarin for years." Aunt Margaret spooned some more vegetables onto his plate. "Will you be able to speak well enough to preach a sermon?"

"I am a bit rusty, but it will come back with practice."

Aunt Margaret turned to Sarah. "I wonder if some of the Chinese families would send their children to the academy."

Sarah pushed a potato with her fork. "I can try calling on the families, but I can't seem to get any of the children in town to come. They are needed at home, or working in their parents' business. Some are even working claims. The only time they are willing to come to town is on Sunday."

Uncle James pushed his plate away. He gave Aunt Margaret a smile of thanks as she poured a cup of coffee for him, and then he looked at Sarah. "Perhaps you should adjust to the people's needs. If the children are in town on Sunday, maybe that's when you should have your classes."

Sarah shook her head. "What kind of learning can they get on only one day a week?"

"More than they're getting now." Uncle James sipped his coffee.

"It could be a Sabbath school." Aunt Margaret poured two more cups and then hung the coffeepot at the side of the fireplace to keep warm. "You could keep teaching the students you have now during the week, but on Sunday have Bible classes for the children."

Sarah toyed with the idea. "Bible classes would be just the thing. The Woodrow children could come, and perhaps some of the others from the community and the outlying camps." Perhaps even Nate's children, if he was willing to let them. After all, Sabbath school wasn't the same as her academy.

"I couldn't believe my eyes last Sunday." Sarah finished her supper and took a sip of her coffee. "All the businesses in town were open, as if it was a Saturday. Doesn't anyone here go to church or honor the Sabbath?"

"That was one thing I found hard to get used to." Uncle James took another slice of bread. "But the miners are scattered all over the area. Most of them have to walk five or six miles or more to come into town, and they work every chance they get. Most don't work on Sunday, so that becomes the day to buy supplies or visit with their neighbors." He dunked the bread in his coffee. "I think you've probably noticed there aren't many who attend church."

"But you think the ones with families would bring their children to school?"

Uncle James dunked his bread again before he answered. "I think it's worth a try. The folks around here don't have anything against education or church, but it isn't as important to them as their work. Most of them came here with nothing, and if they don't work as hard as they can, they'll have nothing when they leave. Or, worse yet, they'll have spent all their resources and end up destitute. They come to Deadwood thinking the gold is here for the taking, but nothing can be further from the truth."

"Surely some have struck it rich, haven't they?" Aunt Margaret put her cup down. "It isn't all some kind of lie to lure people here, is it?"

"Some have struck it rich. There is gold here—in the streams, in the mountains—and there is a lot of it, if the estimates are correct. But like most gold rushes, a few people will get very rich, and some won't make enough to pay their expenses. Most will only pull enough gold out of their claims to pay their way back home."

Sarah drained her coffee cup as she rose to start washing the dishes. It seemed Nate Colby had chosen a wise course when he decided to raise cattle and horses rather than search for gold. Stacking the plates and cups, she wondered how Nate and the children were doing tonight. Were they warm enough? Who cooked their meals? Did Nate remember to tuck the children into their beds?

She set the dishes down on the table. "I'll be right back." Her aunt and uncle were intent on their conversation and didn't notice as she slipped out the door. Dusk had turned to darkness.

Standing at the edge of the rimrock across from the cabin door, raucous singing, gunshots, drums, a trumpet and all kinds of sounds drifted up to her from the town below. The nightly revelries reminded her of the great hopes she had to save the young women down there from their sordid life. But she hadn't made any progress toward contacting them since that disastrous trip to the Badlands. Dr. Bennett had convinced her that the women would flock to her for help, but they ignored her and went on suffering from the unfortunate consequences of their choices. How could she help women who had no interest in making their lives better?

She turned to her left, where she could see the glow of Nate's campfire filtering through the young pine trees. She tried to tell herself that the children were the ones who were the focus of her concern, but it was no good. In her mind, she could see Nate sitting by the side of the fire. Was he finishing a last cup of coffee while the children settled in their beds for the night?

Sarah leaned against the rough, dusky bark of a ponderosa pine. Sometimes the man could be cheerful and friendly, but other times as rough and unyielding as this tree. Would she ever figure him out?

# Chapter Eight

Sunday morning. Nate lay still on his bedroll near the fire, listening to the snorts of the horses as they woke and the light snores coming from Charley's bedroll on the other side of the fire. The birds' morning noises nearly drowned all other sounds as they sang in the treetops. Under it all was the faint roar of the wind in the tops of the pines.

Something was different this morning. Nate cast his mind back, over the picnic the day before, settling the children in when they returned, the usual chores around the campsite. He stretched and sat up before he remembered. There had been no nightmare.

He took a deep breath and whooshed it out. No fighting in the dark, no fires licking at his dreams, no panic. Only a restful night's sleep. He ran one hand through his hair. This was what it would feel like if he were free.

Sounds from the other side of the stand of pines told him the MacFarlands were up and starting their day. A smile interrupted his yawn as he thought about Sarah. What would she be up to today? Maybe they could take a walk up Boot Hill. The white rocks at the top beckoned him every time he looked up there. They could take the children and...

Hold on. It was Sunday. Sarah would be busy with church this morning, and he'd have no opportunity to see her.

Nate rubbed at his whiskers. Unless he went to church, too.

He glanced at Charley, sound asleep under his blanket. No sounds came from the wagon. The girls were still sleeping, too.

Could he show up at church just to see Sarah? Wouldn't she think he was there to listen to the preaching?

He threw his blanket aside and stood up. It was time to start the morning chores, Sunday or not. As he built up the fire, he considered what going to church meant. Once he went, the children would want to continue going, and he'd have to take them. He couldn't bear the disappointment in their faces if he didn't.

But he wouldn't be able to bear listening to some holier-than-thou so-and-so preach to him about God.

Nate shook his head at his own thoughts as he poured a measure of grain into each of the horse's nose bags. James MacFarland wasn't like the preacher back at the church in Michigan, or even the soldier-preachers he had heard during the war. James would be the same in the pulpit as he was sitting on the bench in front of his cabin. He had never met a man with more compassion for his fellow human beings or who spoke of God as if He was an intimate friend.

He slipped the nose bag over Scout's ears and patted

the horse's neck as he munched on the grain. "What do you think? Would it do me some good to go to church?"

He moved on to Ginger, who reached eagerly for the bag in his hands. "So, you think I should go, too, do you?"

Pete and Dan were next, and then Nate eyed the mule. Its ears turned backward at his approach. "We're not going to have a fight about this, are we? You like your grain."

Loretta bobbed her head down and then up and pulled her lips back, looking as if she was grinning at him.

"See, Uncle Nate?" Charley was sitting up on his bedroll. "She's learning to like you."

Nate growled, "That'll be the day." But he couldn't keep a frown on his face. The mule stuck her head into the feed bag and he slipped it over her long ears. She didn't even try to nip at him.

Nate peeked over the side of the wagon. Olivia was still sleeping, but Lucy's eyes were open. She smiled when she saw him. He smiled back at her. "How are you this morning, little bluebird?"

Lucy climbed out of her bed and wrapped her arms around his neck, holding tight. Nate's eyes grew moist as he hugged her back. She was getting better. She was coming out of her shell. Sarah had told him that Lucy had spoken yesterday, though she hadn't said another word after that. But it was a beginning.

He lifted her up and over the side of the wagon so she could go behind some trees where he had dug a latrine for them to use. He'd do anything to help her make more progress. Anything. Even… Nate looked up at the bright blue sky between the tall pines. Even pray? The trees grew blurry as his eyes filled. Yes, even pray.

Wiping at his eyes with the corner of his neckerchief, he reached over the side of the wagon and shook Olivia's foot. "Hey there, sleepyhead. It's time to get up, unless you want me to be Cookie again this morning."

Olivia kicked at his hand and sat up, pushing her hair back from her face and yawning. "No, I'm getting up."

"Hurry up, Olivia," Charley said from his seat by the campfire. "We don't want to eat Uncle Nate's cooking again!"

Nate turned toward Charley, his hands held out from his sides in a pretend gunfighter's stance, straight out of Charley's dime novel. "You try saying that to my face, cowboy."

He snarled, but Charley charged straight at him, knocking him to the ground. As they wrestled in the pine needles, Nate couldn't help laughing right along with Charley.

Sarah smiled at Peder as he dashed through the swinging doors of the former saloon. He grinned and snatched the hat off his head.

"Good morning, Miss MacFarland. I hope I'm not late."

"You're not late at all, Peder. Aunt Margaret is just getting ready to start the prelude." She watched the lanky young man make his way to the third bench from the front, his usual seat. The Woodrows with their five children and twin baby boys took up the fourth bench, and Wilson Montgomery and a couple other businessmen sat on the second but the rest of the benches were empty. A few more stragglers might show up before Uncle James started the sermon, but few people came to church in this town that was so crowded. Even this early in the morning, shouts, brass bands and gunfire were all she could hear from the street.

"Go ahead and take your seat, Sarah." Uncle James joined her at the door. "We'll be starting the service in a couple minutes."

Sarah walked to the front of the room and slipped into her seat on the front bench. She could hardly bring herself to call the old saloon a church yet, when the cracked mirror still hung on the wall behind the bar. But Uncle James was making progress. The piano had been repaired and tuned, and he had built a pulpit and some benches to serve as pews. She glanced up at the soot-stained ceiling. It didn't matter. As Uncle James always said, the church was the people, not the building.

As Margaret started playing a quiet hymn for the prelude, Sarah heard footsteps at the door and whispered voices as Uncle James greeted the newcomers. She resisted the urge to turn around as the footsteps came closer to the front bench but had to look up as Olivia took the seat next to her. Nate gave her a sheepish smile as he and Charley filed past her and took their seats.

They had only just sat down when Uncle James took his place at the pulpit and asked the congregation to rise as he read the call to worship. Sarah was too dazed to hear which verse he had selected. Nate brought the children to church?

Through the service, Sarah tried to keep her mind

on the hymns they sang, and the scripture, but by the time Uncle James started his sermon, she was ready to give up. Even with Olivia on one side of her and Aunt Margaret on the other, she wasn't aware of anyone except Nate sitting on the other side of Charley with Lucy in his lap. The first time she'd stolen a glance in his direction, he'd met her eyes and turned bright red before focusing his attention on Uncle James. The last time she'd looked down the bench, he hadn't noticed. He was listening to the sermon, watching Uncle James intently. Was he having second thoughts about his refusal to believe in God?

A smile forced the corners of her mouth up, in spite of her trying to keep it under control. She had prayed for God to bring Nate and the children to church but hadn't expected it to happen so soon.

After the service, the children gathered around Sarah. "I'm so glad to see you all here today." She gave Olivia and Lucy each a hug and laid her hand on Charley's shoulder. She could hug him in private, but he certainly wouldn't appreciate it here with the Woodrow children looking on. She glanced up at Nate. "Good morning. What brought you to church today?"

Could his face have turned more scarlet? Before he could answer, Lucretia Woodrow was at her elbow.

"Oh, Sarah, I can't tell you how much I appreciate your willingness to teach our children. And now I hear you're starting a Sabbath school? Tell me all about it."

Lucretia hooked her elbow in Sarah's and led her off to the side of the room, leaving Nate to shake hands with Lucretia's husband, Albert. Bernie Woodrow was looking Charley up and down while his sister, Laura, smiled shyly at Olivia and Lucy. Knowing Nate and his family were in good hands, Sarah launched into a description of what she and Aunt Margaret hoped to achieve with the Sabbath school. She was facing Nate as she talked, and she couldn't help glancing at him occasionally. Uncle James joined in the conversation with Albert Woodrow.

Wilson Montgomery, on the other hand, had waited to speak to her until it became clear that Lucretia would continue to dominate her time. Then, with a nod to her when she happened to look his way, he took his leave. Sarah turned her full attention to Lucretia then, thankful she had avoided talking to him. He hadn't made good on his promise to invite her out to dinner yet, and she didn't want to have that discussion with him when Nate was nearby.

Lucretia finally followed her family out the door, with the assurance that her three older children would attend the Sabbath school when Sarah started it in a few weeks. Then Sarah turned to greet the others who had come that morning, but other than Peder, who joined them for dinner each Sunday, only Nate and the children remained.

"Are we ready to go home, then?" Uncle James asked as he and Peder picked up the hymnals from the benches and stacked them neatly on the end of the bar.

Nate cleared his throat. "I haven't had a chance to ask, but I was hoping Sarah would like to come on an outing with me and the children. I thought we'd pack a picnic and go for a walk in the hills."

Uncle James glanced at her. "It's up to you. We don't have any plans this afternoon except to enjoy the delicious meal Margaret has prepared, right, Peder?"

Peder grinned in response. "If Miss MacFarland isn't there, we'll just have to eat her share."

Sarah laughed. "I'm sure you will, Peder. I've never seen anyone who can eat more food than you."

Charley grasped her hand. "Then you'll come? Please say you will."

"Yes, I'll come. As long as you let me stop by the cabin and change into a more appropriate outfit."

Nate leaned close to her as they followed the children out the door. "I can't believe any other outfit would be more appropriate than the one you're wearing. You're beautiful."

Sarah stumbled on the threshold and Nate caught her elbow, sending tingles down her arm. Beautiful? He thought she was beautiful? She looked up at his face, certain she'd see his grin that would tell her he was making a joke, but only saw his warm smile. She smiled back. This afternoon promised to be a wonderful one.

Nate followed Charley up Boot Hill, following the faint trail to the formation of white rocks at the top. In front of him, Sarah walked next to Olivia with Lucy between them, holding both of their hands.

He could kick himself. He shifted the cloth bag holding their lunch higher on his shoulder. Why had he told Sarah she was beautiful?

He hadn't meant to. He had meant to say her dress was beautiful, but whenever he looked into those violet eyes, he lost all sense. At least no one else had heard what he said. He was thankful for that. Watching her now, as she and the girls climbed the last steep slope up to the rocky crown at the top, he thought he might be losing his senses again. All he could think of was how perfect it felt to have her here. Since last fall, when Andrew and Jenny had died, he had tried to make a life for the children. To make a family with them. But it was like eating bread made without salt. Their lives—his life—was tasteless and flat. But when she was here, everything was right.

He couldn't tell her, though. How could he ever ask her to become part of his life when all he touched went wrong?

As they reached the bottom of the rocky towers, Charley and Olivia ran on ahead, and Sarah helped Lucy up the steep slope.

They had today, though. He could enjoy her company today.

He pushed himself to catch up with the others, and they reached the grassy top of the hill together. All around them the white rocks towered above, as if they were standing on a head crowned with white quartz. Charley hoisted himself up on the side of the nearest rock, clinging to cracks in the stone.

"Don't climb up there, Charley."

"Why not?"

"Look how far you'd go if you fell."

Charley looked over the side of the hill. The trail they had climbed was steep enough, but on this side there was a sheer drop to the mining camp below.

Sarah looked and then stepped away from the edge, Lucy's hand firmly in hers. "I think we'll do just fine looking at the view." She turned to the east, where Bear Butte rose above the distant prairie. "Oh, it's so beautiful."

Nate couldn't look beyond her profile. Yes, she was right. It was beautiful.

He cleared his throat. "We should find a spot to have our picnic. It's a bit breezy up here."

Sarah turned to him with a smile, the wind whipping her hair around her face. Her cheeks glowed in the bright sun. "We passed a grassy spot a little way down, and it was out of the wind. Let's go down there."

The simple meal of bread and cheese was finished quickly. Lucy lay down with her head pillowed on Sarah's lap, while Charley and Olivia explored the area around their picnic site.

Sarah stifled a yawn. "If I'm not careful, I'll fall asleep like Lucy." She smoothed the curls out of the little girl's face. "You'll start building your cabin tomorrow?"

Nate leaned back against a tree. "I'd like to, but a corral needs to come first. We can continue living in the wagon, but the horses need space."

She sat in silence for a moment. "Then that means you'll be leaving your campsite soon."

He picked up a twig and broke it in half. That had been the plan all along, but then why did he feel as regretful as her voice sounded?

"We might wait a few days before we move out there. I want to make sure the stream is going to be a good water supply." Nate let his voice trail off.

She leaned back on her hands, careful not to disturb Lucy. "It's going to be a beautiful homestead, the way you described it yesterday."

"Yeah, maybe."

"You don't think so?"

Nate threw the twig away. "I've made plans before,

but they don't work out. Try and fail. That seems to be how I do things. I'll be happy to be able to keep the children fed and clothed." He shook his head. "Sorry. I just don't have good results when it comes to being a success."

"It depends on what you mean by success. I think the only successful life is following God's will. Whether you're successful in the eyes of man or not makes no difference."

"What do you mean?"

"Well, look at Uncle James. You'll have to ask him to tell you about his years in China. While he was there, he had to move from one city to another several times because the mandarins didn't want him teaching about Jesus. The other missionaries avoided him because he believed as Hudson Taylor did, that he should immerse himself in the Chinese society in order to reach the people. And then when his first wife died, he thought God had abandoned him."

Nate's throat tightened. He hadn't had any idea James had endured such hardships. "It looks like he was right, doesn't it? How could he think he was successful in those circumstances?"

Sarah was silent for a minute. Charley and Olivia's voices floated to them from farther down the trail where they were playing.

"I asked him that same question once. He said he spent many hours on his knees, asking God to show him what His purpose was in taking him to China."

"And the answer?"

She looked at him, her eyes moist. "He had gone to China because he thought he would win lost souls for Christ. But what he learned was that God only wanted his obedient spirit and willing heart. Once he learned that, he said his preaching changed. He was no longer trying to do God's work, but allowed God to work through him. He built a church, taught the Bible and trained men to be pastors. His students—all Chinese—started a dozen more churches, in places he would never have been able to reach on his own. By the time he came home, he knew his success wasn't in what he did, but who he followed."

Nate picked up another twig, methodically breaking it into one-inch pieces. How did he fit into Sarah's story? He didn't. His plan wasn't to save souls, it was to keep his family together. He threw the pieces of twig into the grass. And a fine job he had done of that so far. Ma, Pa, Mattie, Andrew, Jenny. He had lost them all. Ashes to ashes, dust to dust.

He dug his fingers into the long grass. "I still think the only way to measure success is if you do the job you set out to do, and my job right now is to get a roof over our heads before winter comes again."

That was success as far as he was concerned. Survival.

Tuesday afternoon, Sarah shooed Alan and Bernie Woodrow out the door to follow their sister home and closed the door. She leaned against it, glad for an opportunity to rest for a minute. Teaching was both energizing and exhausting. Sarah pushed a stray curl back into place with her forearm. As eager as she was to start each school day, she welcomed the quiet at the end of the afternoon, as well. Sometimes teaching the three siblings was more work than a classroom full of students. A sigh escaped as she picked up a book from the nearest bench and added it to the pile on her desk.

She hadn't seen Nate at all yesterday. He had taken the children out to the homestead early in the morning, before Sarah had left for school, and they hadn't come back to their camp until after dark. She had waited to see if he would come to tell her about his day, but as she sat on the bench outside the cabin, the campsite on the other side of the trees had grown silent.

Why was she looking for him, anyway? It wasn't as if he owed her an explanation of his activities.

Sarah took the rag and wiped the chalkboard clean and then straightened the benches. No, Nate would move to his homestead, and there would be no more picnics at White Rocks or long days spent with the children. She took the broom and attacked the ever-present dust in the corners. She wouldn't have the opportunity to see Nate again, unless he continued coming to church. But she couldn't count on that.

Opening the door, she swept the pile of dirt out into the alley.

"Miss Sarah!"

Charley was racing toward her from the street at the alley's head, followed by Olivia. Behind them came Nate and Lucy. He returned her smile before she turned her attention to the children.

"How are you?" She leaned the broom against the wall just inside the door as they all came into the classroom. "Tell me what you've been doing today."

"We've been out to our ranch." Charley had to pause to catch his breath. His face was ruddy from the sun and all three children were windblown and hot.

Sarah shot a look at Nate. His smile made him look

like the proverbial cat that had swallowed a canary. "So you'll be moving out there soon."

"We already started." Olivia grasped Sarah's hand. "We took the wagon out today and set up camp. Uncle Nate started a corral, and he's going to build us a cabin."

Sarah sank onto the nearest bench. "Already?" She put one arm around Olivia. "We weren't neighbors for long, but I'm going to miss you being next door."

She pressed her lips together to keep them from trembling. Lucy came over and Sarah lifted the little girl into her lap.

"You'll have to come visit us." Charley hopped on one foot as he spoke. "We're going to build fences and more corrals and a lean-to for the horses and a big cabin."

"You're going to be very busy. You won't have time for visitors."

Olivia leaned closer to her. "We'll always have time for you to visit. Won't we, Uncle Nate?"

Sarah looked up at him. They were leaving. Nate would be too busy with the homestead to come into town, and she had the school… When would she see him again? This was exactly why she refused to open her heart, so she wouldn't feel the blow when she had to say goodbye, but somehow, it was breaking anyway.

Nate turned his hat in his hands, his eyes meeting hers. "Don't forget, Olivia, we're going to be away for a while."

Away?

Charley stopped hopping. "We're going to Wyoming to buy some cattle. I'm going to be a real cowboy."

Lucy snuggled closer to her and Sarah felt that steel

rod of stubbornness that warned her she was going to interfere. Of all the ideas a man could come up with, this had to be one of the worst she had ever heard of.

"You're taking three children on a cattle drive?"

Nate twisted the hat brim. "Of course I am. They did fine on the trail when we came here from Michigan. Why wouldn't they come with me now?"

"On the trail with a crew of freighters is one thing. You were in a group and had plenty of protection in case of trouble. But this?" She stood, lifting Lucy in her arms. "This is ridiculous. Who is going to drive your wagon? Olivia? And what if the cattle run off, or one of you gets hurt or if the Indians…" A hiccup interrupted her. She couldn't go on.

She met his blazing eyes. He shoved his hat onto his head. "We'll be fine. I'll take care of the children, and I'll hire men to help drive the cattle home."

He didn't lower his gaze, and neither did she. Couldn't he see how pigheaded he was being? But what other choice did he have?

"Leave the children with me. I'll take care of them while you're gone."

"No."

"You know they'll be safer here, and you know I'll take good care of them."

"They're my responsibility, and they're coming with me."

Sarah pressed her lips together. Lucy wiggled in her arms and she lowered her to the floor. She glanced at Olivia and Charley, who were staring wide-eyed at her and their uncle.

The steel rod melted, leaving her trembling. She was just as pigheaded as Nate. "You're right. They're your responsibility. But please, think about what's best for the children."

She sat back down on the bench and looked at the floor, waiting for his decision. He paced from one side of the schoolroom to the other. He stopped in front of her and turned his hat in his hands again. He ran one hand through his hair and sighed.

"I can't help but feel that what's best for the children is to be with someone they love and trust. And that should be me."

Sarah's heart fell.

Nate paced the room again, his boot heels echoing with each step. He stopped in front of her, started to speak and then strode to the window.

After staring out at the sunny alley, he came back and squatted down in front of her with another sigh. One side of his mouth tugged up. "But I don't see any way around it. You're right. A cattle drive is no place for children." His words were soft, only for her. He paused, glancing at the two older children. They still watched him, waiting for him to decide their fate. "If you're willing to care for them while I'm gone, I'm beholden to you. I know I'll leave them in good hands."

"But, Uncle Nate," Charley said, "I was going to be a cowboy."

Nate stood up and faced the boy. "You will be a cowboy, but you need to learn how. I can't teach you and drive cattle at the same time." He laid one hand on Charley's shoulder. "Besides, the trip could be too dangerous for your sisters."

Charley nodded, and Olivia caught Sarah's eye, bouncing a little on her toes.

Sarah's mouth trembled. "And school? Can they attend school while you're gone?"

He shrugged. "I guess they'll have to, won't they?" He looked at the children again and then back at her, his eyebrows knitted together in a frown. "I trust you to do what is best for them while I'm gone."

Sarah nodded. "You don't need to worry. We'll get along fine."

Nate took Lucy's hand and ushered the children toward the door, but then hung back after they went out into the alley.

"I don't want you to think I'd put the children in danger, but I just assumed they'd come with me. They're my responsibility, and I don't take that lightly. It goes against my better judgment to leave them with someone else."

Nate rubbed his chin as he watched the children play. He was having second thoughts.

Sarah touched his arm. Just one touch, but it brought his gaze to hers. "Don't worry about them while you're gone. We'll take good care of them."

He rested his hand on hers, and the warmth of his fingers burned on her skin. "I'll leave at first light tomorrow and bring the children to the cabin on my way out of town, but I'll be back as soon as I can."

She longed to tighten her grasp on his arm, to hold him back, but she couldn't keep him from going. He needed to buy the cattle for his ranch. She put a smile on her face, hoping it looked genuine.

"Take care of yourself, and we'll be looking forward to your return."

# Chapter Nine

Nate shifted in his saddle, studying the cattle Barker's cowboys had sorted out for him. Most were young longhorns, thin and restless after a winter on the range. In the mix a few cows with spring calves cropped at the rich grass. Brown, white, piebald and spotted, they spread out over the prairie east of Camp Sturgis, in the shadow of Bear Butte. The rest of the steers, sleek and healthy, bawled as the cowhands drove them into the army's waiting pens.

"What do you think?" Justice Cooper pulled his hat off and wiped the sweat from his forehead with a practiced gesture.

"I think I'm happy we're at the end of this drive." Nate shifted in his saddle, weary and sore. "And this herd will be a good start for my ranch. I owe Mr. Barker my thanks for letting me put them in with the cattle he was sending to Camp Sturgis."

Coop rode as if he lived on his horse. Nate had the passing thought that maybe the young man had never learned to walk, but started riding as a baby. Coop had become a good friend on the drive, nearly as close as a brother. He hadn't left Nate to himself the way the other Barker Ranch cowhands had, but had sought him out. The cowboy taught Nate the finer points of herding cattle, teaching him to anticipate each animal's next move.

But by the time the Barker herd had reached Camp Sturgis from Wyoming, Nate was dead tired. Driving cattle was a tough job, no matter how you looked at it. Between keeping them moving when they wanted to graze and stopping the young steers from heading up every dry draw they came to, the days were long in the saddle.

The nights were no better. Three times they had to fight off small bands of raiders. Indians or cattle rustlers, it didn't seem to matter. The raiders would edge up to the outskirts of the herd in the dark and drive off as many head as they could. By the time the night guard reached the spot, they'd be gone. They lost a few head of cattle in each incident.

And then one of Nate's cows had died along the way, just as they got into the Black Hills. She lay down while they watered the cattle at the Belle Fourche River near the Devil's Tower and didn't get up again. Cookie had let her calf ride in the chuck wagon, but it was touch and go with the little bull for a while. Nate hoped he'd be able to make the fifteen-mile trip up to the homestead from the military camp.

When the army's steers had been sorted out from the herd and bunched in a corral, the trail boss, Jed Slaughter, rode up to Nate and Coop. Jed's sun-browned face was hard and wary.

"Got bad news for you, Colby. The commissary officer doesn't care if we ran into rustlers, he still wants the full count of cattle he paid for. I offered him a re-fund, but he wouldn't take it when I had cattle stand-ing in front of the man."

Nate watched a couple hands cut a bunch of his steers out of his group and move them toward the cor-ral. He didn't have the practice to count them on the hoof the way Jed or Coop could, but he could tell he was left with far less than the hundred he had paid for.

"How many did I end up with?" He kept his voice low, his jaw tight.

"There are around seventy-five left."

"Am I going to have to take the losses on my own? I paid for a hundred."

Jed shifted in his saddle. "I know that. I'll give you a refund for some of them, but you have to expect a few losses on a drive like this."

"But not the army. Shouldn't they expect some losses, too?"

Coop leveled his gaze at Jed, who shifted in his saddle again.

"I'll refund the money for ten of your cattle. That's all I can do."

"That won't cut it, Jed." Coop edged his horse closer to Nate, still staring at Jed.

"Aw, come on, Coop. I have to answer to Barker."

"But you're asking Nate to take a bigger loss than Barker. You know that isn't right."

Jed leaned forward. "Colby here knew his cattle weren't all going to make it. I think his percentage is fair." He turned toward Nate. "Take it or leave it."

"And if I leave it?"

The trail boss shrugged. "The army will be happy to buy another seventy-five head, and I'll be able to give Barker the full amount he expects." He turned his horse toward the army camp. "Let me know what you decide by morning."

Coop watched Jed ride away. "I'll tell him what I decide. Barker's a fair man to work for, but I'm not going to hang around as long as Jed is the boss. He'd shave his own ma to make a profit." He leaned down to pat his buckskin's neck. "Maybe I'll see what's happening up Deadwood way." He tilted his head toward Nate. "Know any outfits that need a cowhand?"

Nate and Coop both turned their horses toward his herd of cattle. "I'd hire you in a minute, if I had any way of paying you."

Coop plucked a head of grass as they rode and stuck it between his teeth. "Maybe we could work something out. Didn't you say there was another claim next to yours?"

The rest of the mountain meadow, up for grabs to whoever claimed it. "Yes, but I've taken on as big a section as I'm allowed."

"What if I filed on it?"

Nate reined in his horse. "You'd want to settle down? Have the responsibility of a homestead claim?"

Coop shrugged and pulled his horse up facing Nate. He leaned on the horn of his saddle and looked beyond Nate to the foothills surrounding Boulder Canyon and the mountains beyond. "When I look at those hills yonder and think of the country we've been driving the cattle through the last couple weeks, I feel an urge to be part of it." He looked at Nate. "Did you ever feel that way? You take a look and know that you've found the place where you belong?"

The muscles around Nate's heart constricted. Yes,

he knew. From the first moment he had seen his land, he knew.

Coop didn't wait for Nate to answer. "That's how I feel when I look at those hills. Not as high or wild as the mountains farther west, but a man can put down roots in them. Build something to last. That ranch you have in mind, raising horses and cattle, that's something that I can do." Then he looked at Nate and grinned. "And if I decide settling down isn't for me, I'll sell my claim to you after I prove up on it. Until then, we can be partners."

Nate followed Coop's gaze up into the foothills. Could he partner with Coop? Did his friend even know what he was getting into, offering such a thing? Taking up a yoke with him might not be a smart idea for the cowhand. While some people turned everything they touched to gold, for Nate everything turned to ashes.

But all along the trail, as Nate had watched Coop and the other cowhands handle the cattle, he had discovered just how complex a job he had taken on. Herding wild longhorns in this Western land was nothing like taking care of cows in the East. This bunch of his was more like a herd of deer or mountain goats than cattle. How would he ever learn to keep them alive without some experienced help?

Coop was offering more than a chance at gaining the other section of land as part of his homestead. He was offering his knowledge, his experience and his life. At least for the next five years.

Without Coop's help, would he even be able to prove up on his homestead? Without Coop's help, would he ever have a home for the children? A home to offer to

Sarah… He wouldn't let his thoughts go any further down that path.

During the long hours inside his own thoughts on the drive, he had been forced to face the truth. Every time he thought of the future, the homestead and his family, Sarah was always part of the picture. But Miss Sarah MacFarland deserved better than what he could offer her.

He had to admit, though, that he needed the help. He glanced at the cowhand next to him. He not only needed his help, he needed his friendship and the partnership he offered.

With Coop's help, the future he envisioned might become a reality.

Nate stuck out his hand. "Partners."


"Miss Sarah," Olivia called from the church half of the building, "do you want me to clean the windows, too?"

Sarah straightened the last bench in the row and went into the front room where the children had been sweeping. "No, we don't need to wash the windows today, but you can dust the windowsills."

Looking around the large room, Sarah smiled. What had once been a run-down saloon was now a clean and comfortable place of worship. The building had been transformed since she had first seen it, and even Margaret hummed as she polished the walnut veneer on the piano. The poor thing still sounded tinny, but no one complained. Margaret's playing was a blessing.

Margaret gave the piano a final rub with her cloth. "Are you ready for our first Sabbath school, Sarah?"

"I think so. I've chosen the creation story to start with. I just hope we have students."

"We'll have at least three." Margaret tilted her head toward Olivia and Charley as they raced each other to finish dusting the windows. Lucy sat on a bench, holding her rag doll while she watched them.

"And the Woodrow children are planning to come." Sarah ran her dust cloth down the slats of the swinging door and then stopped with a sudden thought. "Uncle James put notices in the newspapers, didn't he? And flyers in the stores? Star and Bullock's store and Furman and Brown's?"

"Yes. Of course, many folks won't see the advertisements until later in the day, but the families who come to church will know about it."

Olivia finished the windows and brought her rag to Sarah. "They're all done. What else do we need to do?"

Sarah glanced at Charley, making a second round of the windowsills with his rag. "We're all finished. Everything is ready for tomorrow, so we'll head home for dinner." Lucy slipped off her seat on the bench and took Sarah's hand. Sarah crouched down to the little girl's level. "Are you hungry, Lucy?"

She waited. Charley's running steps echoed in the big room while Olivia and Margaret chatted about what to make for their meal. Lucy lifted her eyes up and Sarah held her breath. Even though the smiles were progress, Sarah still longed to hear Lucy speak again. But the little girl gave only a nod. Sarah smiled, hiding her disappointment, and gave her a quick hug before standing and following the others out the door.

Nate had been away for three weeks while the children stayed behind. At first, Sarah was afraid Lucy would retreat further into herself again when Nate left, but she seemed to understand his absence was temporary and made herself at home with the MacFarlands.

Sarah both dreaded and welcomed the day Nate would return. She looked down at the little girl next to her as they walked. Somehow, these children had wormed their way further into her heart than she had thought possible. Giving the children back to their uncle would be difficult, but she couldn't keep her affection for them from growing stronger with each day. The longer Nate stayed away, the more she let herself love and enjoy the children as if they would always be together.

But at the same time, she missed Nate. She missed watching him with the children, missed his wry grin when he teased her with pointed barbs and she missed the way his hand felt when he laid it on hers.

At that thought, Sarah's face heated even though they walked under the awning of the Custer House. She swung Lucy's hand a little. Lucy glanced up at her and swung Sarah's hand harder. When Sarah exaggerated the swing even farther, Lucy giggled.

Lucy giggled! Sarah looked to see if the others had heard, but they were walking several feet ahead, and the street was crowded and noisy.

Sarah laughed and repeated the high swing, almost pulling Lucy onto her toes. She was rewarded with another giggle, and she picked the little girl up in her arms and twirled her around.

"I love to hear you laugh, Lucy! You have the prettiest voice."

A hand grasped her elbow and she turned to meet

Wilson Montgomery's frown. He propelled her across the walk and against the hotel's wall.

"Miss MacFarland, you're making a spectacle of yourself." He glanced around them, released her elbow and dusted off his suit.

Lucy's smile was gone, her face blank. She threw her arms around Sarah's neck and turned her face away from Wilson.

No one had noticed Wilson or Sarah, and the crowd around them continued their regular business.

"I don't think playing with a child attracted undue attention, Mr. Montgomery."

"You don't know what people were thinking. I saw several men looking your way just now. Calling attention to yourself is inappropriate for someone of your position."

Sarah bit her lip and counted to ten. Slowly. The one dinner she had shared with Wilson Montgomery last week had convinced her there was no future in their friendship, but he continued to assume a relationship that was nonexistent. For Uncle James's sake, and for Aunt Margaret's, she would be civil to him.

"I will take your opinion under consideration."

Wilson pressed closer to her as a young woman, dressed in bright pink flounces, passed by on the boardwalk followed by several admirers. The woman blew a kiss in Wilson's direction as she passed and then put on a pretend pout when he didn't acknowledge her.

When he spoke again, his voice was low. "I would urge you to control yourself in public. You don't want to be compared with the likes of that woman."

He nodded in the direction of the girl in pink, who had turned around and was teasing the men following her in a bright, ringing voice. Everyone around had stopped to watch her, but she kept glancing toward Sarah—or was she trying to get Wilson's attention?

Wilson took her elbow again and guided her past the crowd, moving so quickly that Sarah was almost running as she clutched Lucy in her arms. He didn't stop until they caught up with Margaret and the other children at the bottom of the Lee Street steps.

Margaret smiled and blushed. "Why, Mr. Montgomery, what a surprise to meet you again."

Wilson released Sarah's elbow and removed his hat, bowing slightly toward Aunt Margaret. "Mrs. MacFarland, it is always a pleasure."

"It is so kind of you to escort Sarah through these crowded streets."

Olivia and Charley stood on either side of Aunt Margaret, but Wilson hadn't acknowledged them.

"May I escort you ladies home? I have business at the bank, but nothing that can't wait for ten minutes."

Sarah saw Margaret's smile start and jumped in with her refusal before her aunt could gush her acceptance.

"We don't want to take any more of your time, Mr. Montgomery. We will have no trouble getting home on our own from here."

"As you wish, Miss MacFarland." His smile didn't go any farther than his thin lips as he bowed toward her and then toward Aunt Margaret. He took his leave, still not glancing at the staring children.

Sarah set the quiet Lucy on her feet and took the girl's hand. Olivia joined them, a slight frown on her face.

"Miss Sarah, is that man courting you?"

"Isn't it wonderful?" Aunt Margaret swept over to

Sarah. "Wilson Montgomery is going to be an influential man in Deadwood very soon, and he is honoring you with his interest. Has he asked you to dinner again?"

Sarah flexed her left elbow, still sore from Wilson's attention. "No, Aunt Margaret, he hasn't." She held up her hand to stop Margaret's protest. "And I don't want him to. He may become an important man someday, but I have no desire to let our friendship go any further." If it even was a friendship.

Olivia let Margaret and Charley go up the steps ahead of them.

"I'm glad," she said, taking Lucy's other hand. "Because I want Uncle Nate to court you."

Sarah felt her face heat. "Your uncle Nate hasn't said a word about courting." She stopped, and Olivia looked at her. "And I don't want you to mention it to him. If Nate Colby wants to come courting, it has to be his own idea, not yours or mine."

Olivia grinned. "Then you do like him. I knew it!"

Sarah started up the path again. "Of course I like him. He's a kind man and takes good care of you children." She glanced at Olivia's triumphant face. "But that doesn't mean I want to marry him."

She laughed as Olivia's face fell. "But don't worry, whatever happens or doesn't happen between your uncle and me, we'll still be friends."

Olivia grinned again. "Forever?"

She stopped, giving both girls a hug. "Forever." She kissed the top of Lucy's head and then Olivia's cheek. "No matter what happens, we'll always be friends."

Sunday morning's service started out like every service of the past month, with a scattering of families filling the rows of benches here and there and Peder Swenson in his usual place in the third row. Sarah smiled at the children she knew and introduced herself when a new family paused in the doorway.

"Good morning," she said, extending her hand to the wife. Her face was drawn, her eyes hollow. "You're welcome to come in and join our worship service."

The wife glanced at her husband and then shook Sarah's proffered hand. "We didn't know there was a church here. We live up in Galena and haven't been to town since last fall."

Her husband stepped closer to the door, peering in as Margaret started playing a hymn for the prelude. "I think we have time, Katherine." He glanced at Sarah, looking her up and down and then at his wife. "But we ain't dressed for church. We'll have to come another week."

"Nonsense." Uncle James met them at the door and ushered them into the building. "You're dressed just fine. Please, take a seat and join us."

Sarah turned to Katherine, smiling at the two boys hiding behind her skirt. "We have a Sabbath school this afternoon for the children. Perhaps your sons would like to attend while you and your husband do your shopping."

Katherine's tired face brightened. "We'd like that. We'd like that fine. I hate to see the boys growing up without Bible learning."

Sarah watched them take their seats on one of the benches, and then turned back to the door. A grizzled miner was standing there, and he snatched his hat off when Sarah greeted him. "Never mind me, ma'am. I'll just find a place. I heard you have good hymn singing here."

By the time Margaret had finished the prelude and Sarah had taken her seat on the front bench with Charley, Olivia and Lucy, three more miners had followed the first. Sarah turned her attention to Uncle James as he read the call to worship from the book of Psalms, silently thanking God for bringing new people to their small church.

After the second hymn, Margaret left the piano and sat next to Sarah. She leaned over and whispered in Sarah's ear, "There's one of those girls from the Badlands outside the door. She's going to drive good people away from the church, don't you think?"

Sarah didn't answer. Aunt Margaret had never understood her need to help these poor women. She had never confided her fears to Aunt Margaret. She knew how fine a line lay between the naive orphan she had been before Uncle James found her and the girls who worked in the saloons. Between the scripture reading and the sermon, while Uncle James was arranging his notes, she glanced back at the door. She could see the top of a girl's head above the swinging saloon doors and her bright red skirt underneath.

She leaned close to Margaret. "I'll be right back."

As the first words of the sermon started, Sarah slipped out the door, startling the girl in red. It was Dovey. She was much younger than Sarah had thought at first, and she jumped like a spooked deer. She clutched a flimsy purple lace shawl around her bare shoulders.

"Don't go." Sarah reached out a hand to stop her as the girl edged away.

She looked down at her dusty slippers. "You don't want someone like me here. I'm sorry I intruded."

She glanced at the open doorway of the church and bit her lower lip.

"You're not intruding." Sarah stepped closer to the girl. "You're the one they call Dovey, aren't you? Is that your real name?"

The girl looked at her then and smiled shyly. Face powder barely covered an old bruise on her cheek. "My name is Maude, but Tom—Mr. Harris—said it wasn't a good name, so he gave me the new one."

"I'm Sarah. My uncle is the pastor here. You're welcome to come in and sit down."

Maude blushed and backed away. "Oh, no, ma'am. I know my place. I just stopped to listen to the singing and then the Word. That's a powerful Word he read, isn't it?"

Sarah's eyes pricked when she remembered the passage of scripture Uncle James had chosen for his sermon that morning, the story of the woman caught in adultery. "You heard Uncle James read the scripture?"

"Yes'm." Her face broke into a smile. "When I heard that Jesus kept the people from stoning that woman…" She blushed again and looked down. "I didn't know the preacher could tell a story about someone like me in church."

"It isn't only a story. It's true. Jesus kept the people from stoning the woman and then told her to go and sin no more. Did you hear that part?"

Maude nodded, her face suddenly sad and hard. "That's how I know it can't be true. Once you're like me, you can never change."

She pressed her lips together, and Sarah waited for

her to say more. Uncle James's voice drifted through the door, preaching the grace of God's forgiveness, but Maude took a step back.

"I shouldn't have come. It's too late for me." She pulled her shawl tight around her shoulders and slipped behind a passing wagon.

Sarah nearly went after her, but she had disappeared into the mass of people filling the streets on this Sunday morning. Between the bands playing in the Badlands, trying to attract miners to their shows and the street preachers shouting in the intersection, the morning was anything but peaceful. She prayed that in all that chaos, God would protect that young woman.

Nate eased out of the saddle, stiff and tired after days on the trail. But now he was home.

He led Scout to the small stream meandering through the meadow and let him drink while Nate tilted his head up to take in the hills surrounding his land spread out in front of him. The cattle were already settling down to grazing on the lush grass. Even the little orphan bull calf pulled at the green carpet.

His land.

He flipped his hat off and wiped the sweat from his forehead with one arm. This was what he had been working toward for years. His own place.

Coop rode up next to him. "They look like they're going to like it here."

Nate grinned at him as he dismounted. "They better like it here, because I'm not taking them one step farther."

"It's a good range with plenty of good water." Coop squatted down upstream from the horses and scooped some of the clear water into his mouth. "Yep. This is perfect." He stood and looked up into the surrounding hills.

"Your claim would start just left of that rock outcropping—" Nate pointed across the valley "—and include the far end of the meadow and up into the hills."

Coop shoved his hat back onto his head. "I like what I see. If you agree, we'll start the partnership right now."

Nate shook his partner's hand, waiting for the churn of regret in his stomach, but there was only the buoyancy of anticipation. "Let's get into town. I've got children to collect, and you have a claim to file on."

They walked their horses toward town, making their way to Two-Bit Gulch and then to the trail along Whitewood Creek. Now that the cattle were settled on the claim, it was time to bring the children out here for good. How had they been during the weeks he was away?

He should have worried about them more, shouldn't he? But every time his mind flew back to Deadwood and the children, he knew they were all right. He could trust James and Margaret to take good care of them.

And Sarah. He urged Scout into a faster walk. Had she thought about him while he was gone? He longed to look into those violet eyes of hers, and perhaps she would even let him hold her hand for more than a brief minute, if he could presume on their friendship that much.

As they rode past the mining claims along the creek, Nate counted only a few men scattered here and there, all of them sitting idle by their claims. One of them reached for his rifle as they rode past, but didn't say a word.

Coop came alongside Nate when the narrow trail widened. "Where are all the miners?"

"It's Sunday. Most of the miners take Sunday off and go into town for supplies and to break loose a little."

Or go to church. Did James still have his small flock attending each Sunday? And Sarah had said something about a school for the children on Sunday afternoon. Olivia would like that. Maybe he should let them continue after they moved out to the claim. He urged Scout into a trot as they reached the edge of the mining camp nestled in the gulch. It would give him an excuse to see Sarah every week, too.

When they reached the trail leading to the MacFarlands' cabin, Nate turned to Coop. "This is where I turn off. The claim office is up Main Street there, about four blocks."

"All right. I'll meet you back at the ranch."

Coop headed off, and Nate couldn't help grinning after him. Ranch? The cowboy was right. With cattle grazing on the green grass, he certainly couldn't call it a claim anymore.

The cabin was empty when he reached it. The MacFarlands must still be at church. He rode back to his old camp, where he had left the horses in James's care. They stood in the small corral, their ears pricked. As Nate dismounted, Scout reached over the fence rails toward the other three horses.

Nate patted each nose in turn. "Hey there, Pete old boy, how are you doing?" He scratched ears and greeted each horse until he reached the long black face with the gray nose waiting for him at the end of the row. Loretta greeted him with bared teeth. He ignored the mule and unsaddled Scout. He turned him into the corral with the others and gave each of them a measure of grain in preparation for the short trip to the homestead. Nate caught himself with a laugh. The ranch.

By the time he had finished caring for the horses, he heard voices on the trail from the mining camp. He left his chore and went to the MacFarlands' cabin to watch the children walk toward him. Lucy and Olivia were both wearing new dresses, and Charley was wearing a tie. Sarah had decked them all out for church. She shouldn't have made new clothes for them.

He looked beyond the children to Sarah and his irritation rose. There was that Montgomery fellow behind her, escorting her up Williams Street as if she belonged to him. The afternoon sun glinted off the watch chain spanning the banker's brocade vest, and his jacket was spotless. The five of them made a right cozy family.

Nate rubbed at his whiskers, weeks old. Suddenly his trail-worn clothes weren't comfortable anymore. He wanted to retreat back to the waiting horses, but Charley spotted him.

"It's Uncle Nate!" His yell made everyone look at Nate, and he was too late to escape their notice.

Instead he put a welcoming smile on his face and waited for the children to reach him. He didn't have time to think about Montgomery anymore as he was grabbed by Charley and Olivia.

"Uncle Nate!" Olivia's voice squealed. "How long have you been here?"

"Only long enough to take Scout's saddle off."

As Sarah reached the group, she stumbled and Nate shot his hand out to steady her, but he was too late.

Montgomery was already there with a hand at her elbow. Nate felt his face turn stone cold at the smile Sarah gave the man.

He gripped Charley's and Olivia's shoulders. "You two go get your things together." He spoke without looking at them. He couldn't take his eyes off Sarah as she exchanged a few words with Montgomery. "We need to get out to the ranch so we can get settled in before dark."

Charley was off to the cabin with a yippee, but Olivia didn't move. He tore his eyes from staring at Montgomery's hand resting lightly in the center of Sarah's back and looked down at his niece.

"Didn't you hear me? We need to get going."

Olivia chewed her bottom lip as she looked from him to Sarah, whose violet eyes were finally turned to him. He could lose himself in her smile, if Montgomery wasn't hovering behind her.

"I'm so glad you made it home safely, Nate." She turned to Lucy, who had not left Sarah's side. "Don't you want to say hello to your uncle?"

Lucy stared at him, stuck her thumb in her mouth and stepped sideways to hide behind Sarah's skirt. His stomach constricted. What had happened to his Lucy while he had been gone?

Sarah turned back to him, her eyes shining. "She's made such great progress while you've been away." She stepped forward and put her arm around Olivia's shoulders. "We've all had a wonderful time, haven't we, Olivia?"

Montgomery stepped next to Sarah, nearly touching her, and held out his hand. "We're happy to see you back safe and sound, Colby."

Nate ignored Montgomery. The *we* in his comment made the situation all too evident.

"Olivia, Lucy, we need to pack up and get to the ranch. Go get your things, right now."

Olivia's eyes brimmed with tears. "But, Uncle Nate, Miss Sarah and I were going to…"

Sarah leaned down with a quiet voice. "We can continue our plans another time, Olivia. Now is the time to obey your uncle."

"Yes, ma'am."

Olivia didn't look at him again, but took Lucy's hand and went into the cabin.

Nate's face burned under caked dust. "Thank you for taking care of the children while I was away."

Sarah's eyes met his, and he felt a smile start. She was more beautiful than he had remembered.

"It was my pleasure. I hope you'll let them come and stay with me often. I enjoy their company so."

Montgomery stepped forward, cupping Sarah's elbow in his hand once more. Was it only his imagination that a look of irritation passed over Sarah's face?

"I'm sure that won't be necessary, dear. Colby is going to be busy, and he'll need the children to help him. I'm sure we won't be seeing much of him from now on." He turned his calm, cool smile on Nate. "Will we?"

The cold rock that had been turning in Nate's stomach turned once more and then dropped. Nothing sounded better than getting out to the ranch with the children and never coming into town again. He turned toward the cabin and stepped forward to take a bundle from Charley.

"We need to get the horses hitched up. Are your sisters coming?"

"Yup. Lucy's crying, though."

The rock turned again.

"Nate," Sarah said. She pulled her arm out of Montgomery's grasp. "You can at least stay for supper, can't you?"

He turned toward the trees screening the old camp. "I want to get out to the ranch before dark."

He heard footsteps behind him and turned when she laid her hand on his shoulder. Her eyes were wide, questioning. Nate let himself swim in them for a second... two...

"Montgomery's waiting for you. You can have supper with him."

He left her standing there and followed the boy. They harnessed the horses in silence, and Charley tied the mule to the back of the wagon. His nephew must have figured out that he was in no mood to talk, and that was good. The way that rock was seething red-hot in his gut told him he wouldn't be civil to anyone. Even Charley.

Finally they were ready. He drove the wagon to the front of the MacFarlands' cabin, where the girls were waiting for him. Lucy clung to Sarah's skirt, and even Olivia was crying as she stood with her arms wrapped around Sarah's waist.

When he reached for the children's bundles to load onto the wagon, Sarah took Olivia's hands in her own. She leaned down to talk to both girls. "You know we'll see each other again."

"But it won't be the same." Olivia hiccupped.

Sarah smiled, but Nate could see the tears in her

eyes. "I'll see you at church next week. Won't I?" She looked at Nate, but he couldn't answer.

Sarah gave both girls a hug and a kiss and helped them into the wagon. "Remember what we talked about? We need to trust God for the future and not worry." Nate twisted the reins in his hands but couldn't watch the last goodbyes. His mouth was as dry as ashes. He shook the reins and the horses started down the trail. He didn't look back. Sarah had made her choice.

# Chapter Ten

Sarah listened until the creak and rumble of the wagon wheels disappeared in the general noise from the mining camp. Suddenly, the clearing was very large and very quiet.

She let the tears fall as she went into the cabin. She had been looking forward to Nate's return, but he was so distant. So quiet. So…angry. Had something gone wrong on his trip? Why hadn't she asked him?

Kicking a chair away from the table, she took a leftover biscuit from under the towel that covered them and sat down. She knew why she hadn't asked. That overbearing Wilson Montgomery. He had insisted on escorting her home. He had even presumed to speak for her when all she wanted to do was welcome Nate home.

But she had had no words when Nate's manner had been so grim. Even though he was dirty, sweaty and trail worn, she had wanted to greet him with more enthusiasm than was proper. Even with the children present, she had almost made a fool of herself. He certainly wouldn't appreciate her being so forward as to give him a welcoming hug. But between his stony face and Wilson's presence, she had resisted the urge.

Could Wilson have been the cause of Nate's mood?

She broke off the edge of her biscuit and popped it into her mouth.

The only reason for that would be if Nate resented the banker for some reason. And the only reason she could think of for him to dislike Wilson was that he was jealous.

The biscuit was dry powder in her mouth.

Jealous because he cared for her?

She rubbed at the tense spot between her eyes. Could it be that Nate cared for her? He couldn't. They weren't more than friends, were they?

Nate Colby was just a friend. That was all.

She swallowed the dry biscuit.

But if he was only a friend, then why did it feel so right when he laid his hand on hers?

She spread her hand on the table, feeling the wood grain beneath her fingers. When she was a young girl, she had decided that she would never love anyone. The pain when her parents died in the boating accident was too much to bear, and she didn't ever want to go through that grief again. But then James and Margaret had amended her decision with their persistent love, and she had made an exception.

Still, to love opened her heart to pain, and she knew that pain so well. It was part of her, like a Gordian knot filling her with its intractable complexity. No one could loosen it. No one could set her free of its bonds.

But somehow, the children had tugged at the cords until she had to admit she loved them, in spite of her resolve. She had no choice but to let them into her heart.

Nate, though, was another matter. If she loved him, the pain would be unbearable when he left. She wouldn't let that happen. She couldn't.

Leaving the table, she went to the dry sink, where a pail of water stood. She lifted the towel covering it and lifted the dipper for a drink. The cool water cleared her throat and her mind.

She had sent Wilson away as soon as Nate had followed Charley to their campsite. Once they were alone, she had turned on him. She rarely needed to be so blunt with a person, but Wilson seemed to ignore her suggestions and hints. She had told him to leave and hadn't let him protest or even apologize. She regretted she hadn't helped him down the trail with a nudge from her foot.

Sarah finished the biscuit and wandered out to the bench in front of the cabin. She and Olivia had planned to look for the next reader among the books Sarah had brought with her from Boston and then climb up the hill behind the house to a grassy spot they had found. All three children had enjoyed the time they spent up there during the warm summer evenings, Olivia and Charley taking turns reading aloud or lying on their backs to watch the sky as the day passed into twilight and it was time to return to the cabin.

And so quickly they were gone. Not only the children, but Nate, too. If he didn't bring them into town to school, or to church, would she ever see him…them… again?

A low-down, thoughtless skunk. That was what he was. He had no right to be angry at Sarah. She could keep company with whoever she chose.

Nate turned the horses off the road up the trail to-

ward his ranch, the noise of the jangling harness finally drowning out the sniffles from the wagon behind
him. They'd get over whatever was bothering them.
He gripped the reins between his fingers, urging the
horses through the rough grass. It was only right that
they'd miss Sarah.

He drove along the creek until he reached the cattle,
still bunched from when he and Coop had left them
earlier in the afternoon.

"There they are." Nate nudged Charley with his
elbow. The boy hadn't said anything on the drive out
from Deadwood. "Seventy-five head of the prettiest
cattle this side of the Missouri."

The rough ground made Charley jostle on the seat
next to him. "Those are the ugliest cows I've ever
seen."

"They're longhorns. You've seen longhorns before."

Charley sighed. "Yeah. I guess."

"It's our ranch, Charley." Nate shifted a glance
sideways toward his nephew. "Aren't you the one who
couldn't wait to be a cowboy?"

"But why did we have to leave Miss Sarah? Why
can't she come out here with us?"

Nate's gut wrenched. If things were different, then
maybe. "Miss Sarah has her own home with her aunt
and uncle, and her school. And her friends."

"But we're her friends, aren't we?"

As they reached the small knoll by the old beaver
dam, Nate pulled the horses to a halt. He couldn't think
of an answer to Charley's question.

"Let's get the horses unhitched." The pole corral
he had put together before leaving for Wyoming was
still in place, and the ring of rocks where they had built

their fire still encircled the gray ashes. It was as if he had never been away, except for Montgomery's possessive hand on Sarah's elbow.

"Come on, Olivia. You and Lucy come on out of the wagon, and we'll get supper started. I'll get a fire going after we take care of the horses."

Olivia climbed out of the wagon and paused, looking back the way they had come. "Someone's coming, Uncle Nate."

Nate followed her gaze. "It's Coop. I hope he has good news for us." He unharnessed Ginger. Charley led her to the corral as Nate turned to Scout.

"Who is Coop?" Olivia was still watching the horseman riding across the grass, skirting the cattle.

"He's a friend I made on the trail. He's going to be part of the ranch."

Charley took Scout's lead rope but didn't move. He stared as the cowboy rode up to them.

Coop nodded toward Nate, then removed his hat and dismounted in one smooth motion in front of Olivia and Lucy. "Now, who are these two lovely ladies?"

"This is Olivia and Lucy. And over here is Charley. Say hello to Justice Cooper."

Charley's mouth hung open until Nate laid his hand on the boy's shoulder. He laughed at Charley's expression but couldn't blame him for staring. Coop looked as if he had just ridden right out of the pages of Charley's dime novel.

"Nate, when you told me you were going to fetch some children, I never suspected they'd be such fine young folks." He grinned at the girls and shook Olivia's hand. "Pleased to make your acquaintance, ladies." He turned to Charley as he replaced his hat. In the two weeks he had known Coop, Nate hadn't seen his head bare for more than a couple minutes at a time. "And you're the cowboy, right?"

Charley stuck out his hand. "Yes, sir. That is, I want to be."

"Your uncle and I will make a cowhand out of you in no time flat."

"How did things go at the claim office?"

The cowboy's grin widened. "I'm a homesteader, thanks to you. Now all we need to do is keep those cattle growing fat and sassy."

Coop's arrival lightened everyone's mood. Before the fire had settled into coals, Nate's and Charley's bedrolls were laid out under the wagon and Olivia had mixed up a batch of corn bread. While it baked, the sky turned to dusky blue. Orange-streaked clouds floated above the hills to the west.

"What's the first thing we need to do to get this ranch going?" Nate asked Coop as they ate the corn bread and canned beans.

"We need to mark those cattle before very much time goes by. Have you decided on a brand?"

Nate nodded. "I've been thinking on it, and I have a design in mind. I'll draw it out for you tomorrow and you can let me know what you think." He sopped up the last of his beans with the edge of his corn bread and stuck the mess into his mouth. "Are all the cows bred, do you think?"

Olivia looked up from her supper. "Miss Sarah said not to talk with your mouth full."

He swallowed and then stared at her. Across the fire, he saw Coop's grin before the cowboy ducked his head. "Did Miss Sarah also say that children should respect their elders?"

"Yes. But that part about not talking with your mouth full is important."

When did she get so grown-up? "You're right. I should mind my manners. Thank you for reminding me." He reached over and squeezed her shoulder. "Now you'll mind your manners and let Coop and I talk. Right?"

"Right. Except..." Olivia pushed her beans around on her tin plate.

"Except what?"

"What about school?" She looked up at him, her eyes wide. "I really want to go to school, and if we're branding cows and all the other stuff, we won't be able to go."

Nate looked from Olivia to Charley. The boy was watching him, waiting for his answer.

Lucy pulled on his sleeve. "I want to go to school, too. I want to see Miss Sarah."

"Lucy! What did you say?"

"I want to go to school."

Not just a word or two. A complete sentence. Nate looked from Lucy to Olivia, and then to Charley. "How long has she been talking?"

Olivia shook her head. "She hasn't been. It just happened."

Nate's empty plate fell to the ground as he grabbed Lucy in a big hug. "You can go to school. Anything you want." Sarah had thought Lucy might start talking all at once like this, but he had given up on ever hearing her again.

Lucy pushed back from him and rubbed at his whiskers. "Can we go tomorrow? Miss Sarah said I could draw a picture tomorrow."

He couldn't contain his grin. "Of course you can go tomorrow." He glanced across the fire at Coop. "I'll take you into Deadwood and order the branding irons while I'm there."

And he'd see Sarah. Could he bear seeing her, after watching her with Montgomery today?

He smoothed Lucy's hair and gathered her in as she settled in his lap. He needed to thank her for helping with Lucy, for whatever she had done, even if she didn't want to see him again.

By the next day, Sarah had convinced herself she wouldn't see the Colby children at school. Even if Nate did agree to bring them, they were still in the process of setting up their home on the ranch.

As she followed Uncle James down the steps to the mining camp, she let her mind drift to Nate's homestead. The one day she had spent there seemed like a dream. Removed from the smells of the town and the noise of stamping mills, the mountain meadow had been a quiet, windswept retreat. More than once during the past few weeks she had let her mind drift to the ranch, but no more. She shook herself and hurried to catch up to Uncle James. That dream was out of reach this morning.

The Woodrow children waited for her at the doorway to the school.

Bernie Woodrow ran to meet her. "Where is Charley?"

"The children's uncle returned yesterday afternoon, and they moved to their homestead."

Laura held Sarah's books as she unlocked the door. "Are they coming to school?"

Sarah forced herself to smile at the girl. "I don't know. Mr. Colby and I didn't have an opportunity to discuss it yesterday." They hadn't had time to discuss anything. She opened the door and took her books from Laura. "Why don't you three water our plants while I get things organized for the morning?" She nodded toward the tomato seedlings the children had planted a few weeks ago. The south-facing window gave them plenty of light, and being in the schoolroom protected them from the crowded streets outside.

Bernie and Alan took the pail from its hook and went out to the horse trough on Main Street while Laura turned the plants to give each one the benefit of the best light. Sarah wrote the date on the chalkboard and below it wrote the Bible verse for the day.

Just as she finished, Bernie came into the schoolroom with Charley. When Olivia and Lucy followed behind them with Alan, Sarah's throat grew tight. It seemed silly that she had missed them so when they had only been gone one night. She hugged the girls, and Lucy clung to her.

"I missed you so much, Miss Sarah."

The little girl whispered the words in her ear so softly, Sarah almost didn't hear them. But they were there. Lucy had spoken!

"I missed you, too, Lucy. I'm so glad you came to school today." Sarah drew back, holding Lucy's hand in her own, and knelt so she was on the child's level. Tears threatened to blur her vision, and she wiped them away with her handkerchief.

Lucy grinned, her dark eyes shining. "Are we going to draw today?"

As if speaking was the most normal thing in the world!

"Of course we are. I brought everything we need, and we'll get out the art supplies after we finish our reading and arithmetic."

A shadow covered the doorway, and Sarah looked up into Nate's eyes, so much like Lucy's. He leaned against the doorframe with his hat in his hands, a half smile on his face as he looked down at the two of them.

"Lucy, why don't you help water the plants while I speak with your uncle?"

Lucy wrapped her arms around Sarah's neck, nearly knocking her over. "I love you, Miss Sarah."

Sarah hugged the girl tight and then released her as Lucy ran off to the window. Sarah had no choice but to stand and face Nate. She walked toward the door, and he stepped back into the alley so they could talk out of the children's hearing.

"When did Lucy start speaking?"

He avoided her eyes. "She joined in our conversation last night at supper as if she had been talking all along. I thought maybe she had started while I was away, but Olivia said she hadn't."

"She was as quiet as ever while you were away. Maybe she's happy that you're home."

Nate curled the hat brim but didn't answer.

"Thank you for bringing the children to school this morning. I'm sure you didn't have time to make the trip in from your homestead."

Nate turned his hat in his hands. "I needed to come to town anyway, and, well…they wanted to come."

He took a step closer. "I wanted to thank you." She watched his hands twist and roll the hat brim. "When Lucy spoke to me last night…" He looked at her then flicked his eyes down to his hat again. "Well, I about fell over. You said she had made progress, but I had no idea."

"I didn't, either."

"I had tried everything I could think of to help her." The hat brim twisted again. "But nothing I could do or say made her better. She just seemed to fold into herself. Some days she wouldn't even look at me, or Olivia or Charley. I was afraid there was something broken deep inside her that I couldn't fix." He shifted his gaze to her face, and her knees wiggled like jelly. "But you reached her, somehow. You reached that broken place and fixed it. What did you do?"

Sarah shook her head. "I really didn't do anything. I just…" She cast about in her mind. What had she done? Only waited and prayed.

"You just loved her." Nate rubbed at his chin with one hand. "You loved her, and she felt safe. I can't let her lose that safe feeling, so if it's all right with you, I'd like to keep bringing the children to school."

"That would be just fine." Her mouth was dry. He stood as if there was a wall between them. "I enjoy them in the classroom, and they've become good friends with the Woodrow children. We're having an art lesson today, and Lucy's looking forward to…"

She let the words drift to a halt. He didn't want to listen to her ramble on. She wanted to retreat to the schoolroom, where the unsupervised children would be more peaceful than the beating of her heart.

Nate turned to leave, but she stopped him with a touch on his sleeve.

"Is everything all right?"

He shoved his hat on his head. "Of course. Everything is just fine. I'll be back this afternoon to pick up the children."

"I know Aunt Margaret and Uncle James will want to see you. Won't you and the children come for supper?"

"I need to get back to the ranch." He took a step away and her hand fell back to her side. "And I'm sure you'd much rather spend your time with someone else." He turned to leave.

"Nate…" He didn't turn but walked down the alley and around the corner onto Lee Street.

Sarah slipped into the noisy classroom and closed the door. Tears pricked at her eyes. Yesterday afternoon, and now this morning. Maybe she had been right about him being jealous of Wilson, but he had no reason to be. None at all.

"Miss Sarah." Olivia tugged at her skirt. "The boys are chasing flies again."

If she didn't bring order to the classroom, the day would be lost. Sarah turned and clapped her hands. The sharp claps broke through the children's shouts, and as they turned toward her, she sat behind her desk. "We need to get our school day started. Please take your seats."

Six sweaty and disheveled children sat on their benches, grinning at her. She lifted her Bible from its place to begin the day with scripture, but the looks on the children's faces stopped her.

"What is it?"

Laura giggled into her hand. Her brother Bernie looked at the floor, his feet scuffing the wood planks. So he was the guilty one.

"Bernie, I want you to tell me what you are all laughing at."

Her back itched. One time the boys had placed a hairy spider on the back of her chair and had watched it crawl up her arm and into her hair before she had noticed the creeping tickle. Bernie and Charley exchanged looks and she jumped from her chair. No spider.

"I'll tell you, Miss Sarah." Olivia stood as if ready for recitation.

"Yes, Olivia?"

"They said you have a beau." At this Olivia collapsed on her bench with her hand over her mouth, giggling as hard as Laura.

"A beau?" They couldn't mean Wilson Montgomery, could they? The children would have noticed his unwavering attention yesterday.

"It's Uncle Nate." Lucy wiggled in her seat.

Olivia finished for her. "Uncle Nate is your beau, Miss Sarah. When are you going to get married?"

Sarah grasped the side of her desk as her face grew hot. How had they ever come to that conclusion?

She cleared her throat and waited for the giggles to subside. "You are all mistaken. I do not have a beau." She took her seat and lifted her Bible again, turning to the Psalms. Olivia's frantic waving called for her attention.

"Yes, Olivia?"

"If Uncle Nate isn't your beau, then why are you always so happy when you see him?"

Sarah put on her best schoolteacher face. "That is

none of your concern." She looked from face to face. "It isn't a concern for any of you." Clearing her throat, she leafed through her Bible until she found the right page. "Children, this morning we're reading from Psalm 91."

As she read, Sarah's mind wandered to Nate. She had never been so confused in her life. Why did she care about this new distance between them? If she didn't know better, she would think he was worming his way into her heart the way the children had.

She reached the ninth and tenth verses in her reading. "Because thou hast made the LORD, which is my refuge, even the most High, thy habitation, there shall no evil befall thee, neither shall any plague come nigh thy dwelling."

Her voice faltered. The Lord was her habitation. The Lord was her only refuge, not any man.

## Chapter Eleven

Nate waited until the corner of the church was between him and the door of the school and then leaned with one hand against the wall. A fool. He was a fool. He had no right, no place in her life. No call to be putting himself forward when she needed a man who could care for her the way she deserved. A man who could provide for her and one she could count on to protect her when danger threatened.

And that man wasn't him.

A footstep thumped on the wooden porch. "Good morning, Colby." Montgomery's voice was ice cold. "What are you doing here?"

Nate straightened, running his eyes up and down the banker. Montgomery held a pair of white kid gloves in one hand and hit them against his palm with a restless motion.

"I brought my children to school." He took a step closer. "And what are you doing here?"

Montgomery sniffed and laid a finger under his nostrils as if some scent had offended him. "I'm here to talk business with Reverend MacFarland. It's none of your concern." He waved his gloves toward Nate. "You can go on your way."

Nate bristled at the other man's dismissive attitude, but he couldn't think of a reason to stand outside the church any longer. He watched Montgomery go into the former saloon and headed toward Main Street. He may not be the right man for Sarah, but that narrow-faced, slicked-up weasel sure wasn't, either. He reached the corner and glanced back toward the church. He'd do anything to protect her from a man like that one.

He rolled his shoulders. The hot sun beating on his back made his scars itch. Was he judging Montgomery too harshly? The man went to church and seemed to be an upstanding citizen, but something about the banker rubbed him the wrong way.

Crossing the street, he passed a familiar figure leaning against the wall of the hotel. Nate turned the face over in his mind as he walked down Main, past the printing office, a bath house and the dry goods store. Nate reached the end of the block before he could place the man leaning against the hotel. It was Tom Harris. The man whom he had nearly fought with over that girl Dovey. Was it only a coincidence that he had seen both Harris and Montgomery in the same few feet?

His imagination was running rampant. The two couldn't be connected. Montgomery was too worried about his reputation to risk associating with someone like Harris.

He passed through the Badlands on his way to the forge where he had left the horses and wagon. As he went by the Mystic Theater, he ignored the scantily dressed women on the balcony calling to him. One on the street, at the corner of the building, drew his attention, though. It was Dovey. Her red dress advertised her profession, but she lacked the brassy demeanor of the girls leaning over the railing above. She stared at him as he walked by, then he heard footsteps behind him and a hand plucked at his sleeve.

When he turned, Dovey pulled at him, toward the alley next to the Mystic.

He pulled his sleeve out of her grasp. "I'm not interested in what you're selling, miss."

"I only want to ask you a question." She peered down the alley to the back of the building and then toward the street. Her pinched face was pale.

"What is it?" Nate was leery of talking to this girl, even if she did remind him of Mattie. Men had been ambushed in alleys like this.

"You know the girl at the church? The one with the dark hair?" She wouldn't look into his eyes, but twisted a worn flounce on her dress between her fingers.

She must mean Sarah. "Yes, I do. But what does she have to do with you?"

Her face reddened. "Shh. Don't talk so loud." She glanced down the alley again. "You just saw her, didn't you? You take your children to the school."

"Yes, she's teaching today."

"She spoke to me once. I stood outside the church and heard the preacher. I can't get the Word out of my head. It won't let me be."

She met his eyes, challenging him. She must have been to the church on a Sunday, and Sarah had spoken to her. "What do you want?"

"She'll speak to me again, won't she? She can tell me what it means."

Nate nodded. If anyone could explain what a Bible passage meant to this girl, it was Sarah.

"Can you tell her? I mean, that I want to see her?"

He had told Sarah that if she wanted to help these girls, she'd have to wait for them to come to her, but he really hadn't thought one of them would seek her out. "I'll give her the message."

She stiffened as the sound of measured footsteps on the boardwalk drifted down the alley, and then pushed him away.

"If you don't want any fun," she said, her voice loud and petulant, "then go away and make room for someone who does."

She ran down the alley as Nate turned and looked into the face of Tom Harris. He held the man's gaze as he brushed past him and then continued on his way toward the blacksmith.

This idea of Sarah's could be more dangerous than she thought.

Sarah tilted the watch pinned to her shirtwaist to read the time. Nearly four o'clock. Her scholars leaned over sheets of newsprint she had begged from the printer, faces serious as they attempted to draw their chosen model. What Lucretia Woodrow would think of three novice artists' portraits of their teacher, she had no idea. What Nate would think? She skirted her mind away from the thought.

The students concentrated as they used her treasured oil pastels. She had instructed them on the proper use and admonished them to take care. As far as they were from civilization, and as expensive as freight was, the pastels may as well be irreplaceable.

At a knock on the door, she glanced over to see Nate waiting outside. She looked at her watch again and beckoned to him.

"All right, children, it's time to go home. If you aren't finished with your drawing, you may place them here on my desk to finish tomorrow."

Olivia lifted her drawing to admire it. "May I take mine home, Miss Sarah?"

"Yes, if you're finished, you may take it home. Let me show you how to roll it to protect it from the wind as you carry it."

As Sarah rolled up Olivia's paper, and then Charley's and Bernie's, Nate opened the door. He stood aside as the Woodrow children burst out of the classroom.

"You three can go out with your friends for a minute. I want to speak to Miss Sarah."

Olivia turned her back to Nate and mouthed the word *beau* to Sarah. Sarah felt her face flush as she gave Lucy a hug goodbye.

"I'll see you all tomorrow."

After they followed their friends out the door, Nate took a step closer to her.

"I have a message for you, from that saloon girl Dovey."

Sarah looked at him, all thoughts of the children's teasing forgotten. "Dovey?" She had included the girl in her prayers but had no idea if she'd ever see her again.

"She said she was here at the church one Sunday and that she hoped you'd explain the Bible passage for her."

"What did you tell her? When can I see her?"

"Now, hold on."

His frown fell on her like a bucket of cold water.

He wouldn't try to stand in the way of this girl learning about God, would he? But even as she faced his stormy expression, her mind flitted from one possibility to another. Where could she meet Maude to talk? What questions did the girl have? What other Bible passages could they discuss?

"You don't really think that girl wants to know anything about the Bible, do you?"

"What do you mean? Of course she does. I could see it in her face the morning she was here—she's hungry to hear about Jesus and to see some light of hope in her life."

"Those girls just want to use people. That's all they do."

Sarah felt her chin lift. "You met her. She has a name. Not Dovey, but Maude. Didn't you see she's different from the others?"

Nate shifted his feet, and his face softened as he considered her words. "You may be right. There was something different about her. But you live in a separate world from her. You can't just have her come to the church like…"

"Like anyone else? We're talking about a young woman, Nate, not some kind of leper."

He took a step toward her. "I know, Sarah, better than anyone. But there is a difference." His soft voice penetrated her defenses. "She has chosen a path that puts her in a place in society you aren't part of. Men look at her differently than they do you. She is welcome places you aren't, and she can't think of going places you take for granted."

"Like church?"

Nate nodded. "Like church. And that's not all. You

enjoy a certain safety, even in Deadwood, because of the kind of woman you are. Even the most hardened ruffian respects a gentlewoman, and you can walk down most streets without fear of being accosted. She can't go anywhere without meeting someone who would use her without a thought. She isn't safe from that anywhere."

Sarah turned away from him. She had never imagined what kind of life a girl like Maude led—no one had ever told her the details beyond the obvious sinful activities connected with her line of work. Her mind flitted back to the orphanage, not long before Uncle James had come to claim her. She had overheard a comment from one of the patrons of the orphanage about her future. The only words of the conversation she had heard were spoken in a tone that told her of the possible shame and degradation that awaited her, an orphan with no means to support herself and no prospects.

"Hire her out to a good family," the woman had said, addressing Mrs. Blair, the matron. "You don't want her to end up on the streets, the poor victim of some man's schemes."

Sarah had hurried away from the open door, mortified that she had been eavesdropping.

How close had she come to living a life like Maude's, or Nate's sister's? Alone and forced to support herself? She shuddered at the thought.

"Maude is someone's daughter. She was a child once, like Lucy or Olivia. Maybe she didn't have someone to love her, like they do. Maybe she didn't have a choice when she…" Sarah shook her head, banishing the thought of what Maude may have gone through to arrive at the place where she was now. What had Nate's sister gone through? No wonder he had spent so many years searching for her.

"If she's asking for help, I can't turn my back on her. I have to try."

Nate stepped up behind her. She felt his hands brush her sleeves, but he didn't touch her.

"No, you can't, can you? You wouldn't even be able to turn your back on a starving kitten."

Sarah's eyes stung. He understood the situation even more than she did.

"I'll help you, Sarah. I don't know what we can do, but you only need to ask, and I'll be there."

She turned around, but his hands didn't move. She froze, his strong chest inches away, her forehead nearly brushing his chin. He closed his hands, grasping her arms, and pulled her close. She couldn't look up into his face, but she couldn't back away, either. Taking a deep breath to steady her nerves, she inhaled the scent that clung to him—leather, horses, woodsmoke. His hands held her gently, his strength restrained. This was Nate, not the man who had kept her at arm's length this morning. She felt his lips brush her forehead, lingering as he breathed in. She wanted to raise her face to his, to let him give her the kiss hovering between them, but he dropped his hands and backed away.

"Just let me know what I can do." His eyes avoided hers. "I'll bring the children to school in the morning." He shoved his hat on and slipped out the door.

Sarah sank down on the closest bench. After all her resolve, she would have melted into his embrace if he had kissed her. She chafed her arms, trying to feel something other than the burning brand of his hands. She couldn't love him. She wouldn't. She shook herself and rose to clean the chalkboard, putting thoughts of Nate out of her mind. She paused her vigorous wiping. It was no use. She would never forget the way she felt in his arms. He held her as if she was something precious.

But she couldn't let her imagination run away with her. Nate Colby didn't have any special feelings for her. He couldn't. She wouldn't let him, not when he could change his feelings at any time. She wouldn't risk his refusal.

She forced her thoughts to another problem. What to do about Maude? She must see the girl somehow, and it wasn't likely to be here at the school or the church. If it was any other girl, any of her friends in Boston, she would call on her one afternoon. She would walk to her house, present her card to the maid and they would spend an hour or so chatting while they occupied their hands with needlework. How many afternoons had she spent visiting with her friends that way?

Sarah gathered the papers scattered on her desk into a neat pile.

Aunt Margaret carried out such visits with the ladies of Deadwood, the few that braved the mining camp to settle here with their husbands. Sarah hadn't been able to accompany her, since her responsibilities at the school occupied her time.

She could call on Maude. Sarah stacked her schoolbooks. She chewed on her bottom lip as she wiped her pen and corked the inkwell. Maude worked at the Mystic, and lived there, too. But she couldn't risk going there again.

The memory of Nate's frowning face loomed before her. Of course he wouldn't approve of her seeking out

Maude. Neither would Uncle James or Aunt Margaret. But would God approve? What did He want her to do?

As she picked up her books to take home, she resolved to pray about it. Prayer had never failed to help her reach the right answer.

A week later, Sarah ate her Monday morning breakfast with only half her thoughts on the sourdough pancakes Margaret had prepared. The rest of her mind was preoccupied with Maude.

Sarah had hoped Maude would come to the church again, but she hadn't. Yesterday's heavy rain had kept most of the families away, at least the ones who lived outside of Deadwood gulch. Nate hadn't brought the children, but she could hardly expect them to make the journey in the storm.

Maude only had a short walk down the block, though. She might have stayed away because she thought she would feel uncomfortable in church. Sarah pushed at a pancake with her fork. What if Mr. Harris was preventing her from coming? She had to talk to Maude.

Every time she thought of approaching the Mystic Theater again, her stomach went into convulsions. She didn't want a repeat of that Saturday afternoon, but how else could she contact the girl?

"It's going to be a beautiful day after yesterday's rain," said Uncle James. He sopped up the last of the sugar syrup with the final bite of his pancakes. "What do you have planned today, dear?"

Aunt Margaret refilled all three of their coffee cups and set the pot back on its hanger by the fire. "I thought I'd do some visiting this afternoon. Mrs. Brewster has a new knitted lace pattern she wants to show me, and I'm going to take her some of that green thread I have left."

"Could you take a few minutes to stop by Star and Bullock's? I need more pipe tobacco."

"Oh, my, no. No respectable woman goes shopping on Mondays. You remember that, surely."

Margaret's tone brought Sarah's attention fully on the conversation. Her Monday afternoons had been spent in the classroom, but she had never noticed anything different about that one day of the week. "Why not? What happens on Mondays?"

Her aunt sniffed, then took a sip of her coffee. "That's when the saloon girls do their shopping." Her eyes shifted to Sarah's. "Remember that. Never go shopping on Monday afternoon."

"I'll keep that in mind."

Sarah let the rest of the conversation continue around her as an idea formed in her mind. This may be her only opportunity to see Maude without going to the Mystic to seek her out. She finished her coffee and started up the ladder to gather her schoolbooks from her bedroom.

"I must be going if I want to get to school on time." She hesitated. "And, Aunt Margaret, I have a few things to take care of after the children leave, so I may be later coming home."

Aunt Margaret started clearing the breakfast dishes. "That's fine, Sarah. I'll see you this evening."

In the loft, she took her second-best dress from the peg on the wall. It was clean and would fit Maude perfectly. She folded it carefully and wrapped it in a bundle. Then she picked up her books and slipped down the ladder and out the door. Now all she had to worry about was if Maude went shopping with the rest of the girls and if she could find her in the busy streets.

That school day dragged. The children behaved well enough, even though Uncle James wasn't in the next room. He spent the day visiting families who lived outside Deadwood.

One disappointment was that the Colby children came into town alone, all three riding on Charley's mule. She hadn't realized how much she was looking forward to the quick hello from Nate to start her morning on the right foot, even though he remained as distant as ever. As if those few moments in the classroom the previous week had never happened. Finally, four o'clock rolled around and she sent the children on their way. Closing and locking the door, a twinge of guilt made her look back through the window to the sunny room. She had never left a classroom without cleaning it first, but today she couldn't take the time. She pocketed the key, took her pile of books in one hand and the bundle in the other and started off for Main Street.

Yesterday's rain had made a miry mess of the streets. Horses walked in mud nearly up to their knees, while the drivers of the wagons shouted curses to keep their teams from stopping before they got to firmer ground.

Sarah crossed Lee Street on the wooden crosswalk and paused on the corner, looking up and down Main. Aunt Margaret had been right. The saloon girls crowded the boardwalks in front of the stores, their bright silk dresses and fancy plumed hats lining the street like a show of exotic tropical flowers. Not one "respectable" woman was in sight.

Finally, she caught sight of Maude's red dress and purple shawl in a cluster of girls outside a peanut vendor's next to The Big Horn Grocery on Upper Main. She hurried across the street on the wooden walk, soaking her kid shoes in the slime as the boards sank into the mud beneath the weight of the crowd doing the same. Thankfully, she climbed the stairs between Lower and Upper Main, out of the mud for a change.

When she approached the group of girls outside the peanut vendor, Maude recognized her right away.

The girl hurried to meet her. "Sarah, what are you doing here?" She glanced at the girls behind her.

"I came to see you. I have something for you." Sarah held the bundle out to the girl, who took it with hesitant hands. "It's a dress. Something you can wear when you want to come to church, or visiting, or anything."

Maude pulled the corner of the wrapping back to reveal the green calico. "It's lovely." She looked at the girls behind them again. "I'll have to keep it secret. Tom, I mean Mr. Harris, wouldn't want me to have it."

"Surely he isn't concerned about what you wear when you aren't working, is he?"

Maude looked at her with a mixture of pity and envy in her eyes. "You wouldn't understand. He says I owe him money for my trip here, and my room and board, and until I pay him back I have to do what he says."

Sarah took a step closer to the other girl. "You mean you can't even leave if you want to?"

Maude shook her head. "Not until I pay him back."

"How are you going to do that?"

"He keeps my earnings and pays for my room and board at the Mystic, and then the rest goes to him."

"How long has it been?"

The other girl bit her lip and glanced behind her again. "It's only been six months."

Six months of slavery. Sarah bit her lip, too, but only to keep back the words she longed to say.

"I'll help you leave this life, if you want to."

"You can do that?"

Maude's face held such hope that Sarah longed to take her hand and run home with her. But over the girl's shoulder she could see that the other girls had noticed them talking, and coming down the boardwalk behind them was Tom Harris with a couple other men. They wouldn't get farther than the top of the stairs leading to Lower Main before they would be stopped.

"We can't talk now, but I will help you. If you can, meet me in the afternoons at the Wall Street steps. School lets out at four o'clock, and I'll pass by there on my way home when I can. Even if we can't talk, at least I'll know you're all right."

"Yes, oh, yes."

"What do we have here?" Tom Harris stepped up beside Maude and draped a possessive arm around her shoulders.

Sarah straightened herself to her full height. She would not be intimidated by this bully on Main Street in the middle of the afternoon. Hours of listening to Dr. Bennett's lectures on the evils of men who took advantage of young women came back to her, and she raised her chin.

"We were just visiting. Women quite often enjoy visiting on a fine afternoon like this."

Harris narrowed his gaze. "You're that preacher's niece, aren't you? The schoolteacher?"

Sarah nodded. "Yes, I am."

He moved Maude behind him and stepped closer. Sarah took a step backward.

"If you know what's good for you, you'll leave my girls alone. Nothing good can come from them talking with you."

Sarah looked from Harris, to the two thugs who flanked him, to Maude, who cowered behind Harris. She had accomplished all she could this afternoon.

"I'll be on my way, if you'll excuse me."

She turned and made her way to Lee Street and the route home. To safety. But would Maude ever find her way home?

## Chapter Twelve

The next several days were busy ones for Nate as he and Coop worked to get each cow and calf branded with the new C Bar C brand they had designed.

Coop had protested using both of their initials in the brand. "I don't know how long I'll be around. What if you find a new partner whose name doesn't begin with *C*?"

Nate had straightened up after releasing the first branded calf and brushed the dust off his chaps. "No matter. *C* stands for Colby as well as Cooper, and someday, if Charley is running this ranch on his own, his initials will fit right into it." He had grinned at Coop. "Besides, I have a feeling these hills are in your blood. You'll find a nice girl, build your house under that rocky outcropping, and you won't be going anywhere."

Coop had shoved his hat back on his head and gazed at the hills surrounding them. "Yep. Maybe you're right. I can't imagine leaving this place."

After the branding was finished, he and Coop started felling trees for the cabins they needed to build before winter set in. As busy as they were, Nate couldn't justify taking the time to escort the children to school when they were able to make the two-mile ride on their own.

Even if Sarah would rather spend her time with Montgomery, he had looked forward to a glimpse of her. By the next Sunday morning, though, he knew he couldn't stay away any longer. He had to see her, even if it pained him.

The morning dawned bright and hot. Just as Nate started hitching Pete and Dan up for the ride into town for church, Coop took over for him on Pete's harness, fastening the traces.

Nate whistled at the other man's shaved face and polished boots. "What are you all slicked up for?"

"It's Sunday, isn't it? You're going into town for church, and I'm going along with you." He grinned at Nate. "Every time we need something from town, you hightail it off the ranch like you were off to see someone special, and I want to know who it is."

Nate felt the back of his neck heat up. "There's no one special. I'm just taking the children to church."

"And I'm coming with you."

By the time Nate had helped the children climb into the wagon, Coop had his buckskin saddled.

"You're coming with us, Coop?" Charley almost fell out of the wagon in his excitement.

"Sure am, cowboy. It's Sunday morning, isn't it?"

Lucy bounced on her seat. "Will you sit by me at church, Coop?"

Coop leaned over and patted Lucy's curls. "I can't pass up an invitation like that."

Nate chirruped to the horses and the wagon started

down the trail through the meadow. It was almost a road already. Coop rode ahead of them, checking on the cattle. When they reached the road to Deadwood, he fell back to ride with the wagon.

"The cattle are looking good. These days on that rich grass is putting some weight on them, and the calves are doing well. That little orphan bull calf is doing just fine, too."

"You were right when you said this was a good herd to start with."

"Tell me about your church. The preaching is good?"

"I've only been there once, but I think you'll like Reverend MacFarland. He won't put you to sleep."

Coop grinned at him. "Good preaching rarely puts me to sleep."

Nate shifted the reins through his fingers. "I never figured you for a churchgoing man, Coop."

"How can you look at all this beauty around you and not know in your heart of hearts that there is a God who set all these things in place? I just figure He deserves my praise every day and my worship with other believers whenever I can."

Nate watched the other man as they rode along. Coop's eyes were turned up to the crests of the surrounding mountains, ignoring the scarred and torn creek side they rode past. From the stories he told around the campfires along the trail, Coop hadn't had an easy life. Nate thought about what Sarah had told him about her uncle's experiences in China. These men had both seen hardships, even tragedy, yet they insisted on worshiping God as if they didn't hold Him responsible for what had happened to them.

No, not that they didn't hold Him responsible. It was

almost as if they thanked God for the difficulties He had put them through.

Would he ever think of thanking God for what he had experienced in the war? For the fire that took Andrew and Jenny? Nate shook the reins to keep the horses moving past a particularly green patch of grass. He couldn't imagine being thankful for that.

They reached the outskirts of town and Coop dropped behind the wagon. Pete and Dan picked their way through the crowded streets. As they passed the Mystic, Nate glanced at the balcony, where a few girls lounged on the rail, but he didn't see Dovey's red dress. He hadn't seen Sarah since he had promised to help her meet the girl. She wouldn't be so foolish as to try to seek out the girl on her own, would she?

He turned the horses down Lee Street and pulled up in front of the church. Several families crowded the boardwalk, greeting each other as they went into the former saloon. He didn't remember that many people attending the last time he had attended the services.

Sarah met them just inside the door, giving Nate a smile before turning her attention to the children.

Charley reached for Coop's hand. "This is Coop, Miss Sarah. He's a real cowboy."

Coop took off his hat and nodded to Sarah. "Justice Cooper, miss."

"It's good to meet you, Mr. Cooper. You're a friend of Nate's?"

Nate cleared his throat, turning her smile back to him. "Coop and I are partners. He's taken the claim adjoining mine. He knew I could use his expert help."

James walked up to the group just as Nate finished. "Did I hear you say the two of you are ranching together?" He shook Coop's hand. "That sounds like a fine idea. Are you from the West, Mr. Cooper?"

He and Coop walked away, leaving Nate to watch Sarah greet the children as if she hadn't seen them in weeks. She bent her dark head toward Lucy's curls. They could be mother and daughter, the way they looked alike and with the love they had for each other. Nate took a step back. It was almost as if they were the family and he was the outsider.

Margaret sat at the piano and the first measures of a hymn flowed into the room.

"It's time to sit down, children." Sarah turned them toward the benches then faced Nate. "Will they be staying for the Sabbath school this afternoon? We start an hour after the service."

He lost himself in those blue eyes. "Yes, of course. They would enjoy that."

Sarah rewarded him with a smile, and then her gaze strayed past him to the door. "Oh, she came!"

Nate turned to see who Sarah meant. Dovey stood just inside the door, as if she wasn't sure if she was in the right place. Her red dress was gone, and in its place was a green dress he had seen Sarah wear often.

Sarah took the girl's hand and brought her over to him. "Nate Colby, I think you've met Maude Brown. This is her first Sunday with us, so I'm going to sit with her. Would you and the children like to join us?"

Nate looked into Dovey's—Maude's—face. She wouldn't meet his eyes. He knew that feeling. She was afraid someone would recognize her—that someone would know who she was and what she was. How many times had he felt that condemning gaze when people knew his cowardice had killed his brother? But here, in Deadwood, he had left the past behind. He glanced at Sarah's face. She held her bottom lip between her teeth, waiting for his reaction. As if he thought this girl was any less deserving of a fresh start than he was. Had anyone ever given Mattie this same chance?

He smiled at the girl and gave her a nod. "I'm pleased to meet you, Miss Brown."

Her face reddened. "You don't recognize me?" Her voice was low, quivering. She glanced at the other people in the room, all finding seats on the benches.

"Of course I do. I'm happy to meet you under different circumstances this time."

Her eyes met his, wet with unshed tears. "Thank you, Mr. Colby," she whispered.

Sarah pressed her hand on his in thanks and then led the other girl to a seat on one of the back benches. Of course she wouldn't sit in front. That would make Miss Brown uncomfortable.

The children filed into the row after Sarah, and then Coop took his seat next to Lucy. Nate sat on the end of the bench. When he spotted Wilson Montgomery two rows up, he felt a warmth of satisfaction. At least the man wasn't sitting with Sarah in church. Yet.

As the service ended, the families of the congregation drifted out of the warm church onto the covered boardwalk in front to enjoy visiting in the breezy shade. Sarah stood with Maude near the end of the building. She refused to think of the girl by her professional name.

"Would you like to have dinner with us? I'm afraid it will be quite hurried, since the children will be coming for Sabbath school before long."

The girl shook her head. "No, I can't. I have to get back before they miss me." Maude grasped Sarah's hand. "I just want to thank you. I never heard what your uncle was saying before today…that everyone is a sinner. I thought…" She bit her lip. When she spoke again, her voice was a whisper. "I thought it was just me."

Sarah leaned her head close to Maude's. "No one is immune to the sin that affects us all. The difference is in what God did to redeem His people. When we understand that, then we know how marvelous God's grace is."

"Do you really think I could be saved?"

"Of course. It isn't a question of whether God is able to do that. You have already felt Him working in you. That's why you came here—why you are looking for Him. And once He draws you to Himself, He will never let you go."

Maude's eyes filled. "But how can He do that when I'm living like I am? He can never forgive me, can He?"

Sarah squeezed the girl's hand. "Of course He can. And He can help you live differently. We'll both ask Him, all right?"

But Sarah could tell Maude had stopped listening. Her eyes were fixed on something…someone…behind Sarah, and her face had blanched. "I have to go." She turned, gathering her skirts. "I'm sorry. I shouldn't have come."

Maude disappeared into the crowded street. Sarah turned around to see what might have driven her away, but she only saw the people from the congregation, gathered in groups as they talked together. Wilson Montgomery stood off to one side, watching her.

When he caught her eye, he lifted the brim of his hat in acknowledgment.

She fixed a friendly smile on her face as Wilson came near. She hadn't seen him since the Sunday afternoon when she had to ask him to leave the cabin. The expression on his face as he walked between the churchgoers who were making their way to their wagons and buggies told her he harbored no ill feelings for her blunt treatment of him.

"Hello, Sarah." His voice was smooth. Cultured. Familiar.

"Hello. How are you this fine day?"

"Excellent." He stroked his clipped mustache. "Do you have plans for dinner? I would be honored to have you dine with me at the Grand Central Hotel."

"You must have forgotten. I'm teaching the children's Sabbath school in a short while. I'm afraid I don't have time for a leisurely dinner." Sarah's stomach twisted at the thought of another meal in this man's company. He was friendly enough, but she certainly didn't want to encourage him.

"I wanted to ask you who that young woman was."

"What young woman?" Why would he be interested in Maude?

"You were just talking to her. She is quite young and pretty. Where does she come from?"

His eyes were daggers, looking past her heated face to the truth behind it. She had the passing thought that he knew exactly who Maude was.

"I think she's new in town." Would he see past her attempts to hide Maude's occupation? "Today was her first Sunday attending church."

He smiled, and she was reminded of a snake. "We'll

have to make her feel welcome if she comes back, then, won't we?"

"Yes. Yes, of course."

Wilson touched the brim of his hat. "I hope you have a good time with your students, Sarah."

"Thank you." She watched him step off the boardwalk and melt into the crowded intersection of Lee and Main, just as Maude had done. She rubbed her hands up and down her arms, suddenly chilled.

"Miss MacFarland." She turned to Justice Cooper, standing next to her with his felt hat in his hand. The cowboy inclined his head in the direction Wilson had disappeared. "Is that man a friend of yours?"

"He's an acquaintance, and a friend of my uncle's. Why? Do you know him?"

"No, ma'am. It's just that I saw him watching you talk to that girl, and then he came over to you as soon as she left. I thought perhaps he was bothering you."

Mr. Cooper's voice was gentle, his manner courtly. He smiled as he spoke, his eyes sharp and surrounded by fine lines, as if he spent his days gazing across the prairie in the bright sunlight.

"Thank you for your concern, but Mr. Montgomery was just…" She paused. Why had Wilson been so curious about Maude?

Nate joined them. He and Coop both towered over her. She had never felt so protected.

"Your aunt asked me to tell you she has your dinner ready."

Sarah glanced at her watch. "Oh my, it is getting late, isn't it?" She smiled up at both men. "Will you and the children be able to join us? I'm afraid we have nothing fancy to offer, just a cold lunch."

Nate backed away. "I have errands to run while we're in town. I'm sure the children will be happy to eat with you, though."

With a tilt of his hat, he was gone, with Coop threading through the crowded street after him.

Nate leaned against the wall of the freight office on Upper Main Street, Coop next to him. He hadn't exactly lied to Sarah. They had browsed through Star and Bullock's store while they waited for the children's Sabbath school to finish, but he could have accepted her invitation to join them for lunch. The sight of her talking to Wilson Montgomery ate at him, so he had left.

Coop shook his head as they watched the crowds surge and flow through the streets of the mining camp. "I never thought I'd see so much humanity in one spot. Where do they all come from?"

"Nebraska, Kansas, Illinois, Minnesota, Montana, Wyoming, Colorado, California, you name it. Once someone let out that there was gold to be found, every man and his uncle showed up for their share."

Coop looked at him. "But not you."

"Nope. Not me. The more I see these poor beggars digging in the dirt for scraps of dust, the more I'm happy to be banking on a sure thing."

"I wouldn't call cattle a sure thing." Coop pushed his hat back on his head.

Nate grinned at him. "Maybe not. But we're not standing knee-deep in icy water or breaking our backs hauling gravel to a sluice to do it, either."

A brass band marched down the street. The banner in front advertised a show at the Mystic that evening.

"Things never stop around here, do they?" Coop nodded down the street toward the Badlands, where a fistfight between two miners had held up the progress of the band. The upstairs girls hung over the balcony rail, calling to their favorites in the fight and egging them on.

"Nope, they never do." He watched Tom Harris push his way through the crowd toward Lee Street. Where was he going?

"That schoolmarm." Coop's voice was nonchalant, but Nate was on the alert. He hadn't missed the way Coop had looked at Sarah. "She's the one, isn't she? The reason you come into town so often."

"Maybe." Harris reached the Custer Hotel on the corner and leaned against the wall.

"If she isn't, you're missing out on something."

Nate turned his attention to his friend. "What do you mean?"

"I tried to get her attention, but when you showed up I may as well have been a bump on a log for all she cared."

"I thought she was pretty interested in you." Hadn't she kept her eyes on Coop the whole time they had been talking? Harris moved away from the corner of the hotel as families with children appeared from the direction of the church. "It looks like the children are done for the day. Are you ready to go home?"

"Yup."

Nate led the way through the crowd toward Lee Street. He had lost sight of Harris. Once they reached the alley next to the church, they left the crowds behind. Their horses stood in the shade of the building, hips cocked as they rested.

As they approached the door, a man's voice drifted out to them.

"Just leave her be. She's no concern of yours. She works for me, and you have no right to use up her time."

Nate opened the door, coming face-to-face with Harris. Behind the thug, Sarah stood straight, tall and trembling. She had Charley by the arm, while the girls hid behind her skirt.

Stepping aside to let Coop into the room, Nate looked from Harris to Sarah. "Are you and the children all right?"

"Yes, Nate. Thank you." Her voice was quiet. She took a step back, pulling Charley with her.

Nate looked back at Harris. "What's going on here?"

Harris grinned through scraggly whiskers. "The lady and I were just having a talk about a mutual friend. There's no harm done."

"A bully like you intimidating a lady? I'd say there's been plenty of harm done."

"I'm just telling her to mind her own business. What kind of lady keeps company with a girl from the Mystic, anyhow? I'd say she's no lady."

"It's time for you to leave, Harris."

"I'll say when it's time." As Harris spoke, he grabbed a pistol from his belt and pointed it at Nate.

But Coop's gun was faster and Harris's hand wavered. "I suspicioned you might try something like that." Coop reached over and pulled the pistol out of the other man's hand. He threw it out the door into the dusty alley.

"I think you had better go now."

Harris spat at Nate's feet. "You haven't seen the last

of me. You don't know who you've tangled with." He pushed past Coop and out the door.

Sarah let go of Charley and threw herself into Nate's arms. "I'm so glad you came when you did."

Nate clasped her close and then held her away so he could see her face. "Did he hurt you? Did he hurt the children?"

She shook her head, tears threatening now that Harris was gone. Lucy clung to her skirts while Coop stood watching them, his arms around Olivia's and Charley's shoulders. "No. No, he didn't come in until all the children had left, except…" She sniffed, and Nate untied the bandanna from around his neck and handed it to her. She blew her nose. "…except yours. And he just came right in the door."

"Who was he talking about?"

Her eyes met his. "Maude. He threatened to hurt her if I didn't leave her alone." She blew her nose again and leaned into his chest. "The poor girl." Her voice was muffled. "How can I help her?"

Nate looked past her to where Olivia stood, staring at them with wide eyes. Even Charley looked shaken. Nate caught Coop's eye.

"Why don't you take the children back to the ranch, Coop? I'll see Miss Sarah home, and then I'll be out to the ranch later."

Charley shrugged off Coop's arm and stepped toward him. "Are you going to find that man, Uncle Nate?"

Nate laid his hand on Charley's shoulder. "A man doesn't have to go looking for trouble. You and Coop need to take care of your sisters and I need to make sure Miss Sarah gets home safely."

"What about that man? Won't he come back again?"

Nate glanced at Sarah. She was pale and shaken. "He might, and if he does we'll deal with him then." He tousled the boy's hair. "Now you get on home with Coop."

As Charley led his sisters out to the alley, Coop stepped in close. "You watch yourself, Nate. I wouldn't put it past Harris to try to bushwhack you between here and the ranch."

"I'll watch my back trail."

The schoolroom was silent as Coop and the children drove past the window and out of the alley. Sarah turned and started cleaning the chalkboard. Nate straightened a row of benches before he heard a sniff.

He moved to the next row of benches, the one closest to the chalkboard. Another sniff.

"You aren't going to let that tough worry you, are you?"

Sarah took one last swipe at the board. "I'm not worried about myself. It's Maude." She turned to him. "What will he do to her when he gets back to the Mystic? Or what has he already done? Maude said he can get violent."

"Was all this because she came to church this morning?"

Sarah nodded. "I asked her to come. I thought that since it was Sunday morning, Mr. Harris wouldn't begrudge her a little time." Her nose was pink from holding back tears. "But she said Mr. Harris watches her every minute. He gets angry every time she…" Her face reddened and she looked at the floor. "Every time a gentleman comes calling. But if she doesn't…entertain them…he threatens to dope her up with laudanum so she won't care."

Her hands were shaking. Nate grasped one and led her to the bench, where he took a seat next to her. As her tears started to fall, he moved closer so she could lay her head on his shoulder, and let her cry.

When her tears subsided, he moved away while she sat up. "I told you that you and this girl were from different worlds."

She nodded and sniffed. "You were right. I had no idea."

He pushed the burning anger down. "I wanted to protect you from this."

"Protect me from knowing about the sufferings of my fellow human beings?"

He wanted to smile at how quickly he had gotten her dander up. "No, you wouldn't put up with that." He looked into her deep blue eyes. "I would protect you from knowing the bare truth of that kind of life. A girl like Maude, well, isn't it too late for her? Maybe you should concentrate on the girls you can help before they fall too far. One of your students would never become a saloon girl."

Sarah shook her head. "No. No, it isn't too late for anyone. Maude came to me. She asked for my help. I can't turn my back on her."

"But will she be able to turn her back on the life she's leading?" Nate studied the boards beneath his feet. "If Harris has been giving her laudanum, that means she could be addicted to it. Just like someone can be addicted to whiskey. It's an awful thing. A snare you can never be free of. How could she turn her back on that?"

"With God's help, she can."

God again. If Sarah had ever seen a person in the

last stages of drug addiction, she might not be so quick to assume God would be able to intervene. But he had talked to Maude. Her eyes were clear, her hands steady. Maybe she hadn't gotten caught in its clutches yet.

Sarah laid one hand over his. "I have to try to help her, Nate. I have to."

He took her hand in his and looked into her face. The tears were gone and her mouth was set in steely determination. He would kiss that mouth if she was his.

"Don't do it alone. Don't visit her on your own, don't try to contact her. I don't want Harris coming after you again. If you need to get a message to her, I'll take it. You need to stay away from the Mystic."

Her firm lips trembled up at the corners. "You'd do that for Maude?"

He squeezed her hand. He'd do it for her, and for Mattie.

# Chapter Thirteen

"I won't be able to say my piece, Miss Sarah. I know I won't."

Sarah looked over her shoulder at Olivia. With pins held tight between her lips and the bunting threatening to end up in a heap on the floor instead of festooned across the front of the schoolroom, Sarah was at a loss. She held the bunting in place with one hand and took the pins out of her mouth with the other.

"You've said it perfectly every day this week, Olivia. You'll do fine tomorrow night." She pinned the bunting in place and slid a step to the left on the bench. Another pin and another swoop of bunting.

"But that was only in front of you. When everyone is here, I know I'll forget. Can you hear me say it again?"

Sarah counted the remaining flounces. "Three more pins, and then I can." She slid another step along the bench. "Are the boys done washing the windows yet?"

"Yes. They went out front to wash the church windows."

A six-week school term was short, but it had been a good start. It was the end of June, and with the weather turning hot, the children were looking forward to a summer break before classes started again in September. Sarah pushed another pin into the soft wood. Not only the children. With no school schedule to keep, she hoped to be able to spend more time with Maude. Despite her best intentions, it was Thursday already, and she hadn't seen the girl since Sunday morning. When she had gone to the appointed meeting place after school, Maude hadn't been there. Had Harris hurt her as he had threatened? She had no way of knowing.

She pinned the last flounce to the wall. Mr. Woodrow had loaned the bunting to decorate the academy for the final exercises of the term. Not only would the children's parents be attending the program, but other townspeople would, too. Perhaps they would help spread the word and more children would attend school in the fall.

"Now, Miss Sarah?"

Sarah climbed down from the bench and sat facing Olivia.

"All right, Olivia. Go ahead."

Olivia stood straight, her hands clasped behind her and eyes focused on a spot behind Sarah's head. "'Tis a lesson you should heed, try, try again."

Sarah held up her hand. "Slower, dear. You aren't running a horse race. If you speak too fast, your listeners won't be able to understand what you're saying."

"All right." The girl took a deep breath. "'Tis a lesson you should heed…"

Olivia's voice went on, reciting the poem from the McGuffey's Fourth Reader perfectly. Sarah let her eyes drift to the table against the wall, where Lucy and Laura put the finishing touches on their art projects. The children all knew their recitation pieces. After saying the poems from their readers, the four older students would take turns relating the events of United States history. The younger ones, Lucy and Alan, would demonstrate doing sums for the audience, and then the evening would finish with a spelling bee. Sarah smiled. It had been Aunt Margaret's idea to have all of the attendees participate in the bee, and it promised to be a lot of fun.

"Did I do good, Miss Sarah?"

"You mean, did I do well?"

"Yes, ma'am. Did I do well?"

"You recited your poem perfectly, Olivia." Sarah checked her watch. Nearly four o'clock. "It's time to gather our things. Will you call the boys in please, Laura?"

Sarah tried to quell the flutter in her stomach. Since the run-in with Mr. Harris, Nate had been bringing the children to school and taking them home again every day. And each day, at nine o'clock and at four o'clock, that flutter told her she would be seeing him soon. But they had little time to exchange more than a short greeting before he had to be off again. He still kept that invisible wall between them.

She smoothed her skirt and turned to the gathered children. "Remember, children. Tomorrow is the last day of the term. You must finish your homework tonight and return it to me in the morning." A step on the porch outside the door drew her attention. Nate removed his hat as he ducked inside the open door and her stomach did a flip. "Tomorrow we will go through your recitations one more time and finish decorating the classroom for our program in the evening." She smiled at the children. "Class dismissed."

"Uncle Nate," Charley said when he saw his uncle, "Bernie and Alan want to show me their new puppy. Can I—" He stopped short and glanced at Sarah. "May I go see it before we go home?"

Nate grinned at Charley. "A new puppy? Do you think Lucy and Olivia would like to see it, too?" He turned to Bernie. "Do you think it would be all right if all of them stopped at your house for a little while this afternoon? I need to talk with Miss Sarah."

"Sure thing."

The children were gone to the Woodrows' house in Ingleside before Sarah could say a word. Her stomach threatened to revolt when Nate looked at her. Why, after all this time of knowing him, were her nerves on edge at the thought of talking to him now?

He ran his finger between his bandanna and his neck. The afternoon had grown warm, and sweat beaded on his forehead.

He pointed to one of the benches with a flick of the hat in his hands. "Can we sit and talk for a minute?"

"Yes, of course."

When she was seated he sat next to her. "I saw Dovey—I mean Maude—today."

All thoughts of her nervous stomach disappeared. "You did? Where? How? Is she all right?"

He didn't look at her, but sighed and set his hat on the bench next to him. "Yes, she's all right. I'm not sure I did the right thing, but I hadn't seen her all week, even though I pass the Mystic morning and afternoon." He turned his gaze toward her. "But today I talked to her, and she's doing as well as you can expect."

"But how did you manage it?"

"I saw Harris leave town, heading toward Crook City, so I knew he'd be gone long enough for me to try to see her."

"What did she say? Does she still want me to help her?"

"She's desperate to leave. She said Harris is watching her day and night. He won't let her out of the building unless he or one of his men escorts her."

"How can we help her?" Sarah's mind went to the Mystic, with the barred windows facing the cliff wall below Williams Street, and the constant presence of armed guards. The guards... "How did you get past the guards to see her?"

His face reddened as he shifted the toe of his boot on the floorboard. "I had to pay to see her. I didn't dare try it when Harris was there, but I knew the others wouldn't recognize me."

Sarah felt her own face blush as she considered the implications of what he had done. She laid her hand on his resting on the bench between them. "You did what you had to. It was providential that Mr. Harris was gone so that you could see her."

"It wasn't providential, it was just good timing, and I don't know when we'll get another chance like that again. But when we do, we have to be ready."

Sarah moved her hand away from his. Couldn't he admit to God's hand in all of this? "Do you have a plan?"

"Not yet. But I'll come up with something."

"I'll be praying."

He leveled his gaze at her, one corner of his mouth

turned up. "You really believe prayer will make a difference in the outcome."

"Certainly it will. It's much better than relying on timing."

Nate stood and she rose along with him. "Maybe you're right." He smiled at her. "I have to admit, something sent Harris on an errand just when I was in town and able to see Maude."

"Do you mean that you might be willing to concede to the existence of God?"

"I had to admit to that weeks ago. Your uncle is a pretty convincing preacher." He paused, searching her face with his eyes. "You're pretty convincing, too."

"Why? What have I said?"

He gave a slight shake of his head. "It isn't what you've said, it's what you've done. I've never known anyone who cares about other people as much as you do. That has to be one of those gifts from God James talked about."

He stopped, as if he was lost in thought. Sarah watched him as his eyes focused on the bunting at the front of the room. With a start, she realized that his scars had faded. The angry scarlet burns had turned to dusky red over the weeks she had known him. He had changed.

Had she changed as much?

His gaze turned to her. "Maude will be ready when the time comes. I want it to be soon, before Harris gets suspicious. I'm afraid for you, though."

"For me? He wouldn't know I'm involved in Maude's escape, would he?"

"Maybe not. But I can't help it." He stood up, ready to leave. "I can't help feeling you're in danger, and I don't know what to do about it."

She smiled as she stood, choosing to remember Dr. Bennett's words. "Don't worry about me. Dr. Bennett always said that those who do right are protected by God."

He reached out and stroked her sleeve with a light touch. "But be careful. Dr. Bennett could be wrong, you know."

Sarah stepped closer to him. The wall that had been between them wavered like a desert mirage. "I know she is wrong, so you be careful, too. And I don't care what you think about it, I'm going to be praying for you."

"Then go ahead and pray." He grinned as he turned and walked toward the door. "We both need all the help we can get."

Nate ignored the children's chatter on the way home. Olivia and Charley couldn't stop talking about the Woodrows' pup, but Lucy leaned against him and slept. He let Loretta pick her path up the trail leading to the ranch ahead of him, the older children both on her bare back. He and Lucy followed on Scout.

His mind drifted from his visit with Maude to Sarah, and back again.

It had been a shameful thing to pay for time with the saloon girl. The knowing wink from the madam had been bad enough, but the leer from the guard patrolling the hall started his blood to boil. The guards were present to keep the peace, they claimed. To prevent jealous customers from doing harm to each other or to the girls. But they were really there to intimidate the girls, Maude had said.

All the girl wanted was to go home to her brother's

family in Omaha, but Harris kept her working on the pretext that she owed him money for her stagecoach passage the previous fall. Nate shook his head. It was hard to believe that so many men had fought and died to preserve the Union and to abolish slavery just a dozen years ago, and yet this scheme of Harris's was just as much slavery as that had been.

And Sarah. Nate shifted Lucy on the saddle in front of him as Scout climbed the last slope up to the rolling grassland of the ranch. The half-finished log house rose out of the meadow at the base of the hill, with the tree-covered slope rising behind it. It was more than a house. It was the fulfillment of his dream of giving the children a home. Being with Sarah gave him a glimpse of what his life could be. A wife, children, a home. He hoped that he could rid himself of this cowardice that seemed to poison everything he touched, but until then he had to forget about a wife. Forget about a future with Sarah.

But before he could think of a future, he had to get Maude out of the Mystic. If he couldn't save Mattie, at least he could help another girl in her position. And he had promised Sarah. He would follow through on that promise no matter what.

Coop had supper ready when they reached the camp. All through the meal and while he helped the children settle for the night, Nate ran possibilities of Maude's rescue through his mind. Having been inside the Mystic—seeing the layout of the place, the number of guards and how they were armed—helped him form a plan.

Darkness covered the eastern sky by the time he poured himself a final cup of coffee. The western horizon still glowed soft yellow above the hills, and pale clouds floated on a northern breeze.

Coop filled his tin cup and settled next to Nate, his eyes on the slowly changing sky. "You've been quiet all night."

"Hmm." Nate took a sip of the coffee. Coop sure knew how to brew a good pot.

"That schoolmarm giving you fits?"

Nate grinned at the smirk on his friend's face. "As a matter of fact, no. But a friend of hers is."

"Maude."

"Yup."

"You're going to try to get her out of Harris's clutches?"

"And as far away from Deadwood as she can get." Nate took a sip of his coffee.

Coop lifted his cup to his mouth in tandem.

"It's either going to take a couple stealthy men or an army, the way I see it." Coop leaned back against a rock.

"I've got a plan. I went to the Mystic today, and I think I know a way I can do it."

"You mean we."

"I'm not dragging you into this."

"You aren't dragging me, I'm volunteering."

Nate took another sip and then turned the cup in his hands as he swallowed the hot coffee. "I need someone to take care of the children and the ranch."

"How long do you aim for this to take?"

Nate set his cup on his knee. "I saw how the guards at the Mystic are armed. I know Harris won't let her go easy." He turned to Coop, keeping his voice low in case one of the children was awake. "This is a danger-ous business. I need someone I can trust to take care of the children and the ranch in case something happens. The land will be Charley's when he's old enough, and I know I can trust you to keep it for him and teach him to work it right."

Coop gazed at the western horizon, where darkness had overtaken the pale light. The moon hadn't risen yet.

"Are you doing this for Maude or for Sarah?"

Mattie's face swam before Nate's eyes, the way she looked when they were children, with her impish grin and her nose peppered with freckles.

"It's something I have to do."

"I hate for you to go in there alone." Coop shifted against his rock.

"If things go right, no one will even know she's gone until it's too late."

"You need God's blessing." Coop sat up and threw the dregs of his coffee in the fire. "And you need to be surrounded with prayer."

"This has to remain quiet. No one can know."

"Then you know I'll be praying, and I'm sure Sarah will. You just be careful, you hear?"

Nate grinned into his cup. "Yes sir." He downed the last swallow.

"When are you going to do it?"

"Tomorrow night, after the school program. I need to act as soon as possible, and Friday night is chaos in the Badlands. I'm hoping the guards may be looking the other way."

Coop rose and dusted off his pants. "Then you know what I'll be praying for."

As his friend went off to find his bedroll, Nate put another log on the fire. Before going to bed, he sat, watching the flames lick the edges of the new wood.

He could pray for the success of this venture. Did God even hear prayers of men like him?

Sarah ignored the trickle of perspiration in the small of her back. Even though the evening air had cooled as the sun lowered toward the tops of the hills, the crowded schoolroom was hot and stuffy. But the program had gone well, and the spelling bee was down to its last two contestants.

Uncle James stood at the front of the room, his eyes on the toes of his boots, as his opponent, Hiram Turner, spelled his word. These two men had spelled down the entire room full of students and guests, and they were head-to-head with every word Sarah put before them. In exasperation, she turned to the very back of the spelling book.

"Uncle James, your word is *mucilaginous*."

Mr. Turner rose up on his toes and down again while Uncle James smoothed his mustache with his fingers. He cleared his throat. *"Mucilaginous. M-u-c-i-l-a-g-e-n-o-u-s."*

"I'm sorry, that's wrong."

The crowd behind her erupted in hoots of delight— from Mr. Turner's team—or groans from the team on the other side of the room.

Sarah faced Mr. Turner. "If you spell this word correctly, your team has won the bee. *Mucilaginous*."

Hiram Turner rose up and down on his toes, waved to his teammates and twirled the end of his mustache between his fingers. Finally he said, *"M-u-c-i-l-a-g-i-n-o-u-s. Mucilaginous."*

"That is correct."

As soon as Sarah spoke, the room rang with shouts

and whistles. Mr. Turner's team surged forward to congratulate him and watched as the two final contestants shook hands.

Aunt Margaret caught her elbow. "Oh, Sarah, this was so much fun. Let me help you with the refreshments."

As they made their way to a table set up at the back of the room, Lucretia Woodrow joined them, holding one of her two-month-old twins. Aunt Margaret stirred the lemonade while Lucretia removed the napkins covering plates of cookies and slices of cake.

"Sarah," Lucretia said, "this evening has been a wonderful success. You have shown this mining camp the kind of civilized entertainment a school can bring to a community. You are to be commended."

"Your children worked hard, and they deserve the recognition. I'm glad so many people attended."

"I'd like you to meet Mrs. Broadmoor, our neighbor."

As she turned to greet Lucretia's distinguished-looking friend, she caught sight of Wilson Montgomery watching her. He stepped forward as Lucretia and Mrs. Broadmoor turned their attention to the refreshments.

He smiled as he caught her hand in his and brought it to his lips for a kiss. "You've become quite a success with your little school, my dear."

Sarah worked to keep smiling as she pulled her hand back. "The children have made it a pleasure, Mr. Montgomery. They have applied themselves to their studies, as I'm sure you could see tonight."

He gave her a mock frown. "How many times must I insist you call me Wilson?"

"Yes… Wilson." She turned to indicate the refreshment table. "Would you like some lemonade and a cookie?"

"I'm afraid I can't stay. I have a meeting this evening, and I'm sorry business has to pull me from your side." He glanced at the crowd pressing around them. "Would you walk with me to the door? I have something I'd like to say to you in private."

Sarah let him take her elbow and guide her through the crowd. She nodded thanks to those who spoke to her, but all the time looked for Nate. Finally she spotted him with Mr. Cooper, standing in a line for refreshments with the children. He held Lucy in his arms, and just as she reached the door, he looked across the room and caught her eye. A frown appeared on his face as Wilson led her outside.

She faced him as he let go of her arm. "What did you want to say?"

It may have only been the glare of the lamplight through the schoolroom window, but it seemed his face changed from affable to cruel for an instant. Then when he looked at her, his usual faint smile was on his lips.

"I have a concern I want to discuss with you. It has to do with some of your activities."

Sarah crossed her arms, suddenly chilled in the fresh air. "What do you mean?"

"You've been seen frequenting—ah, no, visiting— a certain part of town." His smile broadened but his eyes were ice crystals. "A part of town far too crude for your delicate sensibilities."

How could Wilson know of her arrangements to meet Maude in the alley between the back of the Mystic and the Wall Street steps? "I was visiting a friend."

His mouth hardened in a thin line, but his voice remained pleasant. "I don't think it's a good idea for you to venture into the Badlands. And as far as your friend is concerned…"

"Why are you discussing this with me? What concern is it of yours?"

"We can't have the wife of the richest banker in town carrying on in this way, can we? If you want to do charitable work, there are other ways to go about it that won't endanger your reputation."

Sarah's stomach churned. "I'm afraid you presume too much, Mr. Montgomery."

"Wilson, please." He reached for her hand, but she pulled it away.

"I don't intend to marry you, Mr. Montgomery. I wish you would forget the idea right now, before this goes any further."

He stepped forward and grasped her wrist in one quick motion. "I want you to understand. I always get what I want, and I want you for my wife." His voice had lost its soft tone. He twisted her arm, bringing her closer to him. The odor of shaving soap and stale cigars was overpowering. "You will obey me, and you will behave. I won't see you in the Badlands again, will I? And you will forget that girl you call your friend. Do you understand me?"

Sarah gritted her teeth. "I understand you perfectly."

He released his hold, and the smile was back on his face as if nothing untoward had happened. "I must be off. My business awaits." He put his hat on with a smooth motion. "Good night, my dear. Remember what I said."

Sarah rubbed her wrist as she watched him round the corner of the building, heading toward Main Street. She took a deep breath. A step in the doorway behind her made her jump.

"This is where you are."

She turned to Nate, trying to control the quivering corners of her mouth. He had a glass of lemonade in each hand. She twisted her fingers together, wanting nothing more than to throw herself into his arms.

He set the glasses on the windowsill and stepped closer to her, peering at her face in the dim light. His face was set and grim.

"What is it? What has happened?"

She shook her head. Nate and Wilson were already wary of each other. If she told Nate what the banker had said, what might he do?

"N-nothing. Nothing is wrong."

"It isn't nothing. You're upset. Did Montgomery say something?"

"No." Sarah grasped at the first thought that came to her mind. "He only asked me if I'd… We found we have a difference of opinion about something." Nate looked past her toward the street where Wilson had disappeared. "You don't need to be so concerned. Wilson is a pillar of the community. What could he say that would upset me?" She gave a little laugh, hoping he'd forget she had been on the verge of tears a moment ago.

He eyed her, his face pensive. She hadn't convinced him yet.

"Did you bring lemonade for me?" She indicated the forgotten glasses on the windowsill.

"Yes." He handed her one of the glasses and took a sip of his own. "The program went well. Were you satisfied with it?"

"The children were wonderful, weren't they? And the spelling bee was so much fun."

Nate took a long drink of his lemonade and then

paused, turning the delicate cup in his hands. "Tonight is the night, Sarah."

"For Maude?"

He nodded. "There's a stage heading to Cheyenne in the morning. I can get Maude out of the Mystic around midnight, and then I'll need to hide her until she can get on the stagecoach. That will be the crucial part."

"But how will we—"

Aunt Margaret appeared in the open doorway. "Sarah, the ladies are asking for you. Why have you disappeared out here?"

"I needed some fresh air. I'll be right in." Sarah waited until Aunt Margaret had gone back to the circle of ladies just inside the door. "I want to know what your plans are. You know you need me to help you."

Nate sighed, taking her empty cup. "I'll ask Coop to take the children home, and then I'll come up to your cabin later this evening. We'll discuss it then. But you're not going to help me tonight. I don't want you anywhere near the Mystic."

Not anywhere near? Who else would be better able to help Maude get out of Harris's clutches?

"But—"

Nate stopped her protest with a raised finger. "We'll do this my way or not at all. Understood?"

Sarah pressed her lips together to keep from firing back a retort that would ruin any possibility of him including her. No matter what he said, she was going to be part of rescuing Maude.

# Chapter Fourteen

Nate swung Lucy onto the front of Coop's saddle.

"You'll all be asleep before I get home tonight. Behave yourselves for Coop."

He went to help Olivia onto the mule's bare back behind Charley.

"Where are you going, Uncle Nate?" Her voice was sleepy already.

"I need to talk to Miss Sarah and then take care of some business."

Charley patted Loretta's neck. "Are we going to go scout out those wild mustangs tomorrow, like you said?"

Nate couldn't lie to the boy, and he wouldn't make any promises he couldn't keep. "We will if we can, Charley. We'll see what tomorrow brings."

He patted his nephew's knee and then stepped closer to Coop. "I'll be back when I can. If..."

"I know." Coop interrupted him with a nod toward the children to remind him of their listening ears. "You've said all you need to." Coop shook his hand. "My prayers are with you."

Why the sudden catch in his throat? He nodded in answer. Coop's prayers meant something. A Bible verse his mother used to quote came to his mind, swift and sure—*The effectual fervent prayer of a righteous man availeth much.*

Nate turned back to the school, where Sarah, along with her aunt and uncle, were cleaning up after the evening program.

Finally, after they left the schoolroom and made their way to the MacFarlands' cabin, Nate and Sarah were alone. They sat together on the bench by the front door, the quiet of the evening marred by disjointed music and raucous voices drifting up the hill from the mining camp. James and Margaret had gone inside, but not before James had shaken Nate's hand with a nod of approval. Nate's scars itched in the unaccustomed humidity of the evening, and the thought that James assumed he was courting Sarah set his nerves further on edge. But he couldn't tell James the truth of his business here tonight. Not yet.

Sarah gave a tired sigh and sat up straight, rolling her shoulders.

"You're exhausted from the program tonight. You should go in and get some rest."

She leaned back again. "Not until you tell me your plans."

He leaned forward, his arms on his knees. "I don't want you anywhere near the Badlands tonight."

Sarah stood, pulling him up with her. "Let's walk a bit. I don't want Uncle James and Aunt Margaret to overhear."

They walked to the edge of the gulch. Below them, Lower Main Street was brightly lit. The Mystic was ablaze with lanterns in every window and torches along the edge of the wide porch. But behind the building, close under the cliff face below Williams Street, was dark shadow. All the noise and activity was focused in the front of the building. Nate pressed his lips together in a grim smile. It was the perfect setup for his plans.

"Why won't you let me help you?"

"For one thing, my plan is for one man, and one man only. Any more than that will attract too much attention. For another thing, it's much too dangerous for you to be involved."

"But you're involved."

He turned toward her just enough to catch her profile in his vision. Her chin tilted up and her mouth was set in a determined line. Stubborn was only one of the names he could call her. Stubborn and beautiful. He had no guarantees he would succeed in this scheme to get Maude away from the Mystic. In fact, he could almost guarantee it wouldn't work. He had to try, but he didn't want Sarah there to witness his failure.

"I'm a man."

Her head whipped around. "What does that have to do with anything?"

"My job is to protect you, and I can't if you show up at the Mystic on a Friday night. That place draws a rough crowd."

Her gaze drifted back to the camp below them. "I hate the thought of Maude down there when she wants to leave so desperately." She gripped his elbow. "Tell me how you plan to do it."

"Promise me you won't do anything foolish."

She shifted her feet. "All right. I won't do anything foolish."

"My plan is to pay for time with Maude, like I did yesterday."

"What if Harris is there? He knows you. Won't he be suspicious?"

"I hope he'll be too busy to notice who the customers are. There's a different person who takes care of that type of business."

"All right. You pay for your time with her." Sarah paused. "I hate to think about what that means and what it will do to your reputation."

"Never mind that. Once I'm in her room, we'll go out the window and make our way to a hiding place until morning." Nate fingered the pouch of gold dust in his pocket, Coop's contribution to the effort. It should buy enough time that they wouldn't have to worry about anyone disturbing them for a while.

"But aren't those windows too small for you to fit through?"

The windows along the back of the building were tiny and at least ten feet from the ground. They were covered with bars and oiled paper that let no air through and only the faintest light on a bright afternoon. Maude was so slight that she should have no problem going through once he got the bars off, but would he fit? It didn't matter, as long as Maude was safe.

"If I can't get through, I'll have to slip out the other way."

"Someone will see you."

"No one is worried about me. They're only concerned with the girls."

Sarah shifted her feet again. Her profile against the glow of the lights from the mining camp drew him close. He wanted to hold her, promise her everything would turn out fine, but he couldn't make that promise. He pushed away the insistent voice saying that he was no good, that everything he touched turned to ashes. That he would fail tonight, too. He wouldn't be able to face her afterward, to see the look of pity and disappointment in her eyes.

Instead, he scuffed his own foot in the thin layer of dirt. The sounds from the camp intensified. The hour was growing late.

"Where do you plan to hide until the stage comes?"

"Above Williams Street along City Creek. There's a thicket by the creek, and it isn't far from the stage station. We'll wait there until dawn, and then I'll go down to the stage office and buy her ticket."

She turned toward him. "I'd like to say goodbye to Maude. What time does the stage leave?"

"At six o'clock."

"I'll be there then." She looked toward the Mystic again. The tilt of her chin unsettled him.

"I don't want you there." He grabbed her arms, turning her toward him. "Do you understand? It's too dangerous. I don't want you anywhere near the Mystic or the stage office."

"You might need my help."

Of course she would think that. There was every possibility that he would die tonight, and then Maude would be worse off than if he had done nothing. His gut churned. But if he didn't carry out this plan, Sarah would do it on her own. Not even a coward would let a woman be part of this business.

"I won't need your help. And if anything happened to you, James and that Wilson Montgomery would both be after my hide."

Her face stiffened. "Wilson has nothing to do with this."

Nate dropped his hands from her arms and turned to go. "Montgomery has everything to do with this."

As soon as Nate disappeared down the trail, Sarah went up to her loft. How could he expect her to sleep peacefully in her bed while he rescued Maude?

She changed her dress from the lilac one she had worn to the school program to the dark blue calico she had worn the first day they had visited Nate's ranch. Reaching the rear of the Mystic would be hard enough without being seen. Wearing dark clothes would help.

Letting her hair down, she brushed it, then gathered it in a simple bun. She reached for her reticule but stopped and sank onto the edge of her bed. She had promised Nate she wouldn't do anything foolish, and that was exactly what he would think her plans were. But it was even more foolish for him to think he could manage Maude's rescue on his own. She had to help him.

Sarah waited, listening until her aunt and uncle's murmured conversation turned to snoring. She counted to one hundred. Uncle James had to be sound asleep before she tried descending the ladder.

Finally the time came. She let herself out of the cabin, pulling the heavy door closed with a quiet thump. Hurrying down Williams Street, she stopped at the top of the Wall Street steps. Below her, at their foot, was the center of the Badlands. The brightly lit edge of the night's revelries nearly blinded her. She crept down the steps. To her left was the shadowy alley that lay between the backs of the saloons and the cliff below Williams Street. If it hadn't been for the reflected light from Main Street, she wouldn't have been able to see anything.

Behind the first building were three little houses, only large enough for one small room. She had seen them many times, but tonight one door was open, the interior lit by a kerosene lamp. Sarah glanced into the doorway as she went by. A girl, dressed in a gauzy pink gown and with her dark hair tumbled about, lay asleep, or passed out, on a couch. Dark lashes brushed her pale cheeks. An upended freight box next to her held the lamp and a hypodermic needle. Sarah shuddered and hurried on.

Pausing to get her bearings, Sarah stepped into the shadow of the wall. The second story rose above her and raucous laughter spilled out of the windows. Sarah turned her mind from the activities and noises that pressed in from all around.

She had reached the Mystic, but which window was Maude's? Stepping around piles of garbage and a mound of split firewood, Sarah reached the far corner of the building. An alley divided the structure from its neighbor. Sarah drew back into the shadows against the building when a large man stepped to the corner. He glanced along the narrow rear yard and then turned back. His measured paces faded as he walked toward Main Street. Sarah started breathing again.

She stepped back from the building and scanned the row of windows above her. One, the third from the left, was missing its oiled paper cover. Nate's head appeared as he worked to remove the last bar. Then his head and shoulder disappeared into the room, there was a pause and a rope snaked down the wall. Next came Maude's feet through the small opening. Sarah reached to help her down.

Nate poked his head out the window once Maude was through and saw Sarah. "What are you doing here?" he demanded in a loud whisper.

"You need help."

"I told you I don't want your help."

She put her hands on her hips. "You need me. Just admit it."

Nate was silent. His lips pressed together. His hands clenched into iron-hard fists. "You are the most stubborn—"

Sudden pounding on the door behind him interrupted whatever he was going to say.

"Dovey! Dovey, who's in there with you?" The shouts were garbled, slurred. More pounding. "You get out here, Dovey. Now."

Maude clutched at Sarah's arm. "It's Harris, and he's been drinking."

Nate gripped the window frame and tried to force his shoulders through.

"Nate, hurry! Hurry!" Sarah glanced toward the edge of the building. The guard could turn the corner again at any moment.

He pulled at the window frame. A few splinters came off in his hands, but it didn't budge. He backed off and threw his shoulder against the wall, but it didn't give at all. The pounding on the door came again, louder, along with Harris's shouts.

Maude pulled at Sarah's arm. "We have to go." Her whispers were hoarse. Tears streamed down her face. "He'll kill me. He will. I've never heard him this bad."

Nate tried once more to fit his head and one shoulder through the narrow window, but he couldn't do it. "You two get out of here. Now."

Maude fled down the alley toward the steps. Sarah couldn't follow her. Not yet.

"I'm not going to leave you here."

"Yes, you are." Nate looked toward the alley with a wild glance. "Someone is coming. Go. I'll catch up with you. It's Maude they want, not me."

He disappeared back into the room. Sarah couldn't make her feet move. A gunshot rang out from inside Maude's room, loud even against the rest of the night noises. She couldn't follow Maude now. She had to see what had happened. As she backed away, hoping to get a better look through the window, strong hands pulled her back.

"Hold on there, miss. What do you think you're doing?"

The guard. She struggled, but his hands held her in a vise. He pulled her back to the brightly lit alley, then pinned her against the wall at the foot of an outside staircase. She couldn't hear anything above the noise from Main Street. What had happened to Nate?

"Where did you come from? You aren't one of Harris's girls."

She struggled again, but he was too strong.

"Maybe you were looking for a job?" He pinned her against the wall with one hand. His face was shadowed by his hat brim. Sarah closed her eyes as he held her with one hand and lifted the other to stroke her cheek.

"Here, you. Leave that young woman alone."

Sarah's eyes flashed open. She knew that voice.

Wilson Montgomery tapped the guard on the shoulder with his cane. "Let her go. Don't you know who this is?"

The guard backed away. "She wouldn't give me her name, Mr. Montgomery."

Wilson's nostrils flared. "Sarah, what are you doing here?"

Sarah moved away from the wall, toward the back of the building. "I could ask you the same thing."

He glanced up the stairway to the door above. "You don't need to be concerned with my business." His eyes narrowed as he took a step closer to her. "I told you I didn't want you to come here. This is no place for you." He motioned for the guard. "I want you to escort Miss MacFarland home."

Sarah took a step away from both of them. Would Wilson commit her to the keeping of this thug?

"Sure thing, Mr. Montgomery."

She turned and ran, around the corner of the Mystic into the darkness of the back alley. Past the little houses and up the Wall Street steps. When she reached the top, she paused for breath, listening for sounds of her pursuers. She saw them below her, looking between stacks of firewood and behind privies. When they reached the foot of the stairs, she melted into the shadows of the trees.

Both men swore, making her ears burn.

"She's gone." Wilson turned on the guard. "If you see her again, you let me know immediately, do you hear? And no one is to touch her."

"Yes, sir, Mr. Montgomery. Whatever you say."

As they made their way back to the Mystic, Sarah sank down onto a tree stump. Wilson Montgomery was doing business with Tom Harris? The pieces fell into place, one by one. His interest in her friendship with Maude. His mysterious business meetings. And he had to have been the one who told Harris that Maude had come to church. Even his efforts to close down the businesses in the Badlands must have been only an attempt to cut down the Mystic's competition.

Wilson's eagerness to maintain a spotless reputation was only a mask that hid his true nature. He had fooled Uncle James and Aunt Margaret, and he had nearly fooled her, too. But Nate hadn't been taken in by the man's polished manners. He had never trusted him.

A brass band struck up a rowdy tune on Main Street, drowning out all other noises, but the alley behind the Mystic was dark and quiet. Nate knew the plan. He would follow Maude…if he could. The echo of the gunshot rang through her head. If he could…

Sarah hiccupped. She wouldn't cry, not now. Not when Maude's future rested with her.

She stood, peering toward the Mystic through the underbrush on the hill next to the steps. No sound. No movement. Feeling the way with her feet, she backed up the steps, her arms wrapped around her middle. She let herself love him when she knew better. She should have kept to her rule. That was her mistake.

Nate pulled back into the tiny room as the pounding continued. He could try shoving the bed against the door, but what would that do?

Buy the girls time to get away.

The pounding at the door increased. "Dovey, open this door!"

Nate shoved the bed toward the door. Other voices joined Harris in the hall. Voices trying to talk some sense into the bully, from the sounds of it. Wedging the other end of the bed against the door, he leaned on the wall and checked the rounds in his pistol. He could use it if he had to, but these were close quarters for bringing a gun to the party.

"Why isn't the girl answering?" Harris again.

"The man paid for the entire night. Ten dollars in gold," the madam's voice whined.

Nate pressed his lips together at the woman's lie. He had given her at least twenty-five.

A slap. A heavy body hit the wall. Harris growled. "I told you she was mine tonight."

"I thought you'd want the money. You could take another girl." Her voice snarled. Uneven steps stumbled away.

"Who's in there with her? Did anyone see him?"

Silence.

"Get that door open."

A gunshot rang in Nate's ears as a hole the size of his fist appeared where the doorknob used to be. The bed gave way as two thugs pushed it and the door into the room. When they saw Nate, they both trained their pistols on him.

Harris appeared between them. His eyes narrowed. "You. You're the last one I thought I'd find here." He reached over and grabbed Nate's pistol from his hand, sticking it into his waistband. He glanced around the room, crowded with the four men. "Where's Dovey?" He tossed the folding screen aside and then lifted Maude's red dress, discarded on the floor. He glanced at the open window and walked over to look down into the yard behind the building. Swinging his bull head around, he jabbed his finger into Nate's chest. "You

don't think she's going to get away from me, do you?"
He leaned in close, reeking of whiskey. "No one." He
poked again. "No one takes what's mine."

He motioned to the two thugs. "Make him think
twice about coming back. When you're finished, take
him out back with the rest of the garbage. I'm going
after the girl." He pushed his way out the door.

Nate gathered himself. Two against one? He had survived worse odds. But these two were both taller and
heavier than he was, and there was no way to maneuver
in the close quarters. His only hope was to get out the
door before they could do any damage. He leaned his
shoulder forward and thrust it toward the man in the
blue shirt, hoping to throw him off balance. The thug
took the blow and returned it with a fist to Nate's belly.

Nate doubled over, but he drew his fist back for a
punch into the guy's midsection. Before he could deliver, the second thug grabbed Nate's arms behind him.

He was held in the bulldog grip of one tough while
the other one pulled back his fist for a punch to his ribs.
Another one to his kidney. A dim thought that they
were sparing his face drifted by. Another blow to his
ribs. He felt searing pain as one cracked. They didn't
want to risk knocking him out. They wanted him to
feel every punch.

Finally thug number two lifted and dragged him out
to the hall, Blue Shirt clearing a path by tossing the
bed aside and shoving the broken door out of the way.
They pulled him through the outside door and down
the wooden steps to the alley.

Nate's vision swam as he fought to remain con-
scious. He had to follow Sarah. He had to protect her.
A figure stood at the bottom of the steps, watching

the proceedings. The face was familiar, smiling as the thugs dragged him to the refuse heap behind the saloon.

Wilson Montgomery. His presence here was too much of a coincidence.

The thugs dropped him on the pile of garbage, but Nate kept his eye on Montgomery as the banker slipped down the alley. He disappeared into the crowd on Lower Main just as thug two's fist collided with Nate's jaw.

## Chapter Fifteen

Sarah took one step down. She had to find Nate. That gunshot still rang in her ears with all the horrible possibilities it could mean. But if Wilson caught her near the Mystic again… His callous disregard for her safety sent a shudder through her.

She took another step down. Nate or Maude? Which one needed her now?

"Please, God, show me the way."

Even before the breathless words left her lips, she saw the guard on his rounds behind the Mystic. Instead of glancing down the alley behind the saloon, he let his gaze wander up and down, probing every shadow.

With silent steps, she moved back to the top of the stairs. But she couldn't abandon Nate to whatever fate Harris had in mind.

She had to find someone to help. Uncle James.

With that thought, she ran down Williams Street to the cabin. Breathless, she opened the cabin door.

"Uncle James?"

She lit the lamp on the table and called again with a low voice, "Uncle James?"

"What is it, Sarah?"

Oh no, she had awakened Aunt Margaret, too.

"I need Uncle James's help. Nate is in trouble."

That brought both of them out of their curtained-off bedroom, Aunt Margaret tying the belt of her wrapper.

Uncle James ran a hand over his face. "What are you talking about?"

Sarah explained everything as quickly as she could, ignoring Aunt Margaret's gasps.

"I know Nate is in trouble, but I can't help him. He's in the Mystic, possibly hurt—" a sob escaped with a shudder "—or worse. And poor Maude is waiting for me. She thought I was coming right behind her."

Uncle James disappeared behind the curtain to get dressed.

Aunt Margaret pulled off her nightcap and started coiling her long braid into a bun. "I know there's something I can do to help, too."

"You're not going to stop me from finding Maude."

Margaret raised her eyebrows. "Of course not. I'm going to find Peder and have him take me out to the ranch. James will need Mr. Cooper's help, and I'll stay with the children." She gathered Sarah into her arms. "Don't worry. The men will find Nate, and you'll get Maude on that stagecoach out of town in the morning. And we'll all be praying for God's protection."

Sarah returned her aunt's hug. "Thank you, Aunt Margaret."

"You go on now. After the stage leaves, you come back here. By then, the men would have found Nate, and we'll all have a celebration breakfast out at the ranch."

"The stage. Maude will need money for a ticket."

Sarah ran up the ladder to her loft and threw open her trunk. She felt in the corner of the tray for the only money she had—a twenty-dollar gold piece wrapped in a scrap of velvet. She slipped it into her pocket.

She left the cabin and hurried toward the opposite end of Williams Street as fast as she could. She found Maude waiting at the edge of the thicket along City Creek.

"I thought you were behind me, but when you didn't come, I didn't know what to do."

"It's all right." Sarah pulled the younger girl into her arms. "We both got away. Now all we have to do is wait for morning."

They found a downed tree near the back of the thicket where Forest Hill rose steeply behind them. Sarah huddled next to Maude, suddenly chilled. She shut away thoughts of Nate. She couldn't help him now.

Maude rubbed at her nose. "That girl, did you see her? The girl on the bed in the little house?"

Sarah couldn't forget the pale pink gown and the ugly needle. "Do you know her?"

A sniff. "Yes. She's new. Her name is Josie."

"She looks so young. How did she end up here?"

"Tom Harris promised her a job as a maid in his hotel, just like he did me."

"But it was a lie."

"Yes." Maude's voice was hollow. "I wish I could have warned her, but it's too late. She was so ashamed of what happened, of what she did when the men gave her whiskey to drink. She had never had it before." Maude sniffed again. "She said she couldn't live with the shame."

Sarah closed her eyes, the sight of the perfect dark

lashes along the pale cheek rising before her. So many girls could tell the same story.

"Do you think she took laudanum tonight?"

Maude squeezed Sarah's arm. "For some girls, it's the only way they can see. Either to stay doped up on laudanum or use a derringer," Maude whispered. "It could have been me."

Sarah took a deep breath. Such a horror, only a few short blocks from the church and school. What could she do to help those poor girls? "But it wasn't you. And it won't be you."

"How, Sarah? How can I just forget the last year?"

"You'll start over. When you get to Omaha, you'll start a new life."

Maude shivered and Sarah scooted closer to her. Thunder rumbled behind the hill.

"But if I run out of money, or if someone recognizes me from here, or…" She wiped at her face with one hand. "How can I keep from going back to my old life?"

"Shh." Sarah put her arm around Maude's shoulder. "When you belong to God, He gives you His Holy Spirit. The Spirit lives in us, helping us turn our back on sin. All you need to do is ask, and He'll give you the strength you need."

Maude was quiet. The thunder rumbled again.

"Do you think I belong to God?"

"I think He's working in your heart to bring you to Himself. You've wanted to learn about Him, and you've taken the right step in wanting to leave your old life. Have you prayed to Him? Have you asked Him to forgive you for your sins?"

"Yes." She could hardly hear Maude's whisper.

The breeze grew stronger, making the trees above them sound like the waves in Boston Harbor.

"Then you can be sure that God has covered you with Christ's righteousness. When He looks at you, He no longer sees your sin, but only the righteousness of His Son."

Maude sniffed again. "That's a wonderful thing, isn't it?"

Sarah's eyes burned with tears. "Yes, it's a wonderful thing."

"I hate to ask, since you've done so much for me already, but would you help Josie? Help her leave this life before it's too late? Before she does something worse to herself than take laudanum?"

"I will. I promise." She would help Josie, and any of the other girls who needed a way out.

They sat in silence. Sarah's back was stiff and tired. The storm clouds let loose a few large raindrops and then moved on to the east. Perhaps it was raining at Nate's ranch.

Nate. The wall between them was back, as thick and high as any fortress. His face had been hard, his features chiseled as if from marble as he told her his plan for rescuing Maude. And then when he saw her in the alley... Could he hate her that much? She should never have gone against his wishes. But if she hadn't, what would have happened to him? At least now Uncle James and Coop knew where to look for him. With the passing of the storm cloud, the sky cleared. The moon, a bright partial disk just a few days after the full moon, shone in the sky, descending toward the west. Nearly morning. She shifted and helped Maude lie on the log, her head in Sarah's lap.

Sarah blinked to stay awake. The wind following the storm was cool and fresh, but her feet felt like ice. The sky in the east was lightening. She dozed, sitting on the tree trunk.

When the sun was fully up, she woke Maude. Six o'clock wasn't far off, and Nate still hadn't arrived.

"Let's go to the stagecoach office and buy your ticket. The coach will be leaving soon."

The six-horse hitch at the front of the stage stamped their feet, eager to be off in the cool morning air.

Sarah and Maude bought her ticket to Cheyenne, where she would catch the train to Omaha. Maude climbed aboard and took her seat. She leaned out the window. "I wish Nate had come. Do you think he's all right?"

Sarah forced herself to smile. It wouldn't do any good for Maude to worry about Nate all the way to Omaha. "I'm sure he just got held up somewhere."

A movement from the other side of the street caught her attention. Between the horses she watched a man's figure move from storefront to storefront, trying the doors. He peered in the glass-plate window of the Shoo Fly Café, just opening for business, and then turned toward the stagecoach. It was Harris. Sarah's cold feet froze.

"Sarah? What's wrong?"

Sarah couldn't move her eyes away. She didn't want to lose track of him. "It's Harris. He's across the street and looking this way."

The driver came out of the stage office, pulling on his fringed gloves.

"We need to get going." The lanky man climbed onto the driver's box, followed by the guard.

Two more passengers climbed onto the stage while Maude's hand clung to hers.

"Thank you." Maude's words were a whisper, but they echoed in Sarah's heart. "If it weren't for you and Nate…"

Sarah squeezed her hand. "Write to me. Let me know how you're doing."

"I will."

With a "Gee-up" to the horses and a crack of his whip, the driver started the team on their way, south toward Cheyenne. And for Maude, toward the train and home.

As the dust settled in the coach's tracks, swirling in the early sunshine, Harris appeared out of the cloud. Sarah's insides quivered as she turned away from him and started toward Wall Street and the path for home. She hurried faster as she heard his heavy tread behind her on the boardwalk. She stifled a scream as his beefy hand caught her elbow and spun her around.

"Mr. Harris, what do you think you're doing?"

"Who did you put on that stage?"

She looked the man in the eye. "I was saying goodbye to a friend, but I don't see where it's any concern of yours." She pulled her elbow out of his grasp and took a step away from him.

"Dovey has disappeared, and that Nate Colby was involved."

Sarah stopped. Harris had been there when the gun went off.

Harris stepped closer. "I think you helped them. I think you just put her on that stage."

Sarah turned to face him again. "What have you done to Nate?"

"I told my boys to teach him a lesson." A slow grin pulled his face into a distorted mask. "He wouldn't listen to reason any more than you would." She turned away but he grabbed her elbow and spun her toward him again. "But I think you're going to be very useful. You're my ticket to getting even with Colby."

She pulled away from him, running blindly down the street. As she stumbled down the flight of stairs leading to Lower Main, she risked looking behind her. Harris followed, clumping down the wooden steps.

Her chest heaving, she looked all around. The streets were empty of people. Even the shopkeepers weren't around at this early hour on a Saturday.

When she reached the bottom of the Wall Street steps, Harris caught up with her. He clamped a filthy hand over her mouth and seized her around the waist. She struggled against him as he dragged her into the alley behind the buildings of the Badlands, to the three little houses with their doors all closed.

He wrenched open the door of the third house and threw her in. She landed on the cot, and before she could regain her feet he thrust a filthy cloth into her mouth to gag her.

Sarah struggled for breath as he bound her hands and tied them to the metal frame. She gathered her strength and kicked at him with her feet, but he grabbed them and tied them together.

"You wait here and be quiet. Mr. Montgomery will know what to do with you."

Sarah struggled against the ropes but only succeeded in pulling the knots tighter.

Harris chuckled as he watched her until she gave

up, and then walked out the door and locked it with a snick of a padlock. His footsteps faded away.

Sarah adjusted herself to a more comfortable position. Someone was sobbing in the little house next to hers. She tried to remember—which one had Josie been in? She turned on the bed, slipping to her knees on the floor as well as she could with her wrists tied to the bed frame, and started praying. Only God could bring her out of this pit.

"Nate." The voice came nearer. "Nate."

Nate jerked awake, pain radiating through his body. He lifted a hand to his forehead, opening his eyes as he reached up. Only one eye opened. His hand came away bloody.

He tested his other arm. His legs. Nothing broken there, that he could tell, but from the feel of things, at least one rib was cracked. He hadn't been beaten this badly since the time he had stumbled on a Confederate patrol in Tennessee during the war. They had left him for dead. It felt like those two thugs had done the same thing.

"Nate?"

A man shifted near him in the semidarkness.

"James, is that you?"

"How are you feeling?"

Nate lay back against the foul-smelling heap. "Like I fell off a cliff and bounced on the way down." He tried to laugh at his own joke, but ended up coughing in searing bursts of pain.

"Take it easy, there."

Nate steadied himself with shallow breaths. "Where is Sarah?"

"She told me you were in trouble, so I came to find you. Sarah went to make sure Maude gets on the stagecoach, and Margaret and Peder went out to the ranch to tell Coop what happened."

The raucous noise from the street in front of the Mystic made Nate's head ache. Here he was, helpless. The whole plan hinged on him, and he couldn't even stand up and make sure a girl got on the stagecoach. Sarah was in danger because of him. And James was sitting on a garbage heap in the back of a saloon. This was no place for a preacher.

He fought to stay awake. "You shouldn't be here. I can wait for Coop alone."

"I won't leave you, Nate."

Nate barely heard James's words as he drifted away. He had heard those words before, hadn't he? James's voice became Ma's voice, reading from the family Bible. *He will not leave thee, nor forsake thee.*

When Nate woke again, the sky was lighter and the noise from the Mystic had lessened. Coop and James stood near his feet, discussing him. He caught snatches of words but gave up trying to decipher them.

From the look of the gray sky, the time must be near six o'clock. If he could walk, he could find Sarah, send her home where it was safe and take Maude to the stagecoach office. But when he tried to sit up, his ribs burned in answer.

"Whoa, there. Don't try to be going anywhere."

Coop knelt by his side and helped him ease back down onto his questionable bed.

Nate licked his cracked lips. "The children?"

"Margaret and Peder are with them."

James motioned to Coop. "Let's get him to the cabin

while he's awake. It's quiet enough around here this morning that we don't have to worry about anyone from the Mystic bothering us."

With the two men supporting him on either side, Nate found himself standing upright. He swayed, gray lights swirling in his vision, but strong arms kept him from falling. Somehow, he stayed awake as they made their way past the three little cribs behind the saloon, to the base of the stairs and, gritting his teeth at every step, up to the cabin. James and Coop laid him down on the bed and he eased into the warm, soft mattress.

"I'll go get Doc Henderson," James said.

Nate drifted into a half-awake state where Sarah walked at the edge of his vision. Every time he tried to focus on her, she faded away. Coop made him drink some water. Later he smelled coffee brewing. And then pain again as he was brought to a sitting position and his ribs were wrapped tight. The pain eased and he was laid back down once more.

"That should do it." The doctor snapped his bag closed and peered at Nate. "You got banged up pretty hard, but you've seen worse. Those scars of yours tell quite a story." The older man eased a black felt hat onto his head. "Keep quiet for a day or two, and you'll be good as new." He nodded to James and Nate, and left.

Nate propped himself on one elbow. James and Coop were at the table with coffee cups in front of them. He put his feet on the floor and pushed himself to a sitting position. The pain was tolerable.

He grabbed his shirt from the end of the bed and pulled it on, easing his arms into the sleeves. Next were his boots. Shoving his feet in took effort, but he finally got them on. As he pushed the heel of the second boot down on the floor, Coop noticed what he was doing.

"Hold on there. Where do you think you're going?"

"Have you noticed how late it's getting? It's almost eight o'clock. Sarah should be here by now, but she isn't. Something is wrong and I'm going to find out what it is."

Coop and James looked at each other, and then Coop stood and grabbed his hat from the hook by the door. "If you're going to wander around town in that condition, I'm going with you."

"Why should you? I'm the one who made this mess, and I'll be the one who cleans it up."

"Wait a minute," James said, coming to the bed to help Nate stand up. "Why do you think Sarah being late is your fault?"

Nate's head pounded. "I'm the one who came up with this crazy idea, so it's my fault Sarah is involved at all."

"Do you really think you could have stopped her from helping Maude?"

Nate couldn't meet the older man's level gaze. "She can be pretty stubborn when she sets her mind to something, can't she?"

"Whatever happens, or doesn't happen, it isn't your fault, Nate."

Nate started to protest, but James went on. "God is in control of this and every situation. Trust Him to take care of Sarah and trust Him to show you what you need to do. Go find her, help her if she needs help, but don't try to take the blame for something that's out of your control. That's the worst kind of pride."

Nate met his eyes then. "Pride?"

"You think you are more powerful than God? You think you can do anything to change His plans?"

James's point slid into place like a key fitting into its lock. God was the general and he was a private. All he had to do was stay on his mount and follow orders.

He took his hat from the chair at the foot of the bed. "Let's go do what we need to do."

# Chapter Sixteen

Sarah's knees ached when she woke up. She rolled onto the little cot from her kneeling position on the floor.

Breathing slowly to keep herself calm, she looked around the little room. In the growing daylight, it looked the same as the one where she had seen Josie the night before, except there was no needle on the table next to the lamp.

The gag tasted foul and drew all the moisture from her mouth. Her wrists burned where the rope binding them had chafed, and her feet were numb. Harris had not been gentle when he tied the knots.

What would Dr. Bennett think of her now? Tears trickled down her cheeks at the thought. She had been so naive back in Boston, sitting in Dr. Bennett's parlor on those Sunday afternoons, soaking up every word that had dropped from the fiery woman's lips.

Had Dr. Bennett been wrong?

Not completely. Sarah had to believe that education was the way for adults and children alike to improve their situation in life. But Dr. Bennett's high ideas of people—that they would naturally embrace the opportunities presented to them—were so misguided. The woman had lived her life in the privileged areas of Boston and London. Life was different than she had led Sarah to believe.

Aunt Margaret had always maintained that the fault with Dr. Bennett's ideas was that she left God out of the picture. Without God, there was no hope.

Sarah had to admit Aunt Margaret was right.

She twisted her hands, trying to loosen the rope, but it only brought more pain.

A noise made her stop. She held her breath to listen. Voices. Harris was back, talking to someone, and close by.

Then she heard a key in the padlock and the door swung open, blinding her as the sudden morning light streamed in. Two figures stood in the opening, looking at her. Harris and… She tried to flip her hair out of her eyes. It was Wilson Montgomery.

"I put her in here. What else was I going to do?" Harris's voice whined.

"You fool. This isn't some girl out of the saloon. She has family and connections. Connections I wanted to stay on good terms with. What were you thinking?"

"I want Dovey back. I thought Colby would bring her back if I had the teacher."

"You thought?" Wilson smashed his fist on the doorframe and Harris cringed. "You thought?"

A cold shiver ran through Sarah. Wilson leaned over Harris, every word, every motion, out of control. He was an animal.

Wilson turned from Harris to her, running his hand through his hair as he stared at her. He strained to gain control, and with a little shake, he did. He smiled, but the ice blue of his eyes sent panic running through her. She strained at the bonds holding her wrists.

"Thanks to you, Harris, I have to leave Deadwood." His voice was as pleasant and controlled as if he was sitting in a fine parlor. "My lovely wife and I will have to start over in another town." He took a step closer to Sarah. If she didn't know better, she would think he was looking at her with the kindest regard.

His smile grew broader and he stroked her calf. Sarah flinched and his smile froze. He held her in a pinching grasp that shot pain up her leg. "Don't ever resist me, Sarah."

He released his hold and turned to Harris. "I'm calling in your loan. Payable at ten o'clock this morning. You have two hours."

Harris fell against the door. "Calling in my loan? But how am I supposed to raise that kind of money? I'd have to sell the Mystic."

Wilson turned toward the door. "Sell the Mystic, get a loan from another bank. I don't care how you do it. Just have my money ready by ten o'clock." He stepped into the alley and then swept his gaze to Sarah again. "And keep my wife here. I'll come for her soon."

Harris followed him out. Sarah tried to pull her hands free again. She would never leave town with Wilson. Never. She had been afraid of him after the school program last night, but this morning he terrified her.

Her wrists were slippery with blood, but she made no progress. She had an idea. She scooted up on the cot until she could reach her fingers with her mouth and worked the gag loose. By the time she had it out, she was exhausted with the effort. She laid her head on the frame of the cot next to her bound wrists, breathing freely for the first time since Harris had captured her.

Once she had rested, she worked at the rope with her teeth. Only minutes had passed since the men had left her, but the room had grown hot in the morning sun. She finally loosened her wrists, untied the bonds around her ankles with stiff fingers and then stood, trying to work some feeling into her swollen feet.

But she was free. She grabbed the doorknob. It didn't budge. Harris had fastened the padlock again as he had left. Her throat burned from thirst. She slid to the floor, leaning against the unyielding door. There was no way out until that door was opened when Wilson came to claim her.

She curled on the floor and tried to pray. Someone had to find her first. They had to.

Nate leaned a hand against the wall next to the ticket-office window. According to the board, the stage for Cheyenne had left on time. He turned slowly to survey the street as Coop drilled the ticket agent. Saturday-morning crowds gathered in the usual places—in front of the assayer's office, the three banks, the claims office. All the usual business of the mining camp.

But in that entire crowd, he didn't see Sarah anywhere. Maybe he and Coop had missed her, and she was back in the cabin, where James was waiting for her, safe and sound. The churning in his gut told him otherwise.

Coop turned from the window with a sigh. "I don't like this."

Nate straightened, grimacing as pain told him he had moved too quickly. "What is it?"

"The agent said that the girls were here. And he said Maude got on the stage."

Maude got on the stage. His plan worked. She was safe. He rubbed a finger across his forehead, trying to ease the pain. He hadn't failed. He whooshed out a breath.

But where was Sarah?

"There's something you aren't telling me."

"He said Sarah was being followed by a man when she headed down toward Lower Main, and from his description, it could have been Harris."

The familiar lead dropped in his gut. Was James right? Could God be in control, even now?

Nate took a deep breath. "So let's go."

"Where?"

"We follow them. We head toward the Mystic."

Coop's long legs brought him up beside Nate. "You think he caught up with her? Somehow got her to go with him to the Mystic? Isn't that too public?"

"Do you have a better idea?"

"Somewhere away from the saloon, where they wouldn't be noticed."

Nate stopped at the top of the stairway leading to Lower Main. "She's too well-known in town. He'd have to hide her." An accusing voice rang in his head. This was all his fault. He had put Sarah in this danger. He pushed it down.

"We need to think this through, Nate. If we go into the Mystic half-cocked and accusing Harris of kidnapping her, we'd be walking right onto his own turf."

Nate looked down the crowded boardwalk at the

foot of the stairs. A familiar figure caught his attention. Wilson Montgomery emerged from the narrow alley between the newspaper office and the Wall Street steps. He straightened his string tie, adjusted his vest and crossed the street toward his bank. And suddenly Nate was sure the banker was involved in whatever Harris was doing. The two fit together like a pack of coyotes.

But where had he come from? There was nothing back there, except...

"I know one place Harris could hide someone. Behind the Mystic are some cribs. He could have locked her in one of those, and no one would ever know."

Coop's gaze narrowed. "Do you think he would do that to Sarah?"

"The man was out of his mind with jealousy last night, and crazy drunk, to boot. He could have been capable of anything. And I think Montgomery is involved, too."

"The banker?"

Nate nodded, sending throbs of pain through his head. "Montgomery was at the Mystic last night. He and Harris are thicker than thieves. And I just saw Montgomery come out of that alley next to the steps."

Coop looked toward the spot, and they both watched as Harris left the same alley and headed down the street toward the front door of the Mystic.

The cowboy nodded. "All right. Let's go see what they've been up to."

They threaded their way through the crowds and turned down the alley next to the newspaper office. The way between the corner building and the hill was narrow, but it widened out when they reached the Mystic. The privies, the refuse heap, even the open window with no bars that had been Maude's room, all seemed unreal to Nate. Last night's events were of no account next to finding Sarah. Once they were together again, he would never let her go.

The three little houses squatted under the hill, opposite the back wall of the saloon. Nate looked from one to the other. The last one in the row was padlocked.

He pointed it out to Coop, and they walked toward it, keeping one eye out for a guard. Nate tried the padlock and then called in a low voice, "Sarah."

"Nate?"

It was her. Relief flooded through him. He pulled at the padlock again, but it was new and well made.

"You hold on. We're going to get you out of there. Are you all right?"

"Yes. Just hurry."

Coop pointed to the hinges on the outside of the door. Crude and easy to dismantle. Coop took his knife and pried the pins out, wincing as each one screeched in protest, but no one took notice.

Finally, they wrenched the door forward, and Nate slid past it into the hot room. Sarah huddled on the floor. He knelt next to her and pulled her into his arms. It was over, and he hadn't failed. Confident and sure, he held her close.

"I'm here, Sarah. I'm here."

Sarah clung to Nate.

"You're safe. I thought they might have killed you."

Nate stroked her hair. "They tried to, but I don't kill easy."

"We have to get out of here." She pushed away from him. "Harris and Wilson are coming back. Wilson said something about Harris paying him the money he owes him, and then he's leaving town." Her eyes grew blurry. "I'm so glad you found me. Wilson is insane. He thinks I'm his wife." She couldn't control the trembling.

"We'll get you home." Nate grimaced as he stood and pulled her up from the floor to stand next to him. "You're hurt?"

Nate put an arm around her waist and guided her to the door. "Don't worry about it. The important thing is to make sure you're safe."

As they stepped out the door, Coop put out a hand to stop them.

Wilson Montgomery faced them, his usual kind expression belying his purpose. "Colby, I think you have your hands on something of mine." He smiled and held his hand out to Sarah.

"Move away from me, Sarah." Nate's voice was low, close to her ear. "Get behind the bed."

Sarah slipped back into the room and crouched next to the cot.

"We're just on our way home, Montgomery." Nate put his hands on his hips. For the first time since she had met him, Nate had no gun. "And I don't see that I have anything that belongs to you."

Wilson shifted his stance, rolling back on his heels. Sarah's gaze was captured as if he was a deadly snake, ready to coil and strike.

"You might be glad to know I'm leaving town this morning." Wilson nodded at Coop. "And your friend here can relax. There's no call for him to be fingering his pistol like that. I've just come to collect Sarah, and then we'll be off."

"You're not taking her anywhere." Nate took a step

closer to Coop, away from the doorway, and drew Wilson's gaze away from Sarah.

Wilson's smile grew broad. "Of course I am, Colby. She's mine, isn't she?" He smiled at Sarah and she turned away, her stomach roiling. He sounded so calm and sure of himself. Would he convince Nate and Coop that she wanted to go with him? "I thought while we were waiting for my business with Harris to be concluded, we'd stop over at Furman and Brown's and buy a new dress for you. You'd like a new dress for the trip, wouldn't you?"

Nate took a step closer to Wilson. "I told you, she's not going anywhere with you."

Wilson reached into his coat and drew out a pistol. His smile didn't change. "Yes, she is."

He pointed his pistol at Nate, but as Coop drew his gun, Wilson flicked his hand toward the cowboy and fired. Sarah screamed as Coop fell to the ground.

Nate launched himself toward Wilson and threw him to the ground. Wilson's gun went flying, and Nate punched the banker in the jaw.

Sarah ran to Coop as Wilson pushed Nate off and scrambled to his hands and knees. Coop was on his back, bleeding from his right shoulder. He reached toward his gun with his left hand. Sarah picked it up from the ground where it had fallen and handed it to him.

As Wilson scrambled for his pistol, ten feet away, Coop stood up, his gun steady, and aimed at the other man.

"Don't even try, Montgomery. I can shoot just as well with my left hand as with my right."

The snake wasn't done. In spite of Coop's warning, he lifted his pistol with a quick motion and pointed it at Nate. He fired at the same time as Coop. As soon as Wilson fell back, a red bloom seeping through the shoulder of his immaculate vest, Sarah ran to Nate.

He was lying on the ground, groaning, with blood staining his left sleeve.

Sarah knelt next to him and took his hand. "Nate, he shot you."

"It's just a scratch. I'm all right."

Coop checked Wilson and then walked over to Nate. "You're not all right. You're going to kill yourself trying to wrestle snakes with your broken ribs." He handed his pistol to Nate. "If you can keep Montgomery from doing anything foolish when he wakes up, I'll go find Sherriff Bullock."

Nate stood up slowly, keeping an eye on Wilson, but the other man didn't move. Nate reached out for Sarah, and she moved close to him, clinging to him in the dust and dirt of the alley.

"I never want to go through the last twelve hours again. When I didn't know where you were, I about went crazy." Nate held her close to his left side. "I don't know what I would have done if I had lost you."

Sarah smoothed the front of his shirt. "I felt the same way. When I heard that gunshot last night, I was afraid you were gone."

"I never want to risk losing you again, Sarah." He leaned close to her, his cheek brushing hers, and she felt a gentle sigh. She turned and he caught her lips in his for a sweet kiss. When he finished, he didn't pull away, but touched his forehead to hers. She looked deep into his eyes. She shouldn't let him do this. She should pull away from him, refuse to let him kiss her. But she was helpless. Nate's kiss was the blade that destroyed her last defense. The Gordian knot of her fear was gone, vanquished by his gentle touch.

Love for him flooded her heart. It felt so perfect, as if her world had been turned right side up.

"Sarah," he whispered, "I love you. I can't help it."

"Oh, Nate, I love you, too."

She circled her arms around his neck, and with one hand behind her waist he pulled her closer, enclosing her in his strong arms. She rested her head against his chest. She had never known love could feel like this.

"Be mine."

She lifted her eyes to his. "What?"

"Marry me. Be mine. Let me take care of you. Let me love you for the rest of my life."

"Oh, Nate." She threw her arms around his neck. "Yes, yes."

He pulled her close, and she lost herself in his kiss.

# *Epilogue*

The last Saturday in April, Sarah put the loaves of bread into the oven and then straightened, rubbing her swollen stomach. Not long now, and she would meet her own little baby. She glanced at Lucy and Olivia playing with their dolls in a corner of the spacious room.

"Girls, it's almost time for your uncle Nate and Charley to come home. What would you think if we walk out to meet them?"

Olivia looked at her with a frown. "Are you sure you feel like walking that far?"

Leave it to Olivia to guess that she was expecting a baby. At least she hadn't passed the secret on to Lucy or Charley.

"I feel fine. Be sure to put on your coats. There's a cold wind out there today."

The three of them set off across the meadow. Scout watched them from the top of a rise where he could survey the entire ranch and keep an eye on his wives. All twelve of them. Nate kept Ginger and her foal in the corral near the barn, but Scout was in charge of the mustang mares.

They walked as far as the gate before Sarah saw Loretta's ears, and then her head, coming up the trail. Nate followed, driving the wagon. Sarah waved when she saw Uncle James and Aunt Margaret in the wagon with him, and the girls slipped through the gate and ran to meet them.

Tears filled Sarah's eyes. She had been crying more than ever since she knew the baby was coming. Every little thing that filled her heart with thanksgiving brought tears. Every calf born, every mare found to be in foal, every time she stood on her front porch and looked over the land that their grandchildren would call home.

And every time she saw Nate.

The tears were often mingled with laughter when Nate was the reason. Why had she ever been afraid to love him?

Nate pulled the wagon to a stop when they reached her.

"It's so nice to see you!" Sarah climbed into the wagon and gave Margaret a hug. "I'm so glad you came out. Can you stay for dinner?"

"We brought it with us." Aunt Margaret lifted a basket. "And we have enough time for a good, long visit."

"I brought the mail. You got a letter from Maude." Nate's eyes never left hers as he handed her the letter.

Nate drove the wagon up to the house while Aunt Margaret told her the news from town.

"Lucretia Woodrow has a new baby. It's a girl this time, and Laura is so happy after six brothers!"

Olivia caught Sarah's eye and smiled her secret smile.

"And Peder is getting married!"

"He's just a boy, isn't he?"

"Only nineteen years old, but he's doing very well. He sold his claim and is building a little house in Ingleside. He recently took a job writing for the *Black Hills Gazette*."

"Who is he marrying?"

"You know her. Mary Connealy. Her father is the attorney who moved here last September."

Sarah felt the tears starting again. Every little thing. Every little wonderful thing.

Once they were in the cabin, Sarah opened the letter from Maude and scanned it.

"Oh, listen to this," she said. "Maude says there are now six girls in the home." Maude's church in Omaha had established the home, a place for girls to start over once they left the saloon life. Josie and Maude were the house mothers. "She says the new girl we sent to her, Nancy, is doing quite well and is learning to be a very talented seamstress."

"That's wonderful. Do they have room for more young women?"

"She says they have two more beds and possibly another one by summer. The girl who we sent the same time as Josie is getting married."

A yeasty scent reminded Sarah to take the bread from the oven. The loaves were a beautiful brown. She put them on the table and covered them with a towel to cool.

By the time the men came in from the barn, including Coop, Margaret had heated up the soup she'd brought, and they all sat down at the table to a hot dinner.

Once grace had been said and they had all been served, Nate cleared his throat. "There is something Sarah and I have been hoping would happen for a long time."

Both Aunt Margaret and Olivia gave Sarah a knowing glance, but she only smiled back at them. She knew why Nate had gone into town this morning.

"Olivia, Charley and Lucy..." Nate waited until he had the attention of all three children. "I went to see Judge Lessman today, and he has drawn up all the necessary paperwork, so now we only need your approval." He paused and glanced at Sarah. "We want to officially adopt you. Instead of being your aunt and uncle, we would like to be your parents."

Nate paused again, waiting for the children's reactions.

Charley was first. "You mean we can call you Pa?"

"And we can call you Mama?" Olivia asked, turning to Sarah.

Lucy slid down from her seat and came to Sarah. She climbed into her lap, just as she used to, and wrapped her arms around Sarah's neck. "You'll be my very own mama."

Aunt Margaret wiped her eyes, but Coop summed it up.

"I think you've got yourself a family, Nate."

\* \* \* \* \*

Dear Reader,

I fell in love with the Black Hills of South Dakota when our family moved here in 2011. Not only do we live in one of the most beautiful places in the United States, but we're smack-dab in the middle of Western history. For someone who grew up watching television shows like *Bonanza* and *Gunsmoke*, this is paradise.

Deadwood is a real place. I created a fictional church, school and "theater" for my story, but the rest of Deadwood was very much like I describe it in this book. It was a muddy, noisy, wild town with open gambling, drinking and prostitution. But there was another element of society in the mining camp from the earliest days.

Families settled in Deadwood and strove to bring the better aspects of society to the narrow valley in the Hills. Street preachers were drawn here from the beginning of the gold rush in 1876, and churches were soon established. Schools were set up for the children in the town, and societies of all kinds were formed. Ladies spent their afternoons visiting, after the fashion of the day, and many people patronized the Langrishe Theater—a true legitimate theater.

When you visit Deadwood today, you have to look hard to see traces of the mining camp of more than a century ago. Whitewood Creek is confined in a concrete channel under the highway. Casinos are everywhere, as well as stores catering to the tourist crowd. But if you go, don't miss the Adams Museum to get a glimpse of long-ago Deadwood. And stop by the visitor's center for a map of the walking tour of historic

Deadwood. The walking tour is a delight, and you'll spend an hour or so in the twilight world between what was and what is.

While you're in Deadwood, don't forget Mount Moriah Cemetery. Visit Wild Bill Hickok's and Calamity Jane's graves, but don't stop there. Follow the signs to Seth Bullock's grave, on the hill above the cemetery. And then, if you're up for the climb, follow the trail past Seth Bullock to White Rocks, at the top of the mountain. Look east, toward Bear Butte in the distance, and then let your eyes drift to the base of the mountain far below your feet. Imagine for a moment that it is 1877. Do you see the cabin tucked close to the rimrock? The horses grazing in the meadow? Look closely. You may even see Nate and Sarah with their family, enjoying the sunny day.

I would love to hear from you! You can contact me on my website, www.jandrexler.com, or on Facebook at Jan Drexler, author.

Blessings to you and yours,
*Jan Drexler*

# REQUEST YOUR FREE BOOKS!

## 2 FREE INSPIRATIONAL NOVELS
## PLUS 2 *FREE* MYSTERY GIFTS

*Love Inspired* HISTORICAL

---

**YES!** Please send me 2 FREE Love Inspired® Historical novels and my 2 FREE mystery gifts (gifts are worth about $10). After receiving them, if I don't wish to receive any more books, I can return the shipping statement marked "cancel." If I don't cancel, I will receive 4 brand-new novels every month and be billed just $4.99 per book in the U.S. or $5.49 per book in Canada. That's a saving of at least 17% off the cover price. It's quite a bargain! Shipping and handling is just 50¢ per book in the U.S. and 75¢ per book in Canada.* I understand that accepting the 2 free books and gifts places me under no obligation to buy anything. I can always return a shipment and cancel at any time. Even if I never buy another book, the two free books and gifts are mine to keep forever.

102/302 IDN GH6Z

| Name | (PLEASE PRINT) | |
|------|------|------|

| Address | | Apt. # |
|------|------|------|

| City | State/Prov. | Zip/Postal Code |
|------|------|------|

Signature (if under 18, a parent or guardian must sign)

### Mail to the **Reader Service:**
**IN U.S.A.:** P.O. Box 1867, Buffalo, NY 14240-1867
**IN CANADA:** P.O. Box 609, Fort Erie, Ontario L2A 5X3

**Want to try two free books from another series?**
**Call 1-800-873-8635 or visit www.ReaderService.com.**

* Terms and prices subject to change without notice. Prices do not include applicable taxes. Sales tax applicable in N.Y. Canadian residents will be charged applicable taxes. Offer not valid in Quebec. This offer is limited to one order per household. Not valid for current subscribers to Love Inspired Historical books. All orders subject to credit approval. Credit or debit balances in a customer's account(s) may be offset by any other outstanding balance owed by or to the customer. Please allow 4 to 6 weeks for delivery. Offer available while quantities last.

**Your Privacy**—The Reader Service is committed to protecting your privacy. Our Privacy Policy is available online at www.ReaderService.com or upon request from the Reader Service.

We make a portion of our mailing list available to reputable third parties that offer products we believe may interest you. If you prefer that we not exchange your name with third parties, or if you wish to clarify or modify your communication preferences, please visit us at www.ReaderService.com/consumerchoice or write to us at Reader Service Preference Service, P.O. Box 9062, Buffalo, NY 14240-9062. Include your complete name and address.

LIH15

# SPECIAL EXCERPT FROM

*Love Inspired*

*Will a young Amish widow's life change when her brother-in-law arrives unexpectedly at her farm?*

*Read on for a sneak preview of*
**THE AMISH MOTHER**
*The second book in the brand-new trilogy*
**LANCASTER COURTSHIPS**

"You're living here with the children," Zack said. *"Alone?"*

"This is our home." Lizzie faced him, a petite woman whose auburn hair suddenly appeared as if streaked with various shades of reds under the autumn sun. Her vivid green eyes and young, innocent face made her seem vulnerable, but she must be a strong woman if she could manage all seven of his nieces and nephews—and stand defiantly before him as she was now without backing down. He felt a glimmer of admiration for her.

"*Koom.* We're about to have our midday meal. Join us. You must have come a long way." She bit her lip as she briefly met his gaze.

Zack still couldn't believe that Abraham was dead. His older brother had been only thirty-five years old. "What happened to my *brooder*?"

Lizzie went pale. "He fell," she said in a choked voice, "from the barn loft." He saw her hands clutch at the hem of her apron. "He broke his neck and died instantly."

Zack felt shaken by the mental image. "I'm sorry. I know it's hard." He, too, felt the loss. It hurt to realize that he'd never see Abraham again.

LIEXP0915R

"He was a *goot* man." She didn't look at him when she bent to pick up her basket, then straightened. "Are you coming in?" she asked as she finally met his gaze.

He nodded and then followed her as she started toward the house. He was surprised to see her uneven gait as she walked ahead of him, as if she'd injured her leg and limped because of the pain. "Lizzie, are *ya* hurt?" he asked compassionately.

She halted, then faced him with her chin tilted high, her eyes less than warm. "I'm not hurt," she said crisply. "I'm a cripple." And with that, she turned away and continued toward the house, leaving him to follow her.

Zack studied her back with mixed feelings. Concern. Worry. Uneasiness. He frowned as he watched her struggle to open the door. He stopped himself from helping, sensing that she wouldn't be pleased. Could a crippled, young nineteen-year-old woman raise a passel of *kinner* alone?

*Don't miss*
*THE AMISH MOTHER by Rebecca Kertz,*
*available October 2015 wherever*
*Love Inspired® books and ebooks are sold.*

## *Love Inspired* HISTORICAL

*Chivalry demands cowboy Blue Lyons help any woman
in need, so he offers widow Clara Weston—and her
daughters—shelter and food when they have nowhere
to go. And whether he wants it or not, Clara and her
daughters are soon chipping away at his guarded heart.*

*Read on for a sneak preview of
A DADDY FOR CHRISTMAS,
available in October 2015 from Love Inspired Historical!*

Clara turned, squatted and swept Libby into her arms.
"What would I do without my sweet girls?" She signaled
Eleanor to join them and hugged them both.

Blue turned away to hide the pain that must surely
envelop his face even as it claimed every corner of his
heart. That joy had been stolen from him, leaving him an
empty shell of a man.

The girls left their mother's arms and Libby caught
his hand. "Mr. Blue, did you see how full we got your
buckets?" She dragged him to the doorway where they'd
left the pails. Each one was packed hard with snow.
"Didn't we do good?"

"You did indeed."

She looked up at him with blue expectant eyes.

What did she want?

"Did we earn a hug?" she asked.

His insides froze then slowly melted with the warmth
of her trust. He bent over and hugged her then reached for

Eleanor who came readily to let him wrap his arm about her and pull her close.

Over the top of the girls' heads Clara's gaze pinned him back. She didn't need to say a word for him to hear her warning loud and clear. *Be careful with my children's affections.*

He had every intention of being careful. Not only with their affections but his own. That meant he must stop the talk and memories of his family. Must mind his own business when it came to questions about Clara's activities.

She could follow whatever course of action she chose. *So long as it didn't put her or the girls in danger*, a little voice insisted. But he couldn't imagine she would ever do that.

He had no say in any of her choices whether or not they were risky. And that's just the way he wanted it.

*Don't miss*
*A DADDY FOR CHRISTMAS*
*by Linda Ford,*
*available October 2015 wherever*
*Love Inspired® Historical books and ebooks are sold.*